JET XIII

Renegade

Russell Blake

First edition.

ISBN: 978-1976754241

Published by

Reprobatio Limited

CHAPTER 1

Kisangani, Tshopo Province, Democratic Republic of Congo

Antoine Colomet zipped his leather duffel bag closed and looked around his hotel room, whose peeling plaster and blotchy paint were in keeping with the rest of Kisangani. He adjusted the money belt cinched beneath his loose silk shirt, wiped the sweat from his forehead, and adjusted his Panama hat. After thirty-six hours in the miserable city, he was more than ready to leave, as he was every time he traveled there. Between the mosquitoes, the heat, and the squalor, it was unpleasant in the extreme, even to a hardened African veteran like himself.

He did a final quick check of the drawers and then paused at the window, its rusting iron bars silhouetted against the beige of the dingy curtains. A neon light outside, behind high walls topped with razor wire, blinked intermittently from faulty wiring. He peered through a gap in the drapes and surveyed the road – the only vehicle in sight was a taxi waiting in front of the entrance, where an armed hotel guard chatted with the driver leaning against the open door, smoking.

Antoine stepped away from the window. He glanced at his watch, hefted his bag, and made for the door, its edges degraded from jungle rot.

The hall reeked of stale perspiration and the pervasive aroma of sewage; the town's infrastructure was as primitive as its dwellings. Antoine held his breath and made for the lobby, resisting the impulse to break into a run. When he reached the front desk, he handed the clerk his key and then pushed through the doors and out into the humid night. The air was redolent with vegetal decay and exhaust and

1

the muddy swirl of the nearby river.

The guard straightened as Antoine's hiking shoes squished in mud that had accumulated on the flagstone walkway from a recent cloudburst and threw him a lazy salute. Antoine nodded to the man, who motioned to the waiting cab.

"Your taxi is here," the guard said in French, the national language, a remnant of centuries of colonial subjugation.

"I see. Thank you," Antoine replied in kind.

The guard stepped aside and shifted the sling of his rifle to a more comfortable position on his shoulder. Antoine brushed past him and eyed the driver, who was sucking on his cigarette like it contained the antidote. The driver leaned over and stubbed it out with care, and then pocketed the half-unsmoked remainder for later enjoyment.

"You headed to the airport, right?" the cabbie asked, taking in Antoine's duffel.

"That's right. Where else?" Antoine replied, obviously annoyed by the stupid question. Where else would he be going at that hour with luggage?

"Just so," the driver said. "Bag in the trunk?"

Antoine glanced into the interior of the taxi. "No. I'll keep it with me."

The driver nodded. Antoine opened the back door and lowered himself into the decrepit vehicle. The vinyl bench seat was dusty and cracked, the headliner rust-stained and mottled.

"What time's your flight?" the driver asked.

"Just get me there as quick as you can," Antoine said, making clear his lack of interest in small talk.

The driver grunted and twisted the ignition key. The motor stuttered and caught, and Antoine studied the surroundings as the man fiddled with the gear shift. The hotel was a dump, located in a run-down area just off the city center, the streets painted with muddy runoff and the gutters clogged with trash. Few lights burned at the late hour in the commercial neighborhood. There was no traffic in evidence except for a few bicyclists gliding like wraiths in the darkness and a lone motorcycle a block away, its dim headlight bouncing as it approached. Antoine patted the money belt again, the fistful of diamonds it contained his reason for traveling to the godforsaken place, and smiled at the thought of watching the city disappear beneath the wings of the last flight out.

Antoine had been doing the run every month for over a year, but he felt as uneasy as on the first trip; the pilgrimage was never an easy one for him given the cargo he was carrying. If there had been any other way to get the stones from the Congo, he would have done so, but the supplier would only deal with principals, so Antoine was stuck making the journey.

The stigma of transporting blood diamonds extracted by slave labor didn't bother Antoine. He was a businessman, not the world's babysitter, and he felt no qualms about the illicit trade in which he engaged. The locals had been abusing each other since time began, and if he didn't benefit from it, someone else would. It was just the way of things, a problem not of his making.

He shifted in the seat and the driver pulled the car onto the road. Darkened buildings blurred by as the taxi accelerated, a sad procession of poorly built husks with pocked façades and barricaded windows and doors. Antoine retrieved his cell phone from the breast pocket of his shirt and frowned at the lack of signal – another constant irritation of the trip.

The driver turned onto what passed for a major artery, nearly sideswiping a bicyclist in the process, and navigated around pools of rainwater collected in bathtub-sized potholes. Tribally inspired pop music pulsed from the car radio, and the driver hummed along with the din, bouncing over ruts with enough force to dislodge fillings.

Antoine scowled when the car veered onto a smaller side street. "This isn't the way to the airport."

"Main road's being repaired," the driver explained. "The crews work mainly at night. An annoyance, but what can you do?"

The headlights of a pickup truck swung onto the road behind them, and Antoine glanced at the glare in the side mirror. The truck sped toward the cab's rear bumper, and the driver swore and stepped on the gas.

"Idiots. Out joyriding. Probably drunk or something," he growled, and then slammed on the brakes when a Mitsubishi SUV pulled from between two buildings and stopped in the middle of the narrow street. "What the—" he blurted, and Antoine braced his legs against the front seats to avoid being hurled through the windshield.

The taxi skidded to a halt, leaving long grooves in the mud-coated pavement.

"You okay?" the driver asked, and then his eyes widened when two men climbed from the SUV with machetes in hand.

Antoine twisted to look out the rear window.

"Back up," he ordered. "Floor it. Get out of here."

The driver jammed the shifter into reverse, and the tires spun before gaining traction. The car rocketed backwards, and then the driver stomped on the brakes again as the pickup truck loomed large in the back window, blocking the way.

"Keep going," Antoine yelled, but the driver shook his head.

"I'll hit him."

"Then hit him," Antoine cried. "I'll pay, whatever the damage."

"I—"

"Go. Now!"

The driver accelerated again and yawed to the left, but the truck pulled forward at the last second, and the taxi slammed into the front fender, sending the car into a spin and knocking the truck sideways.

The cab pinwheeled like an amusement park ride on the slick asphalt. Antoine held on for dear life until it ground to a halt. The rear end was crumpled, and the smell of gasoline rose strong in the cabin. The driver gripped the wheel with white knuckles. And then the men materialized a dozen yards away, trotting toward the taxi, their blades glinting in the moonlight.

"Get going! Hurry!" Antoine screamed.

The driver complied, but a tortured grinding sounded from the axle, and the engine died. Antoine threw open the rear door and bolted from the car, leaving the duffel behind, and raced for a dark alley down the block.

He paused for an instant after rounding the corner and heard the pounding of sandaled feet behind him. He drove himself forward, legs protesting the unaccustomed exertion, his heart a jackhammer in his chest. A trio of black rats scuttled from a heaping mound of refuse at the far alley mouth, and he followed them onto the street beyond.

Antoine sprinted to the right, away from the downtown area, the maze of shanties that ringed the area ominous shapes in the gloom. A dog barked on his left, and he made for the shadows of an automotive parts warehouse, where a security guard watched his approach from behind a barred door. Antoine slowed and called to the man. "Call the police," he demanded, his breathing labored. "Open up and let me inside. I'll pay whatever you want."

The guard peered over Antoine's shoulder and then hurried back toward the building. Antoine kicked the bars in frustration. "Please. They're going to kill me," he begged.

If the guard heard him, he didn't react and instead disappeared through the warehouse door, leaving Antoine to his fate. Antoine bolted across the road and between a pair of huts with corrugated tin roofs, ignoring the stench of garbage as he crashed through piles of refuse.

Another street stretched beyond a string of lean-tos, and he spotted a motorcycle's taillight breezing through an intersection. He urged himself to greater speed, the tentative safety of a populated quarter his only hope at the late hour. A hurried look over his shoulder as he neared the street put the machete crew thirty seconds behind him – if he got lucky, he might be able to lose them in the narrow streets.

Antoine had no illusions that he hadn't been sold out. This wasn't an ordinary carjacking or robbery. Opportunistic thieves wouldn't dog him as these men were doing; they'd have been long gone once the taxi had collided with their truck. Someone had to have tipped them off about the diamonds, which meant the danger was far greater than if he'd been randomly targeted by one of the local gangs because of the hour. Men would gladly kill for half a million in stones. The reward would justify virtually any risk, and he had no doubt that if he faltered, the men would hack him apart like a sacrificial lamb.

Antoine's legs pumped like pistons as he raced along the street. There were no cars to hide behind, only more shuttered storefronts framing the road, with the occasional sputtering streetlight barely illuminating the way.

He cursed under his breath. If he'd been able to bring his gun on the trip, his would-be executioners would have posed little problem for him. But because of the last minute notice he'd received for this shipment, he'd had to fly commercial rather than his usual private charter, and smuggling his pistol hadn't been an option.

Another glance behind him told him that his pursuers were gaining on him, their relative youth and endurance enough of an advantage that they'd eventually catch him. The wail of a distant siren encouraged him to a final burst of speed; the intersection ahead offered another chance to duck them.

He turned the corner and nearly plowed into a pair of men walking toward him.

"Please. Help me," Antoine gasped, his eyes frantic.

The man on the right offered an ugly smile, and his companion swung the axe he was carrying at Antoine's head.

Antoine tried to dodge the blow but was an instant too slow. The blade caught the side of his skull as he ducked, and sliced through bone and tissue. Blood clogged his nose and throat, and the night exploded in a supernova of agony, and then Antoine's legs buckled and he crumpled to the sidewalk, dead before his body hit the ground.

CHAPTER 2

Givat Ram, Jerusalem, Israel

Journalists packed the conference facility at the Ministry of Foreign Affairs. Reporters from national newspapers and a few international publications jammed into the theater seating that ran front to back of the twenty-meter-square room. The ministry's spokesperson, Levi Arenson, was finishing up his prepared statements about a recent U.N. decision on Israel's settlements in the Golan Heights – a condemnation that had caused considerable controversy over the last week and pitted political factions against each other as they jockeyed to use the issue to their advantage.

"It has long been our established position that the settlements do not violate Article 49 of the Fourth Geneva Convention, and nothing has changed in the official view," Levi said. "That said, the rumors of further settlement in the Heights are unfounded, and we respectfully reject the U.N.'s assertion that more settlements are planned. For whatever reason, someone has been leading that august body astray."

Levi looked around the room and smiled. "That's all we have on that topic. We'll now open the floor to questions, and then we'll adjourn."

A woman in the front row raised her hand, and Levi did his best not to cringe. Sarah Horowitz was the bane of his existence, routinely taking the most adversarial position possible to whatever official narrative he'd advanced, and spinning even the most innocuous issues in a negative light.

"Yes, Sarah. Always a delight to take your questions," Levi said, keeping his tone even.

Sarah's smirk did little to set his mind at ease, and he knew he was in trouble seconds into her question.

"Then you're especially lucky today," she began. "Does the ministry have any comment on the recent document dump that confirms plans to establish more settlements, in contradiction of your statement?"

Levi blinked twice. "I'm unaware of any document dump, Sarah. What specifically are you referring to?"

"HonestyInternational recently published at least a half dozen ministry documents on its website – mostly correspondence with contractors who've already been awarded bids to develop specific new plots in the Heights."

Levi swallowed hard. She was deliberately blindsiding him, and if what she said was true, had done so with spectacular success.

"When did they do this?" he asked, maintaining his composure. "I haven't seen anything."

"About four hours ago, Levi. I printed them for your reference. As you'll see, the signatures on the emails and the documents are those of the highest-ranking ministers. So either the ministry is lying, or you've been misinformed. Do you have an official statement about which it is?"

"Let me see those," Levi blurted, his normally polished veneer cracking.

Sarah's smile reminded him of an alligator. "Sure, Levi. Here you go," she said, handing him a sheaf of papers. "It's fascinating reading, because it appears you're planning the next ground breaking within the month."

Levi rifled through the documents and, after several moments skimming the cover pages of the two top ones, nodded to Sarah. "This is the first I've heard of it. Given the source, I'll have to get verification of their authenticity. I highly doubt they're genuine." He paused for effect. "You of all people should know you can't believe everything you read on the web."

"Then you're saying they aren't genuine? That they're forgeries or fake news?" she pressed.

Levi affected a bored expression. "No, I'm saying that until they have been verified, I can't comment on them. Anybody can type up anything they like and make wild claims. Frankly, the ministry doesn't have the time or the resources to rebut every unfounded assertion. It would be a full-time job."

Sarah nodded in understanding. "I can appreciate that, Levi. But let's not talk in generalities. These particular documents show the ministry entering into binding contracts with two firms to build eighty-seven homes, beginning in twenty days, and you're here telling the world that you have no intentions of doing so. Can you make a quick call to someone and put this to bed? If it's a lie, that should be simple for you to confirm, shouldn't it?"

Levi's tone hardened. "Again, Sarah, we have an internal procedure we follow. I'll alert you when we have a statement." He looked over the audience and chose another raised hand. "Yes, Adam. What can we do for you today?"

"I'm afraid you're not going to like this, Levi. I too downloaded the docs, and I contacted the two firms. They have no official statement, but they didn't deny that the documents are genuine. Instead they referred me to the ministry. That's the sort of response we would expect if they're real, not if they're fakes." He hesitated. "I also have a connection at one of the companies, who told me in confidence that they're legit. So I'd say you have a problem, Levi."

Levi fell back on his best bureaucrat speak and waffled while refusing to say anything more until the ministry had had a chance to examine the documents. By the end of the question and answer period, which he cut short after three more queries, it was obvious to everyone in the room that the ministry had been caught with its pants down. When Levi left the podium and exited into the hall, he was seething, having been hung out to dry by his superiors and made to look like a fool by the journalists, who clearly smelled blood in the water.

Levi glared at his assistant, who was waiting in the hall with a grim expression.

"This is a disaster, Talia," he said, waving the documents over his head. "How the hell do they know things we haven't been briefed about? I can't run interference if I don't have the facts."

"I don't know," she said. "But I just got pinged. The deputy minister needs to see you immediately. He was watching the briefing."

Levi nodded, his expression dark. "The documents are genuine, aren't they?"

Talia wouldn't meet his eyes. "I have no way of knowing."

"If they were fake, he would have told you."

She pursed her lips. "Probably," she agreed.

The deputy minister's office was upstairs, on the other side of the building, well away from the publicly accessed areas. When Levi arrived, the deputy minister's secretary ushered him into his office.

Eli Lieberman was a compact fireplug of a man in his late fifties with the weatherworn face of a field hand, except for a pair of penetrating mahogany eyes that radiated intelligence. He sat back in his chair and stared at Levi for a long beat, and then gestured for him to sit, and waved away his secretary. When the door closed behind her, he shook his head.

"I saw the show. They came at you hard," he said.

"I know. I was there. The question is whether they had it right, or whether I can volley back and tell them it's all lies."

Eli sighed heavily. "Those documents were never supposed to see the light of day."

Levi nodded slowly, his expression unsurprised. "So they're real."

"Yes. But the real issue is who leaked them. How did they wind up on the internet?"

Levi studied the older man. "You have an idea?"

"No. But I've already called our friends at the Mossad. We're going to meet to discuss it in an hour."

"You saw the conference. There's no way they're going to let this go."

"I suppose not. Which complicates things. We can either move forward on schedule, or deny the veracity of the documents and scrub this phase. Obviously, if we choose the former, we're caught in a blatant lie, so I'm going to recommend to the committee that we put this settlement on hold, at least until the furor dies down. But in the end it's not my decision."

"It would be far better for our credibility if we put it on hold."

The observation earned the younger man a dark look. "Tell me something I don't know." Eli checked his watch. "I'll have an answer for you by day's end. In the meantime, avoid any calls and don't talk to anyone."

"I looked like a complete liar out there, didn't I?"

Eli laughed, the sound harsh, like a crate scraping against rough asphalt. "Goes with the territory. Don't worry. Even though they used you for a punching bag, they know you're just the messenger. Tomorrow it'll be some new crisis. Whatever sells papers."

"Sarah was really enjoying herself. You could tell she knew she had me dead to rights."

Eli nodded again. "Everyone gets to win sometimes. Now, if you don't mind, I've got some messes to clean up. I'll keep you apprised of what's decided."

"I'd love to be able to go out there tomorrow and rub her nose in it. Say it was a hoax that she fell for."

"I'll convey your preference to the others," Eli said dryly. "Anything else?"

"No," Levi said, standing. "I'll go hide under my desk until you call."

"Wise man."

Levi gave him a skeptical look. "If you say so."

CHAPTER 3

Nairobi, Kenya

A black Mercedes AMG G63 SUV rolled to the curb on custom twenty-four-inch rims outside a nightclub in the upscale Westlands district, trailed by a Land Rover with windows tinted so dark they were opaque. The crowd on the packed sidewalk parted when the vehicles' doors swung open and four large bodyguards, shoulder holsters bulging beneath their jackets, stepped onto the curb, followed by a leviathan of a man from the Mercedes draped in a hand-cut ivory linen suit, and finally, a smaller, younger man wearing four-hundred-dollar Japanese PRPS lightweight denim jeans and a Versace shirt.

The big man from the Mercedes was easily three hundred pounds in his stocking feet, the black beret on his head more like a beanie given his size, and his coal black cheeks wobbled like a drunk on an escalator as he took in the scene. The bodyguards formed a protective entourage around him and his companion, and they walked together to the club entrance, above which an elaborate electric sign emblazoned with the word *Zeno* blinked on and off.

Dubstep blared as a bouncer swung one of the doors open, and the men disappeared inside, leaving the crowd of young partygoers murmuring among themselves as the two vehicles roared away.

The interior of the club was all mirrors and black velvet and flashing lights. The music was deafening, and the dance floor was packed with the children of the city's prosperous performing their nocturnal mating ritual, fueled by alcohol and chemical fortification. The big man pushed through the throng to the rear of the club and a door beside the DJ booth guarded by a massive bouncer with arms the size of tree trunks and a glare to match. The guard nodded to the new arrivals and stepped aside, and the big man twisted the doorknob and pushed into a dimly lit hallway. His young companion trailed him, and the four bodyguards remained with the security man, their eyes roaming over the crowd, searching for threats.

They entered an office, and the booming bass from the oversized club speakers faded to a dull rumble when the young man closed the reinforced, sound-deadened door behind him. He looked around the room, taking in the tribal totems on the wall alongside framed posters announcing this international DJ or that singing sensation, and a smile spread across the big man's wide face. This was only one of his operations centers, but it was near to his heart, one of the first in a network of businesses he'd built over the eighteen years he'd been active in Nairobi.

Adami Kimobwa was one of the most powerful crime lords in Kenya, responsible for a toxic enterprise that spanned half the city in addition to numerous smaller towns and surrounding villages under his control. His legitimate holdings included a handful of nightclubs and bars, as well as half a dozen hotels, all useful for money laundering and as distribution hubs for gunrunning and narcotics. His son, Yaro, was his second-in-command now that he'd grown into a man, learning the family business at his father's side. The disparity in appearance between the walrus-size father and the slender son would have been more amusing had it not been for the ruthless viciousness in their eyes – a sociopathology that ran in the family.

Adami lowered himself into a throne-like seat behind a hand-carved mahogany desk, and Yaro pulled up a chair.

"When's the call supposed to come in?" Yaro asked, checking an ostentatiously bejeweled Hublot watch.

"In about six minutes," Adami replied, glancing at the clock on the wall. "You want a drink or something?"

Yaro shook his head. "No. I'm good."

Adami shrugged his elephantine shoulders and raised a cell phone to his lips. Two minutes later, one of the bodyguards appeared with a large glass brimming with dawa, the Kenyan national cocktail fashioned from vodka, lime juice, and honey. The guard deposited it on the desk and left without a word, leaving father and son to wait for their call. Adami took a long, appreciative sip, and then with a cloth handkerchief mopped off the sweat that beaded on his brow in spite of the air conditioner's frigid blast.

When the desk phone rang, it sounded like a fire alarm. Adami reached for it with a hand the size of a skillet and stabbed the line to life, leaning forward toward the speakerphone.

"Adami," he announced, his voice a deep baritone in keeping with his stature.

"Are you alone?" the caller asked in English.

"My son, Yaro, is with me. You can speak as though it were just you and I, though," Adami replied, his words grammatically precise with British pronunciation, but tinged with a singsong Swahili accent.

"Very well. I have confirmation of the dinner for tomorrow night. It will be the three executives and a hostess."

"Security?"

"Six guards. But lightly armed. Handguns only. Their instructions are to be discreet at all times. They are not to alarm the guests." A pause. "There will also be a chef and three helpers, as well as two servers, but it would be best if they weren't harmed."

"I can't make any promises about the guards."

"They shouldn't put up a fight. They're hired for the night. Locals."

"What company?"

"Vanguard. Do you know it?"

Adami smiled. He had influence all over the city; he was familiar with the firm. "I do. They hire ex-military and some unemployed mercenaries. I'll see if I can make an arrangement. Nobody in their employ would be willing to die for what they pay."

"There can't be any way to trace this back to you."

Adami exchanged a look with Yaro and laughed, the sound deep and genuine. "This is not, as the Americans say, my first rodeo. Don't worry." He paused. "Do you have a figure and a split in mind?"

"The going rate would be a million dollars per head, delivered alive."

"That sounds about right. And the split?"

"Down the middle."

Yaro frowned and shook his head. Adami exhaled loudly. "We're doing all the work. I was thinking more along the lines of seventy-thirty."

The caller didn't say anything for several beats. "Perhaps I made a mistake – I was clear from the beginning that this would have to be equitable. Sorry to bother you. Maybe we can do business another time."

Adami scowled and sat back. "Sixty-forty would be the best anyone would give you. There's considerable risk, and the logistics won't be simple. There will be a manhunt to contend with. Palms to be greased, favors to be bought."

"I have financial responsibilities as well. It's either fifty-fifty, or I take the offer elsewhere."

Adami didn't know where the dinner would take place, so he couldn't simply agree to disagree, and then perform the kidnapping anyway, keeping all the money for himself – which was tempting, but once he gave his word, something he'd never do. News would inevitably leak out about his actions, and nobody would bring him deals anymore, which would be disastrous. In addition to his weapons and narcotics trade, Adami ran a thriving protection racket and dabbled in high-dollar kidnappings as well as murder for hire – the latter two requiring that those bringing him the opportunities trust him implicitly. Adami had a reputation as ruthless but trustworthy, and no one transaction was worth destroying a lifetime of honorable criminality.

Yaro shook his head again, but Adami waved a hand in the air in dismissal of his input. "You drive a hard bargain. But I suppose two million is better than nothing."

"It's a lot of money."

"After expenses, not as much as you might think. But if this goes down as you've outlined, it should be worth it."

"They're businessmen. Israeli. Their company will pay without question. It will be the easiest payday you've ever had."

Adami's brow creased. "Nothing in Africa ever goes exactly as planned, but it doesn't sound particularly difficult." He slapped his palm against the table. "Fine. You win. Fifty-fifty. Where is the dinner going to take place? Time? I need all the details."

The caller gave Adami everything he needed, and then the line went dead.

Yaro glared at his father with disapproval. "We could have stuck to our guns on sixty-forty. There's nobody else who could do this on such short notice."

"Maybe. Or maybe one of our competitors would have jumped at the chance of two million for a few days' work. I would rather have the two than lose it over a few hundred thousand."

Yaro chewed his lower lip. "It feels like we left money on the table."

"It should feel like we just made a fortune. Or rather, we will if things go according to script."

"I can head up the snatch party," Yaro said.

"No. We'll have Jaali do it."

"But—"

Adami fixed Yaro with a hard stare. "You're far too valuable to risk in the field on something like this. You will soon be a general, my son, not a lieutenant. And generals don't get their hands dirty. They lead and give orders and count the money. You send soldiers to do the grunt work."

"I could do it," Yaro insisted petulantly.

Adami's face softened. "Of course you could. Nobody would dispute that. But we have far more pressing matters to attend to, Yaro, and I can't afford for you to be entangled in the logistics of one kidnapping. I'm sorry. Those days are over."

Yaro sighed but nodded slowly, his expression unhappy but resigned. "As you wish."

Adami drained his dawa and pushed the glass away. "We don't have much time to coordinate this. We'll need a seasoned group of ten fighters who can be trusted not to lose their heads. Getaway vehicles. A technician to ensure nobody's wired. A location to keep the captives until the ransom is paid. Communications gear."

"I'll call Jaali."

"Tell him to be here within the hour. I want no discussion of this on cell phones. No electronic communications." Adami stood. "Use the landline," he said, unbuttoning his coat and shrugging out of it, his face glistening with sweat again from the effort.

Yaro stood, checked his cell phone contacts for a number, and then dialed the desk phone, his fingers drumming an impatient tattoo as the call connected and began to ring.

CHAPTER 4

Mokombe River region, Democratic Republic of Congo

Mist rose from the rainforest floor as the last vestiges of a morning rain converted to steam beneath the sun's glare. A three-room shack fashioned from local mud brick, its thatched roof bleached from the elements, sat at the edge of a red dirt road that meandered from the paved highway many miles to the south through jungle so dense it appeared impenetrable. A hand-painted sign that hung to the side of the entrance featured a red cross, and the plywood door that had been hastily mounted to bar the entryway stood open.

A woman coasted an ancient bicycle to a stop before the hut and leaned it against the porch railing. Her eyes were wild and her face was animated with fear, her movements jerky as she mounted the steps and hurried to the doorway. A tall man blocked her way and regarded her with a stern expression.

"Yes? What is it?" he asked.

"My village. Something terrible is going on. My husband and my three children are all so sick they can barely stand. And it's not just them. There are other families with the same problem. Some have already died."

"Slow down. What do you mean, sick? What are their symptoms?"

"They're weak and can't keep food down. And they have bad diarrhea."

"Where are you drawing your water from?"

"The river. Like always."

"Do you boil it like I've told you to do?"

Her eyes darted away. "Most of the time."

The man shook his head. "'Most of the time' isn't enough. I've

18

explained why. If your family is sick, it's because they've been drinking untreated river water."

She shook her head. "No. That's not it. I know what that's like. This is far worse. You have to do something. You have to help."

"There isn't much I can do if they've been drinking from a polluted source. Other villages upstream use it for their waste. You're drinking their sewage. It's not safe."

The woman's eyes were defiant. "Give me some pills or something."

"I can't just hand out pills without knowing exactly what's wrong. That will take blood tests, a physical examination…"

"Their eyes are all turning yellow."

The man's face didn't change. "You should pour salt into several liters of water and boil it. The salt will help them stay hydrated."

"Hy…hy-rate-ed?"

"It will help them keep water in their systems and help their livers and kidneys to filter out whatever is bothering them."

"Nothing's bothering them. They're dying. I came to get you, Dr. Mutati."

"I'm not a doctor. I've told you a million times. I'm just a physician's assistant. I administer vaccines, stitch up cuts."

"You're as good as a doctor to us," she said solemnly. "My family needs help. Please."

Mutati frowned. The woman was persistent, and he could see she wasn't going to go away without him. He checked his watch and then sighed. "How long did it take to get here this morning, Dira?" Mutati knew the village well and understood that it could take any length of time, depending on the condition of the dirt track that led to the river and traced along its bank.

"Maybe an hour on the trail. It's muddy in a lot of places."

"I have work to do here. I can't just drop everything…" he protested in a last-ditch effort to avoid the unpleasant trek.

The woman's eyes brimmed with tears. "You have to help us. You have to."

Mutati nodded and glanced at her bike – a community conveyance that was the village's most highly prized possession. The situation had to be dire for Dira to have talked the village chief into allowing her to take it. "I'll put together a bag and be right out with my bicycle."

Five minutes later Mutati emerged rolling a cheap mountain bike, a sun-faded backpack over his shoulder. He pulled the plywood barrier into place and locked it using a padlock and chain passed through a hole in the wood and wrapped around the right support pole. When he was satisfied the hut was secured, he carried the bike down to where Dira was waiting and swung a leg over the seat.

"You take the lead," he said, his tone making plain his annoyance at being dragged into the wilds on an especially hot day.

Dira straddled her bike and pedaled off, the handlebars wobbling until she picked up speed. Her nearly bald tires slipped in the mud, making for slow going on the stretch that led to the river, and by the time they reached the water, Mutati's worst fears had been realized — the trip was going to take forever.

The air was muggy, even beneath the shade of the trees that lined the bank, and within half an hour they stopped to rest, their clothes soaked through with sweat. Mutati leaned his bike against a tree trunk and, after examining the ground and the surrounding brush, sat on the ground in the tree's shadow while Dira disappeared into the jungle to relieve herself.

An object bobbing along in the slow current caught his eye, and he squinted to better make it out. After a few moments of peering at it, he drew in a sharp breath. It was a body. A baby, by the looks of it no more than eight or nine months, bloated and floating facedown.

The water a few feet away from the infant wrinkled and swirled, and Mutati struggled to his feet as a long, dark bronze form appeared in the sunlight. It disappeared, and Mutati blinked, the sun blinding on the water at the angle. He'd practically convinced himself that it was a submerged branch or some other flotsam washed into the river by the rain when a pair of wickedly powerful jaws thrust from the water, clamped onto the body with a snap, and pulled it beneath the surface.

The river returned to an untroubled stream, dented by the hot breeze that blew from the north, any evidence of the grisly apparition gone to the bottom of the river.

Mutati felt for the pistol holstered on his hip, fearful that the big Nile crocodile's hungry companions might be lurking nearby. Judging by the creature's size, that wasn't a bad bet – it was smallish, so not a dominant male, which explained why it was willing to scavenge rather than hunt live prey. Which meant that there were likely more in the vicinity; it was the habit of the social animals to throng together in their preferred sun-basking and feeding areas.

Dira reappeared, and Mutati composed himself. "You ready?" he asked, his tone neutral.

She nodded. "Yes."

"You see anything strange on the ride down?" he asked, his words casual.

"Not really. I was riding quick as I could, so I wasn't sightseeing."

Dira climbed aboard her bike and began making her way along the trail, and Mutati followed her at a greater distance than before, figuring that if there were a famished male croc nearby, the space would give him a chance to flee to safety while it attacked the unfortunate woman. It was unlikely, given the bicycles, but he didn't want to chance it; the grim feast he'd witnessed was the jungle's reminder that nothing in the Congo was safe for long, and if he let down his guard, it could be the last thing he ever did.

Eventually the village materialized from the foliage, and Dira led him past cooking fires and dozens of huts to her dwelling. The villagers watched their arrival with gaunt faces and saucer eyes, their expressions betraying nothing but resignation to as harsh an existence as any on the planet.

Dira motioned for Mutati to enter the hut, and he did so after waiting just inside to allow his eyes to adjust. Flies buzzed around three prone forms in the corner on a blanket that occupied a third of the single room, and his nose twitched at the odor of sickness wafting from them.

He crossed the room and unslung his backpack, and the man's

eyes cracked open, revealing jaundiced whites. Mutati gave his best encouraging smile and tried to avoid gagging at the smell.

"Dira tells me you're not feeling well," he said, his tone upbeat.

The man shook his head. "No."

"When did this start?"

"Couple days ago," Dira answered for her mate. "The kids, maybe three days."

"Let me take your temperature, and we'll see if we can figure out what to do about it," Mutati said, and held up an old mercury thermometer. "I need to put this under your tongue for a minute and take your blood pressure."

The man looked uncertain but nodded weakly in agreement. Mutati slid the glass tube into his mouth and then removed a frayed blood pressure cuff from the backpack and strapped it to the man's left arm. He drew a stethoscope from the bag, inserted the earpieces, and pumped the cuff tight and timed the faint pulses with his watch. When he was done, he offered another smile and nodded encouragement. "Almost done," he said, and after a few more moments, checked the thermometer. "Looks like you caught a bug. Best thing for it is to drink plenty of clean water and wait it out. I'll draw some blood to take back to the clinic, but it will be a week before we get the results. In the meantime, the best thing for it is to flush your system and get plenty of rest."

Mutati straightened, withdrew his cell phone, and took photos of the man's face and eyes and then his bare torso, which appeared to be blistered with a rash. He did the same with the children, who were listless and seemed unaware of his presence, and removed a packet of sterile needles and drew their blood into plastic test tubes, which he labeled quickly and slid into a thermal pouch.

"That's it?" Dira demanded. "Drink plenty of water? There's nothing else you can do for them?"

"I told you – I can't treat them until I know what I'm treating them for. The river's full of bacteria and parasites. It could be anything. If I try a broad-spectrum antibiotic, that won't do much for some classes of parasites, and it would just further strain their systems."

"People are dying, Dr. Mutati. They don't have a week."

He shrugged. "It's all I can do." He cast a quick look at the children. "I'm sorry. I really am. I wish there was more, but there isn't. All I can ask is for the lab to put a rush on the results."

"It's that damned vaccine, isn't it? The water's a lie," she spat, her mouth a thin line.

He shook his head. "We've been through that, Dira. The vaccines are necessary to prevent diseases. They wouldn't do this." Mutati was part of the routine inoculation team that the government had approved to inoculate the rural area populations, but he knew that the villagers distrusted the shots and had heard countless rumors and gossip that verged on the hysterical.

"So you say," she snapped. "All I know is my family's always been healthy, and now they aren't." She paused. "We need more pills, like you gave everyone before."

"Those were for something different. I can't just hand out pills to you, Dira. Again, I don't know what to give you because I don't know what's wrong with them."

Mutati pushed out of the hut and found himself facing the village chief, his face lined, the thin crown of hair on his head graying. At forty-four, he was one of the elders.

"Lot of misery here, Mutati," he said, his voice low.

"I see that," Mutati acceded. "How many?"

"Sixteen," the chief said, the word a whisper.

"That's...unfortunate."

"That is all you can say?" the chief countered.

Mutati pursed his lips. "Perhaps we should discuss this someplace quiet?"

The chief nodded and led him to another hut, this one empty.

Ten minutes later Mutati emerged, and the chief watched him return to his bicycle, the fistful of violet ten-thousand franc notes the medicine man had slipped him safely tucked away in his store of valuables. Mutati waved to the villagers and pedaled back along the trail, leaving the chief to attempt to console his tribe the best he could in the face of an invisible enemy whose origin he would pretend not to know.

When Mutati reached the clinic, he continued riding past it, to the road that led to an outpost six kilometers away, where he would make a coded call to alert his superiors that a problem had surfaced. Based on the population size in that one village, he expected up to a five percent total mortality rate unless something changed. He would forward his memory card with the photos of the afflicted in the pouch with the blood for study, and would impress on his bosses that action needed to be taken immediately or he wouldn't be able to keep a lid on the problem, which would invite unwelcome scrutiny none of them could afford.

CHAPTER 5

Nairobi, Kenya

The night air was balmy on the outskirts of the city, the sun having dropped behind the western hills hours before, though its heat lingered on. Night birds signaled one another in the trees ringing the grounds of the Kenyan Museum complex. The main buildings were dark, but bright lights glowed from a structure on the periphery. Music drifted on the breeze from the colonial-era mansion where a dinner was in progress, the meals served on fine china, delivered on starched tablecloths by uniformed servers that harkened to a bygone era.

Sentries stood at the exterior perimeter of the home, watching the gloom around them with bored expressions. Coils from concealed microphones trailed from their hairlines into their jacket collars. Four of the six men were stationary, one at each corner, and two patrolled the grounds, orbiting the mansion with tedious regularity. A catering van sat near the rear entrance, and the cobblestone driveway leading from the parking area by the main buildings was roped off to traffic, blocking the approach.

A group of three men and a young woman sat at a banquet table inside the house, enjoying a "farm to table" sampling of local delicacies accompanied by fine French wine. The men's voices had strengthened as the dinner progressed, and now that the group was on its sixth bottle of Bordeaux, every utterance was loud, and laughter echoed from the high wood-beam ceiling and through the open windows. Overhead fans spun with dizzying speed throughout the mansion, and a centuries-old chandelier illuminated the dining area, its crystal beads glowing teardrops as a recorded violin concerto that emanated from hidden speakers reached a crescendo and then quieted.

"I must say, Shira, you've outdone yourself," one of the diners complimented the woman.

"Why, David, thank you. I try to tailor these events for the audience. I'm glad you're enjoying it," Shira replied, smiling, painfully aware that, as the lone female at the table, she was the center of the inebriated men's attention. Being young and beautiful opened many doors, but in a testosterone fest like this, had notable drawbacks as well.

"Keep the wine coming and we'll enjoy it even more," Noam, on David's right, bayed. His companions laughed as though his comment was hysterically funny, and Shira smiled again and chuckled politely.

"We have a special sauterne for after dinner," she said. "One that rivals Yquem, I've been told," she assured them. "The sommelier we work with is from Paris. He never steers me wrong."

"He knows his job," David agreed. "And the food! My God, I can't remember the last time I ate so much."

"Then you hated it?" Shira asked.

"Obviously," he said with a grin.

A server materialized at David's elbow and refilled his wineglass before moving around the table to pour for the others. Shira held her hand over her goblet, and David frowned. "You're hardly drinking," he complained.

"My supervisors don't like me getting drunk on the job," she explained with an eye roll.

"Oh, come on. A little wine never hurt anyone," Noam said. "And a lot never did, either!"

More laughter, and Shira surreptitiously checked her watch. As the hostess of the dinner, she was expected to be charming and fun, but over the course of several hours, the job began to wear on her. She'd been conducting dinners as part of her company's VIP tour packages for a year, and she vastly preferred them to the safari outings, but they were still tedious, especially so if the diners were corporate executives like these, who would insist on discussing business throughout the proceedings no matter how diverting the meal and company.

"So you've been in-country for almost eighteen months?" asked Gabriel, the third executive, from over his half-finished main course.

"That's right," Shira said.

"Takes some getting used to, huh?" he pressed.

"It's definitely different from back home," she agreed politely. "Then again, most things are, aren't they?"

David nodded. "True. There's no place like home."

A muffled cry sounded outside one of the windows, from just beyond the veranda, and the servers looked up in puzzlement. Noam took a long pull on his wine and grinned. "Sounds like somebody twisted their ankle or something."

"Or maybe it's a snake," David opined. "They have some pretty deadly ones here, don't they?"

Shira nodded. "You bet. They're nothing to sneeze at, although they tend to avoid areas around big cities like this." She paused. "But out in the rainforest, you have to really watch yourself. Step on the wrong thing and it could kill you."

Gabriel held up his glass in a toast. "I hear good red wine will–"

A dozen gunmen burst through the mansion entrance and spread through the living and dining rooms, their rifles trained on the diners. The servers backed away from their positions by the table, and one of the gunmen pointed at the kitchen. Two of the thugs rushed to the door and burst through it as the lead gunman studied the diners with leaden eyes. A cry of protest from the kitchen was cut off by the sound of a blow, and the lead gunman nodded to the man on his right and said something in barely audible Swahili.

The shooter motioned to the servers with his rifle. "Into the kitchen," he ordered.

"Please," the nearest waiter said, hands up, his eyes frightened. "We just work here…"

The Kalashnikov's wood stock slammed against the server's skull. He crumpled to the ground, and the lead gunman jabbed the other waiter with his rifle barrel. "The kitchen, or you're next. Drag him out of here and don't make any trouble."

The man obeyed as the diners looked on in horror. The lead gunman turned to glare at them.

David half stood. "You can have all our money," he volunteered.

The gunman laughed and shook his head. "You're being kidnapped," he said in accented English. "There are two ways this can work. The easy way, and the...unpleasant way. You can either walk out of here or be carried out."

"Kidnapped!" Noam blurted.

"That's right," the gunman snapped. "Put your hands on your head so my men can search and bind you."

Gabriel exchanged a glance with Shira, and the gunman caught it. "This isn't a game. You want to lose some teeth, try to stall. Hands on your head, now, or you'll be sorry."

"Me too?" Shira asked in a small voice.

The gunman looked her up and down. "Oh, definitely you. You'll fetch a pretty penny, I'm sure."

Shira swallowed hard and complied, as did the executives. Three of the gunmen snapped handcuffs on the men. When they were done, the lead gunman did the same with Shira, who winced at the pinch of steel. She tried not to make a face at the sour aroma of dried sweat that overpowered her when the man was close, and held her breath until he was finished, her expression wooden and eyes unfocused as she endured his touch.

"Where are you taking us?" David asked.

The leader ignored him. "Here's how this is going to work. You don't ask questions. You don't cause trouble. You don't do anything we tell you not to do. If you're good, and your company pays, you go home with all your fingers and toes, and this is just a story to tell over drinks. You decide you're going to play hero, you'll be dealt with swiftly. Your ransom will be paid whether you're missing pieces or not, so it's up to you how this goes." He paused. "Hopefully your company will see the wisdom in cooperating. If not... Well, let's not be pessimistic, right?"

The gunmen returned from the kitchen and joined the rest, and the leader barked orders in Swahili. He offered the hostages a predatory grin. "All right. Time to move. You're going to be gagged so you don't make any noise. Again, fight it and it won't go well. My advice is not to."

Two of the men tied bandannas across their mouths, rolling the cloth so they made effective gags. Once everyone was muzzled, the leader escorted the prisoners down the mansion's front steps, where the security detail was sitting, also gagged, bound to an old hitching post off the veranda.

The leader directed the procession away from the driveway into the dark tree line nearby, the faint glow of the moon lighting their way. They walked for six minutes and then arrived at a clearing by a road, where a pair of black vans was waiting. The leader nodded to one of his men, and he strode to the van and slid the side door open.

"Inside," he growled at the prisoners. They shambled forward to the van, and two of the kidnappers helped them aboard. The leader slammed the door closed as the shooters loaded into the other van, and then he hoisted himself into the passenger seat and rested his AK against the floorboards.

The engines roared to life and the vehicles rolled onto the road, their headlights dark. They moved stealthily through the gloom, the drivers navigating by moonlight until turning onto a smaller road. Once on that tributary, the driver of the van filled with gunmen switched on the headlights and drove at a moderate pace toward the Nairobi suburbs while the other vehicle continued on the original road, the kidnapped diners bouncing on the hard steel cargo bed, the van filled with the stink of fear.

CHAPTER 6

Tel Aviv, Israel

Jet faced Hannah, who was stubbornly refusing to eat her breakfast, the expression on her face one of infantile intractability Jet recognized increasingly of late. Hannah had dug in, taken a stand over her meal, and now it was a battle of wills between mother and daughter.

Matt entered the kitchen, sized up the standoff, and smiled at Jet. "You should just tell her that if she doesn't eat, she goes hungry until lunch."

Jet frowned. "I love it when you come in and advise me on parenting. Really, I do."

"Zero-negotiation policy," Matt intoned. "Your way or the highway."

"The problem is she's got a mind of her own, and she needs to eat. We can't just starve her into submission."

Matt's left eyebrow rose. "Why not?"

"She needs to learn to obey me because I'm her mother, not because she's fainting from hunger," Jet snapped.

"How's that working?" Matt asked.

Hannah pushed her bowl away and looked out at the skyline through the kitchen window. Jet sighed and knelt beside her daughter. "Mama loves you, honey, but if you don't eat your breakfast, we're selling you to the gypsies."

Hannah seemed unfazed by the threat.

Matt smiled. "Maybe monsters would work better?"

"So now we're going to scar her for life to get her to eat?" Jet paused and then looked back at her daughter. "Hannah, that's all the food you're going to get. If you don't want to eat it, that's fine, but when you're hungry in an hour, that's your problem. Do you want to be hungry in an hour? Because all I'm going to give you until lunch is that same bowl. Eat it now, or later, or never. Up to you."

Hannah considered the mush in her dish and made a face. Matt cocked his head and Jet shook hers.

"She doesn't look convinced," he said.

"Stubborn as a mule."

"I refuse to say it runs in the family."

Jet gave him side-eye. "You're part of the family now."

"That's how I know I speak the truth." Matt looked up at the television in the living room, where a newscaster was reporting on the disastrous press conference where the government had been caught misstating its intentions. He shook his head. "Sounds like they have a leak on their hands."

Jet nodded. "Sure does. I wonder if it's an issue of the entire comm system being hacked, or an insider leaking documents, like Snowden." She thought for a moment. "If the ministry's confidential communications have been breached, that doesn't bode well for my gang's network."

The phone on the kitchen counter rang, and Jet and Matt both frowned at the sound. There was only one person who had that number.

Jet moved to the phone and lifted the handset to her ear.

"Gorgeous morning for coffee. See you in a half hour?"

The voice was anonymous, a generic male speaking in Hebrew. But the code was a clear summons.

Jet sighed and replied, "Sure. I'd love a cup. Usual place?"

"None other."

The line went dead. Jet set the phone down with the delicate precision of a surgeon making an incision. Matt waited by Hannah, hands on his hips. She eyed his razor-cut hair and suntanned features and forced a smile.

"His master's voice," she said, her tone bitter.

"It's only been eight weeks since the last one," Matt said. "I thought this was going to be a once every year or two thing. Wasn't that the deal?"

Jet shrugged. "So did I. That's how it was sold. Imagine that people lie."

"You can always say no," he pointed out.

"Of course. If it's ugly, I will."

Matt looked down at Hannah. "You think they'd turn us out?"

Jet shook her head. "No. But I'd hate to be wrong. I don't want to have to uproot Hannah again. She's doing well with the stability."

"Except for eating," Matt observed.

"Will you watch her? I have to run out and see what they want."

"Of course," Matt said, giving Hannah a hard stare. The little girl beamed at him, her eyes radiating innocent joy, and he shook his head. "Can we just make this easy? Just this once, Hannah?"

Jet tiptoed and kissed Matt on the cheek. "You're the best. Try not to strangle her while I'm gone. Although I'd understand."

Half an hour later, Jet was sipping a cup of tea at a coffee shop two blocks off the waterfront on a side street that saw little traffic and no tourism. A brown sedan stopped thirty yards away, and the distinctive form of the director stepped from the passenger side, along with two young agents in windbreakers and sunglasses. The director lit a cigarette as he approached Jet, and the pair of agents took up positions on either side of the café, eyes roving over the nearby buildings and parked cars.

"I see you've recovered from your last outing," the director said by way of greeting and took the seat across from Jet.

Jet nodded, waiting for him to tell her what he wanted. He took a drag on his cigarette and studied her.

"What are you drinking?" he asked.

"Tea," she said.

He grimaced and waved at the waitress. She approached and he held up a finger. "Cup of coffee, black, and an ashtray," he ordered, and waited until she left to begin speaking. "We've got a situation."

"I figured this wasn't a social visit." She paused. "Is it related to the ministry leak?"

He shook his head. "Lord, no. Although that's an ongoing headache. No, this is a sensitive problem that arose in Africa. Kenya." He blew smoke at the sky. "A kidnapping."

The waitress returned with his drink and a tray with sugar and sweetener on it, and set them and a glass ashtray on the table before returning to the interior of the café, the director's eyes following her inside before fixing on Jet.

She didn't try to hide her puzzlement. "A kidnapping? I'm hardly a hostage negotiator. Don't you have specialists in that?"

"It's gone beyond the negotiation stage. Three pharmaceutical company bigwigs were snatched by a local group, as well as the daughter of the ambassador's attaché. The drug company has agreed to cough up the ransom. But because of the daughter's involvement, as well as the fact that the executives are Israeli, we want a presence there to oversee the exchange."

"You want me to fly to Africa to hand over a briefcase full of money? Why? A trained monkey could do that."

"We don't have a lot of confidence in the people on the ground. I gave my word to someone I can't name that we'd put a trained operative in place, but I don't have anyone I can send on short notice." The director finished his cigarette and stubbed it out before trying the coffee and making a face. "I wish they'd start using better beans. This tastes like tar."

"That's all there is to this? A flight, supervise the exchange, and bring the hostages back home?"

The director nodded. "It's a milk run for someone like you. Frankly, your skill set is overkill for the mission, but I'd rather have someone who can think on their feet than a less qualified operative. The situation's been described to me as 'fluid,' which tells me the left hand doesn't know what the right is doing. And with the locals being, shall we say, a question mark, I thought all concerned parties could benefit by some adult supervision watching out for our interests."

"How old's the daughter?" Jet asked.

"Twenty-three. I'll get you a full package on all the players if you agree to take it on."

"Anything you're leaving out?"

He coughed twice and tapped another cigarette from a worn pack. "You say yes, then you'll know everything I do."

"When do you want me to go?"

"There's a flight tomorrow morning, first thing."

"How much is the ransom, and do they have it in Kenya yet, or are they going to have to transport it there?"

"Four million dollars. It should be in Kenya this afternoon. Went out early this morning via private jet."

"Who's holding it?"

"The drug company's office in Nairobi."

"You have an identity worked up for me?"

He nodded. "Of course. Your passport is in process. French. We're going with security consultant for the pharmaceutical group."

"Weapons?"

"You shouldn't need any, but we'll instruct the station chief in Nairobi to make himself available to you." The director lit his cigarette and blew a gray cloud at the sky. "His name's Elon. A good man."

"But not good enough to handle this?"

"He's not a field agent; or at least, he isn't anymore. Getting a little long in the tooth for that sort of thing." He laughed and then grew serious. "As are we all."

Jet finished her tea. "When can I get the package and my papers?"

"We can have them delivered to your apartment in under four hours."

She hesitated. "You seem confident I'll agree."

"Hope springs eternal."

"Any idea of the identity of the kidnappers?"

The director frowned. "Could be any of fifty miscreants who pull scams in the region. Rebel groups. Warlords. Gangs. Factions of the military out for easy money. Could be any of them, or any combination. It doesn't really matter. What does is that it's not our money, and the kidnappers have no reason not to turn them loose once they've collected it." He gave a small shrug. "Does this mean we have a deal?"

She sighed. "If I said no, would you let me walk?"

His expression didn't change. "Of course. But I'm hoping you'll agree. You won't be gone for more than a few days. It's really not that demanding an assignment, but if you think you aren't up to it..."

"Don't insult my intelligence. This is something any of a hundred agents could easily manage."

He grunted assent. "And the first time something went off the rails, they'd be on the phone asking for direction rather than making things happen. I need someone capable of acting autonomously."

"And who's completely deniable."

He nodded and drew hard on his cigarette. "There's another dynamic, of course. Because of the culture, women are underestimated. So you'll be viewed as a pretty face, nothing more. That could work to your advantage if things go sideways."

Jet regarded the director's gray complexion, the loose folds of skin hanging from his face lending him the appearance of an old dog on its last legs. If he was telling her the whole story, the mission would be uneventful; but she knew better than to go into anything overconfident. She'd believed that she'd buried her identity in an untraceable manner before moving to the islands, and that had proved a near-fatal mistake. If anything had been drilled into her by life, it was that she would always need to be prepared for the worst.

Still, it was hard to see much risk in the assignment, and after a few moments of consideration, she nodded. "Fine. I'll do it. I'll need a budget as well as access to weapons."

"Elon can arrange for whatever you need. I'll alert him of your imminent arrival." He paused. "You're to coordinate with the locals, but be careful. Africa's a snake pit, and we can't assume competence or loyalty from anyone."

"That's my baseline assumption about everyone these days," Jet said.

He smiled, revealing nicotine-stained teeth. "Probably wise. You'll have the package shortly."

Jet watched him rise and hesitate before pulling a few bills from his pocket and laying one on the table. "Tell them to get a new brand of coffee. Seriously. It's a wonder they stay in business."

He shuffled back to the car, bodyguards in tow, and Jet slid the bill beneath her cup and rose, waiting until the director was out of sight before making briskly for the apartment, anxious to maximize her remaining time with Hannah and Matt.

CHAPTER 7

Republic of the Congo, Africa

The sun was an angry red ball rising into a plum-colored sky as a long line of men and children, some no older than six, filed toward one of the hundreds of illegal diamond-mining operations that dotted the landscape. This outfit was run by a brutal chieftain who paid the workers a dollar a day for twelve hours of backbreaking work, sifting through riverbed gravel for stones. A group of security guards lounged by an old fluoroscopy scanner that all the workers would have to pass through at the end of the shift, but which was inactive now, its generator silent as the guards enjoyed their breakfast.

Child labor in the mining efforts was a constant, from the Congo to Angola to South Africa, where conflict diamonds were a substantial part of the underground economy. The government officials responsible for stopping it were routinely paid off; the workers were desperate peasants willing to endure the harshest of conditions to earn a pittance – and the chance to augment their income through theft of some of the diamonds they found. The mines were on constant guard against pilfering, but human nature in countries where poverty was endemic meant that a substantial number of stones made it through the cracks; the risk of termination or death was one many were forced to take in order to feed starving families or provide desperately needed medical care to relatives.

The child labor of this particular mining effort ran a third of the workers under the age of ten, and a full sixty-five percent younger than sixteen. Conditions were backbreaking: the job consisted of being bent over throughout the day, sifting gravel through mesh while watching for the telltale glint of stones, and many of the young workers graduated to the dangers of the mines after a few years, preferring the danger of cave-ins or death from a host of causes to a ruined spine. There were no schools for the children, who were from destitute families in the local villages, so they would grow up illiterate and unable to find any work outside of the mines, ensuring that they would have short and brutal existences, as would their offspring.

A fourteen-year-old boy prodded his two younger siblings, one six and the other ten, as the line of miserable humanity inched toward the guards. The boys carried plastic lunch pails and bottles of boiled water mixed with fruit juice to sustain them through their shift. The guards barely glanced at the workers, preferring to concentrate on their food and their card game, and the trio of boys passed the scanner and made their way toward the river, the oldest already stooped with the distinctive posture of someone who'd spent most of his life in an unnatural position, his knee joints swollen from autoimmune inflammation.

"I don't know, Dany," Francis, the ten-year-old, said to his older brother. "I have a bad feeling about this."

"You just keep cool, little man, and everything will be fine. We'll soon have enough so we never have to come to this cursed river again."

A rustle sounded from the youngest boy's lunch pail, followed by a series of scratches. "They don't like it in there," Yavan, the smallest of the bunch, said.

"They don't have to like it," Dany snapped. "If we're lucky, they'll be free soon enough. Remember what Father told us: hide the smaller stones under your fingernails until the guards aren't watching, and then put them in your mouth. When we take morning break, meet me and give me the diamonds, and I'll deal with the rest. If you're smart, nobody will see anything, and by the end of the day we'll have worked our last day in this place."

Yavan didn't look convinced. "I hope you're right."

Dany snuck a look over his shoulder at the guards and nodded. "Me too."

The morning's work started as the foreman handed out pans to the laborers, and the guards took up position every fifty feet, watching over the workers with focused attention. The operation was one of the most draconian in terms of penalties for theft, and it was a regular occurrence that a laborer was hauled off to be questioned and never seen again. Even the use of the scanner demonstrated the operation's priorities, with the system on for all shifts, versus the periodic use in other mining groups. The ongoing exposure to radiation was an occupational hazard and worth it to the operator if it saved it millions of dollars in lost stones each year. Diamonds were easily identifiable under X-rays, so the typical scheme of swallowing stones or inserting them into body cavities didn't work – which still didn't stop some theft, but kept it at a manageable level.

Two hours into the shift, Dany had managed to ferret away a promising two-carat example he'd been hiding in the brush for almost a month, and Francis had three one-carat stones of his own he had collected over the prior week. When Yavan joined them for a ten-minute hydration break at nine o'clock, he slipped Dany a one-and-a-half-carat stone he'd told them about the day before, which he'd hidden beneath a flat rock on the bank. Dany didn't look at it, but put it with the others, and then leaned into his brothers and spoke in a whisper.

"Go relieve yourselves, and then make your way back to the river. I'll deal with the birds."

Yavan looked frightened. "Shouldn't you wait until the end of the day?"

"What's the point?" Dany hesitated. "Don't worry. This will work. And we'll be rich by the time the shift is over."

Their father knew of a man in one of the larger towns who would pay thousands of dollars for stones over a carat, depending on the quality, and far more for colored stones of any size. Between what they'd managed to hide from the bosses, they had enough to support the family for a decade, maybe more, and to move from the daily hardship of jungle life to the city, where food was available whenever you wanted it and nobody had to work unless they felt like it.

At least that was what their father had said. Dany privately wondered how he knew what he claimed to know, but would never challenge him. He, like his brothers, had to trust that his father knew what he was doing, which seemed a safe bet given the ingenuity of the smuggling scheme he'd come up with.

Two of the lunch pails contained homing pigeons his father had systematically trained to return to the village, and for which he had fashioned small harnesses with pouches to accommodate stones. Everyone was searched on the way out of the area at the end of each day, but nobody bothered on the way in, and his father had hit on the plan after months of thinking about how to achieve the impossible. Once he'd trained the birds, the boys had collected stones as they could, turning in most of their finds but opportunistically concealing what today would fly from the mining area to their father, right under the noses of the guards. It was perfect, and Dany could feel the excitement building in his chest as he surveyed the area, confirming that none of the guards was close enough to see what he was doing.

He removed the first bird from the lunch pail. The pigeon was startled by the sudden light and relief from the heat of the enclosure, and Dany stroked its head for a moment to calm it. He then slipped two of the stones into the leather pouch and slid the harness over the bird's head, tightening the small strap with trembling fingers. When he was confident that it was secure, he rose and walked farther into the trees, and when he was out of sight of the guards, released the bird. It flapped up toward the canopy, shot through an opening, and disappeared from view, its treasure trove on its way to the village.

Dany returned to the lunch pails and repeated the maneuver, and was ready to carry the second pigeon into the jungle when a voice cried out from the river.

"You. What are you doing there?"

Dany froze, bird in hand. He dared a look over his shoulder; one of the guards was pointing at him, Kalashnikov in hand. Dany's mind worked furiously for some plausible excuse, but he'd never been a fast thinker, and under pressure his faculties failed him completely.

"What? I found a hurt bird," he called, stalling for time.

"Don't move. I saw a pigeon take off a few minutes ago. Stay where you are."

The man began walking toward him on the sloped gravel bank, but then lost his footing and stumbled to catch himself. Dany seized the opportunity and let the pigeon go, and it tore toward the branches by the river in an attempt to find open air.

"It got loose," Dany yelled, figuring that he couldn't be blamed if the bird managed to escape.

The guard cried out to one of the others, who came at a trot, carrying a pump shotgun. The pigeon was frantically flapping into the sky and was almost over the canopy when the big gun boomed and the bird dropped in an explosion of feathers, a few of the double-aught buckshot from the blast ending its flight.

Dany didn't wait to see what happened next, and instead took off at a run into the jungle. His only chance was to put distance between himself and the river before they found the bird and discovered his treachery. He heard Yavan cry out in alarm behind him and cringed as he yelled at his older brother.

"Run, Dany. We're right behind you."

Dany crashed through the brush, forging a path through the undergrowth, terrified for himself and his brothers, aware that the penalty for what he'd done would be extreme – probably summary execution. Nobody would take pity on his brothers because of their age. They would be viewed as vermin to be exterminated and would be shot without hesitation.

Shouts followed them into the jungle, and then the shooting started, confirming his worst fears. Rounds whistled through the leaves around him, and several snapped past his head, narrowly missing him. He ducked down and kept going, committed to trying to make it past the perimeter guards who formed a human cordon around the river mine; he didn't want to think about how he would slip past them with his brothers in the rear.

His bare feet hurt from sharp branches that were decaying underfoot, and he grunted twice as particularly sharp ones stabbed through his calluses and drew blood. The shooting continued and he zagged right, and faint hope was beginning to grow when Francis called out.

"Yavan's down. He's hit."

The thought of his six-year-old brother shot in the back made Dany's throat tighten, but there was little he could do for him under the circumstances.

"We have to leave him," he hissed, slowing.

"No. You can carry him, Dany. Please. We have to save him."

Dany's chest was heaving from the effort of the run, but the shooting had died down now that there were no obvious targets. A few volleys of automatic rifle fire seared through the brush to their left, but nothing came close, and Dany decided to chance returning to where Francis was pointing.

When they reached Yavan, Dany swallowed hard and blinked away tears at the sight of his baby brother gasping for breath, his shirt slick with blood.

"Ak...ach...ungh," Yavan managed, his voice a rasp, his eyes disbelieving and glazed with pain.

"Shhh," Dany said, and turned Yavan over so he could see the wound. A bullet had clipped him in the upper shoulder and exited below his collarbone, taking a chunk of flesh the size of a golf ball with it. Dany didn't know how to help his brother, but Francis ripped off his shirt and pushed it against Yavan's chest.

"Hold that there. Can you pick him up, Dany?"

Dany nodded and lifted his brother, surprised at how little he weighed. Yavan coughed and moaned in pain, but held the rolled-up shirt against his wound. Dany fixed Francis with a determined expression.

"Follow me, Francis. And no matter what happens, keep going until you're with Father."

"What do you mean, no matter what? We'll make it. They stopped shooting."

"We still need to get past the other guards, Francis. They'll be alert. They have radios."

Francis's eyes widened and his shoulders slumped as he realized what they were up against. Tears rolled down his cheeks and a strangled sob escaped from his throat. Dany exhaled impatiently and peered into the brush ahead. "There's no going back. We have to keep moving or they'll get us."

Francis nodded, his chest shuddering as he cried, and Dany took off at a trot, his brother's body in his arms making it harder to push through the brush. He tried not to make noise as he cleared a trail for Francis to follow, but to his ear it sounded like a herd of wildebeest at a full run.

Twenty minutes later they reached the edge of the trees where the guards were stationed. Both of them crouched in the grass, watching the area for signs of life. After several moments Dany pointed to his right, where three armed men were sweeping the area with their rifles – which thankfully didn't have scopes.

Francis looked up at him and whispered softly, "What are we going to do?"

"I think we have to crawl across this field and hope the grass hides us."

"Can't we wait until it gets dark or something?"

Dany shook his head. "Not with Yavan like this. Besides, they'll probably bring more men and do a search of the area if we haven't shown soon. We'd never make it."

Francis absorbed his older brother's words and nodded, his eyes moist and his lower lip quivering. "I'm scared, Dany."

Dany didn't answer for a long beat. "I am too. I…I love you, Francis. And, Yavan, I love you too."

Yavan had lost consciousness somewhere on the trek and had begun shivering as shock fully set in. Dany wiped sweat from his brother's brow and inspected the ugly wound, and then replaced the sodden rag of a shirt and took a deep breath.

"Come on," he said, his voice quavering. "Help me put Yavan on my back. Then I'll crawl ahead. You follow after a few minutes."

"Why wait?"

"In case they see me."

Dany was halfway across the field when Francis screamed from behind him, a high-pitched shriek of pure terror. Dany stopped and listened, his ears straining, and then a single pistol shot rang out. A flock of birds rose into the air from the trees, a dark cloud of fast-moving wings drifting up into the heavens, and then the field fell silent. Dany gritted his teeth and pushed himself to continue, pulling himself along on his belly, and was almost to the next tree line when a voice called out from behind him.

"There he is!"

The stutter of AK-47s from only a few yards away was deafening, and Dany barely had time to offer his God a prayer when the rounds found home, ending his suffering and that of his brother in a burst of lead.

CHAPTER 8

Nairobi, Kenya

The situation room at the Nairobi headquarters of the Diplomatic Police was three-quarters full, and the expressions of the men gathered in front of a bank of monitors were grim. Superintendent Abdi of the Kenya Police Force fidgeted with the two-way radio in his hand; his second-in-command, Femi, stood patiently by his side.

It was late morning, and a call had come in to the pharmaceutical company three hours earlier, delivering instructions on how to hand off the ransom for the pharmaceutical executives and their hostess. The operative who'd been manning the phone with the Algernon Pharmaceuticals representative had attempted to stall for time, but the kidnappers were having none of it, somehow having discovered that the money had been delivered the night before. Abdi theorized that they'd had someone watching the drug company's headquarters and had seen the armored truck pull into the underground parking garage and made the connection – assuming they didn't have someone on the inside feeding them information, which was always a possibility.

The caller had been calm and reasoned in his instructions, but had refused to negotiate on the exchange. The prisoners would be released in an undisclosed location, unharmed, once the ransom had been paid. There was no other deal being offered, and the kidnappers had refused to entertain a simultaneous swap. The police operative had pointed out that they had no way of knowing that the kidnappers would actually release the hostages, to which the caller had agreed, but refused to offer any assurances beyond cutting off body parts and sending them to the company.

Painted into a corner, Algernon had agreed to send the money and had shipped it to police headquarters shortly thereafter. Abdi had been waiting, and switched out the cash for high-quality counterfeit bills seized in a raid two months earlier, and planted a tracking device in the delivery bag, sewn into one of the seams and virtually undetectable.

The counterfeits were a risk, but not a big one – they would fool anyone but a bank, and by the time the kidnappers realized they'd been tricked, the hostages would be free. Abdi saw no reason to allow four million dollars to fall into the hands of criminals when it could be safeguarded by him, and it wasn't like the kidnappers could contact the papers to complain they'd been swindled. If all went according to plan, he'd walk away from the day considerably richer, and the kidnappers would be brought to justice. Abdi had an armed team awaiting his command to descend on the kidnappers and free the hostages if it looked like anything was going wrong, so he'd taken out insurance to make sure they wound up safe. He hoped it wouldn't come to sending the team in, because in that case he'd have to return the money, but he thought he understood the kidnapping mindset well enough not to have to. First and foremost, kidnappers were businessmen who wanted to exchange their asset – the hostages – for a big payday. They likely didn't want to hold onto the prisoners any longer than necessary and wouldn't butcher them and bring down a nationwide manhunt on their heads. They wanted money, not attention, and had made no other demands than to receive the cash that morning.

An unmarked sedan had left headquarters a half hour earlier, with a plainclothes police officer acting as the drop agent. The kidnappers had instructed the company to issue the representative with a communications device so final instructions could be transmitted from the head office to the representative when the kidnappers called back. They were now waiting for the call as the vehicle made a lazy navigation of the downtown streets.

"Call coming in," the technician at the monitor bank said.

"Put it on speaker. It's muted, right?"

"Mic is disabled. They won't hear us," the tech confirmed, and flipped a switch. A moment later, the operative at the drug company's voice answered.

"Yes?"

"There's a stone fountain in Ibori park. Across from it are two garbage bins. Leave the money in the one with a blue paint swatch near the base, and clear the area. You have ten minutes."

"I... It's going to take longer than that. We're not anywhere near there."

"My instructions were for you to be prepared to make a drop downtown. You have ten minutes."

The call disconnected, and another technician shook his head. "Too short to get a trace."

"Damn," Abdi muttered, and then held a radio mic to his lips and murmured instructions to the sedan. When he was finished, he looked over at the first tech. "The tracking signal is coming in clearly?"

"Yes, sir," the tech said, tapping a screen where a blinking red dot was drifting across a map of downtown.

Abdi turned to Femi. "Move the men into position. I want the vans a couple of blocks away. But no sirens, and maintain radio silence. We don't want any attention."

"Will do, sir," Femi said, and raised a cell phone to his ear. Twenty hardened officers in full riot gear, armed to the teeth, were crammed into a pair of unmarked delivery vans, waiting for the go-ahead.

"They're not to make any moves unless I give the order. I just want them ready."

"Of course, sir. I'll make it clear," Femi said, and then walked away several steps so he could relay the instructions in relative peace.

"Will he make it in ten?" one of the attendees asked.

"Maybe a few more minutes, but the kidnappers will wait," Abdi said, his voice assured. "They're not going to walk away from that kind of money to prove a point."

Nairobi saw its fair share of kidnappings, and Abdi was an old hand at them. He knew the criminal mind well. All of the tight deadlines and inflexible instructions had been to establish control, but in the end, the kidnappers wanted to get paid and move on to their next scheme. Hostages were almost never killed because killing them was bad business – a dead hostage was of no value and would limit the success of future kidnappings; if the parties being extorted had no reason to believe they would get their loved ones back, they were less likely to pay.

At least, Abdi hoped that would be the case in this instance. The ransom was larger than most, with the usual demand being a hundred thousand dollars or so for a safe return. He guessed that the kidnappers had done their homework and figured a rich foreign drug company wouldn't be price sensitive – which was correct. What they probably didn't know was that the woman they'd snatched was the family of a member of the diplomatic corps. If they'd known, they would probably have left her at the museum. Nobody needed the kind of heat an international incident would bring. A nice, tidy ransom from a pharmaceutical concern, nobody would notify the press, and the abduction would go unsolved, if Abdi's track record was any indication. It was a nearly perfect crime, and Abdi was reassured that the transaction had thus far been professionally managed. It made him confident they would soon have the hostages returned, safe and sound, and he would have safeguarded his retirement.

His radio crackled and he turned up the volume. "I'm at the park. Damn. There's a uniform patrolling the area."

"Stand by," Abdi said, and turned to his men. "Get dispatch on the horn and pull whoever that is. I can't believe we didn't already do it."

"We didn't know the location until a few minutes ago," the second tech said as he reached for a handset.

"Just do it. I'm uninterested in excuses."

Tense seconds ticked by as the tech spoke to the desk. After a small eternity the radio crackled again. "He's leaving."

"Wait until he's out of sight and make the drop," Abdi ordered.

"Roger that."

Tension hung in the situation room while the radio hissed faint white noise, and then the voice came back. "It's done."

"Get out of there," Abdi barked.

"I'm getting into the car. I'll be out of the area shortly."

"Good job."

Abdi watched the blinking dot: it remained stationary for twenty minutes and then began slowly moving southwest. He looked to the men gathered around him and nodded. "Game on," he said in a low voice, and pressed closer to the screen.

"Looks like he's on foot," the technician said. "Too slow to be anything else."

Abdi was about to respond when the rate of movement increased. He leaned forward and stared intently at the screen. "Looks like he's got wheels now."

The tech nodded.

Abdi leaned into Femi and spoke in a low voice. "Get the chopper on top of him, but stay back a few blocks and keep high. See if we can get a visual, but don't spook him."

Femi relayed the message, and they shifted their attention to a video feed from a camera mounted on the underside of the helicopter. Rooftops blurred by as the helo picked up speed, and then it slowed as it neared the kidnappers' vehicle. The technician studied the image for a moment and then tapped it with his index finger and sat back.

"It's got to be that black van," he said.

"Run the plate," Abdi ordered. "Can we zoom in and capture it?"

The technician smiled. "Stand by."

The van grew in the screen until they could make out the numbers. The tech froze the frame and did a screen capture, and Femi called it in as the image returned to live.

"Looks like he's slowing down," one of the men said.

Another nodded. "He's heading into that industrial area by the river."

"Get the strike force moving. Just in case," Abdi ordered.

They watched as the van wended through the narrowing streets and finally pulled to a stop in an alley framed by warehouses, beneath a tarp overhang that blocked their aerial view.

"Damn," Abdi whispered.

"Now what?" Femi asked.

"Now we wait to see if they release the hostages."

"The strike team will be in the area within ten minutes," the second technician reported.

"Have them wait on the perimeter of the district," Abdi instructed. "We don't want them seen in case the kidnappers have lookouts in position."

Minutes dragged on, but nothing happened. Femi exchanged a glance with his boss. "You think they have the hostages in the warehouse?"

"Seems likely, doesn't it? Otherwise why go there?"

"What if they don't?"

Abdi frowned in annoyance. "This isn't the CIA we're dealing with. It's a gang of scum. There's a limit to their resources. You know how they operate. They're probably counting the money, and they'll release them shortly."

An hour later, everyone's patience had been exhausted. The van hadn't reappeared, and there had been no sign of anyone going in or out of the building. Abdi hated to order the strike team in, but he didn't see any way around it. Too much time had gone by. Something was wrong.

"Get the team in there. No shooting unless they absolutely have to," Abdi ordered. One of the technicians had pulled up a blueprint of the warehouse from the city planning department, so they knew there were only two exits – one on the alley and one on the street that ran parallel to it.

"No sign of lookouts on the roof," Femi said. "That's a plus."

"I don't like it. It's too quiet," Abdi muttered, watching the helicopter feed.

The two delivery vans full of police commandos turned onto the frontage street, and one cut a corner and made its way to the alley. The other van disgorged six men, who ran to another entry point to the alley, putting the kidnap van into a pincer, with both ends of the alley blocked. The first van waited until the men were in position, and then made the turn and crept down the narrow lane toward the warehouse.

Abdi's radio crackled. "We're closing on the van," a voice reported.

"We have you on visual," Abdi replied, the tension in his tone obvious.

The room collectively held its breath as the officers converged on the warehouse as those on the main street approached the front entrance from down the block, where the delivery van had blocked off the street. The onscreen image vibrated in spite of the stabilization system as the helicopter's blades beat the air, and the technician slowly zoomed out so they could better see the entire area.

The delivery van in the alley exploded in a ball of orange flame, followed nearly instantly by a rapid series of explosions from both sides of the warehouse. Abdi watched in horror as his men flew through the air like ants smitten by the hand of an angry god. Clouds of black smoke obscured the helicopter camera as more blasts rocked the street.

The radio shrieked to life and a panicked voice emanated from the speaker, its words hard to make out over the sound of automatic rifle fire. "We're taking fire. RPGs and hand grenades. Half the men are dead—"

Another big explosion from the front of the warehouse, and the transmission abruptly ended. Abdi swallowed hard as only four of the twenty officers attempted to retreat, firing at the warehouse as they went, and were cut down by a hail of bullets from the building.

Abdi turned to Femi and screamed at him, "Get everything we have over there. Cordon it off. Call in the army. I don't want a mosquito to be able to make it out!"

Femi was dialing a number when a smoke trail appeared on the helicopter video feed; a moment later the screen went to static. The men looked at each other in horror. The technician tapped some keys and then shook his head.

"We lost them. Looked like a rocket in that last frame."

Abdi depressed the transmit button on the radio and demanded an update, but when he released it, only a faint hum of dead air answered, the operation having suddenly turned catastrophic in the blink of an eye.

When air support arrived ten minutes later, the scene was one of a war zone. The warehouse was engulfed in flames, and the wreckage of the helicopter was burning in the street, which was littered with the corpses of Abdi's elite fighting force and the smoldering skeletons of the vans that had carried the men to their death.

CHAPTER 9

Nairobi, Kenya

Adami hung up the telephone in his office at a transport company he owned on the outskirts of the city and glared at Yaro, his eyes hard as flint.

"It was counterfeit. Tamu confirmed it with a bank test. And of course the bag was equipped with a tracking chip." The crime boss shook his head. "They must believe they're dealing with amateurs."

"You think it was the company or the police?"

"Does it matter?" Adami asked, pushing himself to his feet and pacing the length of the office.

"What do we do now?" Yaro asked.

"Tamu took out the attack force. That's going to make it difficult to move around the city for a while. There will be checkpoints. Roadblocks."

"Which we'll know the locations of in advance," Yaro said with a grin.

"Of course." Adami paid a network of informants in the police, army, and the ministries, and would know of any countermeasures before the top brass did. He'd gotten tipped that the police would be involved in the drop, which had enabled him to be ready for them, although he took no satisfaction from the carnage that had ensued. Adami tried to keep his activities under the radar, and a sensational battle like the one that had just played out would bring unwelcome attention, even if the police kept it largely out of the news, which he suspected would be the case. "But I think it's best that we move the prisoners out of the city. We can't risk someone talking or stumbling across them."

Yaro regarded his father. "Do you have anywhere special in mind?"

"I do," Adami said, and mentioned a location.

Yaro nodded once. "They'll never find them there."

Adami smiled. "That's the idea."

"I'll tell Tamu. But how are we going to deal with the drug company?"

Adami thought for a moment. "We'll double the ransom. And let them know that we're doing so because of a double-cross on the first try. They need to know that we figured out that the money was counterfeit – that they brought this on themselves. That should keep them from getting bright ideas the next go-around."

Yaro grinned at the idea of eight million dollars. "You think they'll pay?"

"Of course. They probably have insurance that will cover it, so it's not their money anyway. But even if they don't, they'll still have to – otherwise nobody will ever work for them again. Not if they know the company will abandon them in the event of trouble." Adami returned his son's grin. "But the next time, we need to be more careful and expect them to try to screw us. We'll arrange for the drop to take place outside of town – someplace desolate, where our men can disappear without a trace."

"Are we going to let the hostages go?"

Adami stopped walking and looked thoughtful. "I don't see any reason not to. We gain nothing by killing them. They'll have served their purpose."

"It's not a good sign that they tried to pawn off counterfeit bills to us."

Adami frowned. "I'm not convinced that was the company. They have no reason to take such a risk with their employees – if we killed the hostages because of that, it would be a nightmare for them." Adami checked his watch. "No, that feels more like someone here trying to be clever. Someone who thinks he can pull a fast one without getting caught."

"The damned police, then."

Adami nodded. "It's to be expected. I don't blame them. I would have done the same thing. Let's just hope they continue underestimating us. It will make our job a lot easier." Adami felt in his shirt pocket for his phone and checked the notepad, which was filled with reminders to himself. "Have Tamu take the scanning device into the field. I expect they'll try to use a tracking chip in the next drop, too. But this time, rather than using it to lure them into a trap, I want to end the trail at the drop point."

"And the money?"

"We'll ensure that the location is remote enough to give us time to check the bills. If they try to double-cross us again, we'll send pieces of their executives to the home office and notify the press of what's going on. If keeping this quiet doesn't work in our favor, we can turn it into a media circus to put pressure on the company." Adami frowned again. "One way or another, they will pay."

Yaro stood, and Adami eyed him with a mixture of pride and concern. "You're going to have to stop dressing like a street hustler if you want the men to respect you, Yaro. That's fine if you're a pimp or a dealer, but as a boss you need to present a more serious image."

Yaro scowled and looked down at his red T-shirt and expensive jeans. "What's wrong with this?"

Adami pulled a wad of high-denomination bills from his pocket and thumbed off a fistful. "Here. Get yourself three or four suits. Use Mogambu. He'll custom tailor them for you."

"I don't like suits."

Adami nodded as though sympathizing. "Did I miss where I asked what you liked?"

Yaro swallowed hard at the icy calm of his father's tone and walked over to accept the money. Adami handed the cash to him and patted his cheek. "You're a man now. Stop dressing like a pimp. Leave that to your subordinates."

"Understood," Yaro said, doing his best to hide his resentment at being scolded like a schoolboy.

Adami's voice hardened and his eyes narrowed. "Son, I have limited patience, and if you're not willing to do whatever it takes to become a leader, there are many who would kill for the chance. I'd prefer that you grow into the position, but I won't tolerate disobedience or attitude. Am I clear?"

"Yes," Yaro said softly, and met his father's gaze without flinching. "Is there anything else?"

Adami held his stare for several moments and then shook his head. "No. Tell Tamu to prepare for at least a week in the rough and to outfit his men accordingly. He's to tell no one where he's going. I want him ready to leave within the hour." He gestured at the phone. "I'll make some calls and find out what route will be best to take out of the city. In the meantime, make sure he understands what he is to do."

Adami watched his son depart, and then walked to the window to look out at the Nairobi skyline, his beefy countenance troubled. He hoped he hadn't made a mistake with Yaro, expected too much from him. But the boy was twenty, and by his age Adami had already been running a street gang and building his empire. Either Yaro would adapt or he'd be cut out of the business. There could be no third option. How he handled this episode would tell Adami much about Yaro's chances.

If he could hack it, fine. If not, he'd ship him off to France, where he could live with his mother and collect an allowance, chasing models and amounting to nothing, but at least not a liability one of Adami's competitors could grab and use for leverage.

He took his seat and thumbed his contact list onto his phone screen, and then began making calls that would clear his lieutenant's journey into the bush, well away from any search efforts the Kenyan police could mount; any such efforts would be as wasted as the attempt on the warehouse had been.

CHAPTER 10

Mokombe River region, Democratic Republic of Congo

Mutati rode in the passenger seat of the old Toyota Land Cruiser as it bounced along the dirt road to a village halfway between the vaccination clinic and Dira's hamlet. Two heavily modified ambulances brought up the rear along with a split-axle military truck with a green cloth covering draped over the bed. Mutati's driver was a middle-aged man with the features of a hawk, his chocolate skin scarred from childhood acne and one cheek puckered from an old injury that to Mutati looked like a knife scar.

It had been an ugly few days, with more of the villagers along the river complaining of worsening symptoms and a climbing death toll. Mutati had done what he could to reassure those who had shown up for whatever assistance he could muster, but his powerlessness had shown in his eyes, and they had left empty-handed, often to watch their loved ones suffer and die.

Help had arrived that morning in the form of the caravan, and Mutati had agreed to accompany the team to the villages so they could clean up the mess. The driver, Afua, had shown Mutati a satchel stuffed with francs to be distributed to the survivors, with a promise of more to follow. Mutati had nodded, but his distaste had shown, and Afua had climbed behind the wheel and shrugged.

"Best we can do," he'd said.

"Won't bring anyone's kids back," Mutati had observed.

"I know. But it's what we have to offer."

The drive had been hot and uncomfortable. The SUV's suspension was on its last legs, and the ride over the ruts jounced only slightly less than a mechanical bull. Mutati gritted his teeth the entire way and exhaled in relief when the thatched roofs of the first huts appeared after they'd rounded the last bend.

The procession rolled to a stop in a cloud of dust, and Mutati and Afua climbed from the Toyota. A wizened man wearing a stained orange button-up dress shirt and a pair of ragged shorts approached, his expression sour. He narrowed his eyes at Afua distrustfully and shook his head before turning to Mutati.

"It's bad," he said. "We've lost nine so far, and there's six more that don't look like they're going to make it."

"Where are the dead?" Afua asked.

"That's all you care about?" the man demanded. "What about the living? The ones still throwing up blood and wasting away?"

Mutati stepped between them. "I brought help. These men are from a big health concern. They'll take the sick, as well as those who passed. Every family who lost someone will get compensated."

The man nodded slowly. "Compensated," he repeated. "Four of the dead were children. How am I supposed to explain to their mothers what the price for their child's life is?"

"You don't have to. I'll talk to them," Afua said, his voice indicating that he'd had that discussion many times before. "Show us to the dead, and we'll deal with the sick after."

The old man led Afua to a lean-to by the river, where bodies were stacked like cordwood. Their appendages had swollen in the heat, and a cloud of flies darkened the air around them. Afua eyed the corpses for a long moment and then made his way to the ambulances and held a radio to his lips.

Four men emerged from the back of the first ambulance and made short work of pulling on yellow hazmat suits. When they were fully enclosed, they walked like spacemen to the improvised mortuary, followed by the truck, which could only make it halfway before its wheels began sinking into the soft earth. It stopped on the spongy soil, and the men continued to the improvised shelter and dragged out the nearest body – a young boy. One took the arms, the other the legs, and they carted the corpse to the rear of the truck and tossed it into the cargo bed with the casual ease of men practiced at their job.

Mutati didn't wait to see any more and instead accompanied Afua and the village elder to what served as the village square, where a host of women were waiting, some crying, all staring at the new arrivals with fearful, long-suffering expressions. Afua stepped into the midst of the women and began speaking well-rehearsed words, his tone reasonable. Mutati tuned out, uninterested in whatever he had to say, sickened by the extent of the casualties and his role in them.

When Afua finished, some of the women turned away, crying, clearly repulsed and disgusted, while others pressed nearer, looking expectant. Afua reached into the satchel and addressed the elder, and then counted out fifteen bundles of currency and handed them to him, making a show of it.

Mutati moved back to the Land Cruiser, his stomach churning and his chest tight. Afua appeared by his side a minute later, his face a blank, his eyes unreadable.

"You think they'll stay quiet?" he asked Mutati.

"These villages don't see any strangers. Even the missionaries stay away. So who would they tell? They'll entrust their funds to the elder, who will take the community bicycle to the trading post and convert them to goods, keeping a healthy percentage for his trouble and not telling them. In a few months they'll be done mourning the dead, and life will go on as it has for thousands of years. They'll have no idea what happened. We'll blame it on the water or on a virus, like Ebola, and they'll eventually thank me for bringing help." Mutati paused. "Who did you tell them you're with? And where did you say the money came from?"

"The United Nations. Nobody seemed interested in why these are private vehicles."

Mutati sighed. "They don't know any better. You could have said you were from Mars. You'd have gotten the same reaction."

Afua looked away. "Yes. I keep forgetting that this is Africa."

Mutati studied Afua's profile. "You're local. I recognize the accent."

Afua stared at the river, as though he hadn't heard Mutati, before answering in a soft voice, "I left for a while. Not long enough, apparently."

The elder returned and regarded Mutati with knit brows. "They're asking about the pills," he said, in a low voice.

"Those had nothing to do with this," Mutati lied. "There's a problem with the river water. It's bad. All up and down this stretch. They need to take care to boil it well before they drink it."

"I told them. But some don't believe it."

Afua's lips compressed into a thin line. "Make them believe. We'll be back in a week, and there's more money where this came from. They trust you. As far as they're concerned, it's the water. End of story."

Afua palmed a thick sheaf of banknotes and slipped them to the elder, who checked over his shoulder to confirm that the women had dispersed. The money disappeared into his shorts and he nodded. "I'll do what I can."

"That's the spirit," Afua said.

The workers in hazmat suits had finished their grim chore and were carrying the sick on stretchers to the ambulances. When all had been accounted for, they removed the outfits and climbed into the cabs, where the drivers were sitting in climate-controlled comfort.

Afua and Mutati retraced their steps to the Toyota, and minutes later were bouncing back down the trail, leaving the nameless village behind. Any trace of the blight that had descended upon it was gone, and their tracks were covered. A trio of hopeful buzzards wheeling over the caravan gave the only sign of their passing, the brown wash of the river silent save for the straining engines and the crunch of tires on patches of loose gravel.

Afua glanced over at Mutati. "How many more of these do we have?"

"There are four more villages. I haven't heard from them for a couple of days, but we can expect the same results."

Afua spoke into his radio, listened as a tinny voice answered, and then turned the volume down. "We'll unload the ambulances back at your clinic. There's a bus en route for the sick and a garbage truck for the dead, which will be incinerated. We'll dump our load and then head to the next one." He paused. "You going to make it?"

"Yeah," Mutati managed. "You aren't worried about the authorities? Patrols?"

"We've covered those bases. Nothing to worry about."

Mutati rubbed his face and winced as the Toyota jolted over a particularly nasty bump. "It's just...nobody warned me this could happen."

Afua nodded. "It's unprecedented. We didn't expect it. Obviously."

Mutati grimaced and stared through the dusty windshield at the strip of copper dirt that passed for a road. His intake of breath conveyed all of the fatigue and frustration that had accumulated over the last week, and he looked like he was going to vomit. His jaw clenched and his mouth worked, as though it were an effort to choose his words, and then he closed his eyes and leaned his head back against the seat.

"Obviously."

CHAPTER 11

Nairobi, Kenya

The road from the airport was clogged with traffic, a steady stream of panel vans, wildly overloaded trucks, automobiles that would have been at home in a demolition derby, and thousands of motorcycles and bicycles darting through openings without concern for safety or the laws of physics. The air was thick with exhaust and a layer of beige smog that, combined with the pervasive red dust that coated every surface, burned Jet's nose and lungs.

The taxi driver had explained apologetically after they'd left the airport that his air conditioner had given up the ghost only that morning – an obvious lie, she suspected, but not one worth battling over. She kept her window only a quarter rolled down, willing to endure the stifling humidity of the cab rather than provide any would-be carjacker an invitation. The car crawled past a scattering of shanties with tin roofs and walls crafted from discarded wood and crates, the air tinged with an odor of rot. A dizzying array of clothes featuring every color of the rainbow hung from any available support, and impoverished shoppers shuffled along in the dirt while urchins with wild eyes and mouths stretched with laughing smiles ran between their legs.

The taxi pulled to a stop at a traffic light, and a beggar with no legs rolled himself along the line of cars in a wheelchair that looked like it had seen duty in the First World War. The driver shook his head in disapproval as a man so gaunt he looked like a cadaver brandished a grimy rag and a soda bottle half full of filthy water, offering to smear the dust on the windshield away for a tip. The driver snapped at the man in Swahili, and the window cleaner moved to the next car, shambling like a zombie in the afternoon sun.

The taxi lurched forward when the light changed, but not soon enough to avoid a symphony of outraged honks from behind it. The driver smiled at the sound and shrugged as he eyed Jet in the rearview mirror. The beggars and vagrants dodged the oncoming traffic to retreat to the safety of the muddy shoulder, and Jet had the same sense of wonder she'd had in other densely populated areas, like Thailand and Buenos Aires, where the locals seemed to navigate using a form of hive mind to avoid collisions.

The slums slowly transitioned to a skyline of high-rises as the taxi approached the downtown area, but even those seemed coated with a veneer of maroon dust that dulled their sheen in the subtropical sun. She waved away a persistent fly that had entered the car at the last light, and reminded herself to reapply a liberal spraying of insect repellant to safeguard against the disease-carrying mosquitos that called Africa home. Even though Nairobi was at an altitude where those that transmitted malaria were relatively rare, the illness wasn't unknown, and when things like dengue fever and Rift Valley fever were tossed into the mix, it was best to avoid being bitten.

Jet had the taxi drop her off at a hotel near the Israeli embassy and checked in using her new French passport, which identified her as Claire de Vauvre. The hotel, modern and clean, offered a stark contrast to the squalor she'd driven through, with air-conditioning so crisp it felt arctic against her skin. Her room was on the fourth floor, and once she'd hurriedly unpacked and rinsed off, she placed a call to the Mossad chief on the satellite phone that had been part of her kit.

Elon answered on the second ring. "Yes?"

"You were expecting a package to be delivered today?" Jet asked.

A brief pause. "Ah. Yes. I'd expected it earlier," he said, completing the simple code.

"Things ran late."

"Yes, well, they can do that." Another pause. "There's a coffee shop a block from our facility. Fine Kind Grinds. I'll be wearing a tan jacket. Fifteen minutes?"

"Perfect."

Jet hung up and did a quick web search for the shop. After orienting herself, she saw that she was only two blocks away. She inspected her reflection in the full-length bathroom mirror and nodded in approval. Lightweight black cargo pants, a long-sleeved black shirt with breast pockets, and dark brown hiking boots and an innocuous outfit. Her hair pulled back in a ponytail gave her the appearance of a university student, albeit a striking one, with her caramel complexion, high cheekbones, and emerald eyes. She slid on a pair of inexpensive sunglasses and offered her doppelganger a flash of teeth before making for the door.

The café turned out to be little more than a single-wide slot between two office buildings, with three chairs placed on the sidewalk beneath a blue canvas awning. Jet took a seat and was considering the blackboard menu at the entrance when a short, balding man in a flyweight tan dress jacket sauntered up with a smile in place.

"Claire! You haven't changed a bit," he said cheerfully.

"Clean living," Jet said, using the words she'd been instructed to answer with.

Elon looked around and his smile faded. "Follow me."

Jet stood and did as instructed, accompanying the station chief down the sidewalk until he paused at a crumbling brick storefront. A steel roll-up shutter covered in graffiti blocked the window over a barred iron door set into the dark cavity of the entry. He looked both ways down the street and then slipped a key into the jailhouse lock and swung the door inward. "I'll be right behind you," he said. Jet pushed her sunglasses onto her head and stepped into the dank passageway, and Elon relocked the door behind him and brushed past her. "This way," he whispered, and led her into the bowels of the building.

Jet trailed him into the gloom, ignoring the refuse scattered along the length of the hall and the aroma of decay, and turned a corner into a large empty storeroom. Elon crossed the floor, stepping over rubble, and stopped at an ancient steel wood-burning stove in a corner of the room, easily half the size of an economy car.

He felt along the underside of the lip and then slipped a key into a hidden slot. A loud click echoed off the brick walls, and the stove swiveled on tracks hidden beneath its base, revealing a hole. He reached down and flipped a switch, and a string of LED lamps glowed to life in the gap. Jet could make out the steel rungs of a ladder descending what looked like two stories below.

"You first," he said. "This leads to the embassy."

Jet lowered herself down the rungs without a word, and Elon followed her after pressing a button at the top of the ladder that swiveled the stove back into place. Jet waited for him in the tunnel, and he pointed down its length. "It's five minutes along this stretch. I hope you're not claustrophobic."

They walked together, the passage wide enough to accommodate them both. She could feel mild vibrations from heavy trucks on a road somewhere overhead, and eyed the concrete walls and ceiling with trepidation. After what she guessed was three hundred yards, they arrived at a heavy steel door with two industrial deadbolts. Elon unlocked them and pushed it open, and Jet saw a spiral iron staircase leading to a trapdoor twenty feet overhead.

A minute later Jet was standing in an anonymous office with a government-issue desk and racks of file cabinets. She wiped away dust from the desktop and regarded Elon. "Doesn't see much use?"

"Good guess," he said flatly. "The ambassador is waiting for us with the attaché."

Elon escorted Jet from the office and down a carpeted hall to a conference room. Inside were two men, one in his sixties, heavyset, with longish gray hair slicked back off his forehead, and the other at least a decade younger, with brown hair and steel spectacles that failed to hide the concern etched into his brow and the sleep-deprivation discoloration beneath his eyes.

The older man indicated a chair to Jet, and she sat, her face expressionless.

"You're going to help us with this situation?" the ambassador asked.

Jet lifted a brow at Elon, who remained standing by the door. "That's right. What can you tell me about it that I don't know from reading the file?" she asked.

"There's been a complication," the ambassador said. "We just heard about it. You were in the air when it happened."

"When *what* happened?" Jet asked.

Elon cleared his throat. "The local cowboys decided to try handling this on their own this morning, with disastrous results." Elon gave them a brief rundown of the botched ransom drop and finished with a sigh. "The company got a call this afternoon from the kidnappers. Needless to say, they aren't happy. They've doubled the ransom and have a whole new set of conditions they want met for the drop-off."

The younger diplomat shifted in his seat. "It couldn't have gone any worse. They didn't tell us anything until after it was over."

Jet's eyes narrowed. "You're Shimon Ahrens? The girl's father, correct?"

He nodded. "Her name's Shira. She does have a name, you know."

Jet held his stare. "Any word on the hostages?"

"The kidnappers reported that nobody was hurt," Elon cut in.

"Has anyone asked for evidence? How can the company be expected to pay, what, eight million dollars now, if there's no proof they're unharmed, or even alive?" Jet asked.

"That isn't our problem. The company isn't happy with having already lost four million due to the Kenyans' incompetence, but they're committed to seeing this through," Ahrens said. "We have an open line of communication with them. Although they're troubled at the accusation by the kidnappers that the money was counterfeit and that a tracking chip was planted in the bag. Apparently that's what set this entire disaster in motion – the realization that the money was bogus."

"What do you make of that?" Jet asked Elon.

"It could have been switched by the police. Or it could be a lie – apparently the money, genuine or fake, was incinerated in the firefight, so there's no way of knowing for sure." He hesitated. "That's just one more reason to be...skeptical...of the local authorities."

"Are there any leads on the kidnappers' identities?"

Ahrens shook his head. "No. Although based on the battle with the police, it's got to be a sophisticated organization."

"There has to be a way to track that down."

"You would think," Elon said. "But there are numerous criminal syndicates operating in Nairobi, a half dozen of which could easily pull this off. The police have assured us they're pursuing all leads; but again, all this just happened, and I have my doubts about their competence, as well as how deeply compromised they are. It seems like half the city's on the take or running a sideline of some sort. We have to assume that nothing is as it seems, and nobody's trustworthy."

"Although your liaison with the Kenyans is a good man," Ahrens interjected. "Name's Jabori. He's worked with the embassy for a long time."

"Employee?" Jet asked.

Ahrens shook his head. "No. Ex-military. Runs his own security company. But he's a fixer. Gets things done, knows where the bodies are buried, and is willing to do what it takes to make things happen."

"So an outsider," Jet said. "Another unknown."

"I just told you he's not an unknown. I trust him," Ahrens said. "As much as I trust anyone here."

They discussed the attack and the fallout until it was obvious Jet had exhausted any new information they might have, and the meeting adjourned. The ambassador left, and Ahrens approached her, his eyes hunted. His hand locked onto her arm, his grip uncomfortably intense. "Please get Shira back. She's my only child. I...I love her more than life itself," he said, his voice cracking on the last words.

"Doesn't sound like I'm going to be very involved if the drug company's going to pay. But I'll keep an eye on everyone and ensure they behave." She paused. "I'm sorry you're having to go through this."

"It… I can't tell you what it's like to have your daughter taken from you."

Jet simply nodded, her pulse throbbing in her ears as she remembered exactly what it felt like with Hannah – like having her guts pulled through a meat grinder inch by painful inch.

"I'll do what I can," Jet assured him, trying to keep her words from sounding hollow.

Elon cleared his throat again. "We should probably get going. Jabori's waiting to meet you."

"Where?" Jet asked.

"At the pharmaceutical company's Nairobi complex. Management's been briefed on your arrival and that you'll be representing them in the exchange. You'll have carte blanche."

"And my equipment needs?"

"Call me with your requests, and I'll see to it."

"You have a pistol for me?"

Elon nodded. "As agreed. H&K VP9 with two extra fifteen-round magazines. A carton of fifty rounds. Easy-release belt holster and a shoulder holster."

"Excellent."

Elon looked to Ahrens. "If you'll excuse us…"

"Oh. Of course. Do what you have to do."

The Mossad station chief escorted Jet back to the dusty office and opened a file cabinet. He withdrew a black nylon backpack and handed it to her. "Exactly as you specified. The ceramic knife, gun, cartridges, magazines, holsters."

Jet spread the contents on the desk and did a quick check, and then loaded the magazines with deft fingers and slapped one into place in the pistol butt. She hefted the gun's weight with approval and then packed it into the backpack along with the rest of the items. When she was done, she slipped one of the bag's straps over her shoulder and nodded. "Perfect."

"I'll drop you off at the pharma company's offices, but that's as far as I go. There can't be any connection between you and the embassy."

"I understand."

The Algernon Pharmaceuticals building was one of the newer ones in the downtown district, all chrome and bronze-tinted glass and futuristic design. Elon stopped a block away, and Jet turned to him. "You know this Jabori?"

"Yes. We've used him on occasion. Nothing overly sensitive, though. I think Ahrens's faith in him is greater than ours."

She nodded.

He studied her profile for a few seconds and then looked back at the building. "Ask for Ben Sokoloff," Elon said. "He's the local VP who runs the place. He'll have all the logistics on when the money will arrive, the details of the kidnappers' demands, and so on."

"Ben Sokoloff," Jet repeated. "I'll call you if I need anything."

"Good luck," he said.

"Thanks."

Jet stepped from the car into the heat, which enveloped her like a sodden blanket, and walked to the building, one of dozens of pedestrians on the late afternoon sidewalk. She gave her assumed name to the guard at the reception desk, told him that she had an appointment with Ben Sokoloff, and he dutifully phoned the corporate offices.

"Someone will be down for you shortly," he said, and returned to whatever occupied his time behind the counter, apparently uninterested in the new arrival. Jet took a seat in one of the black leather chairs across from the elevator bank and waited until a tall woman in a severe navy blue suit emerged from one of them and approached Jet with a professional smile.

"Miss de Vauvre?" she asked. "This way, please. Mr. Sokoloff is waiting for you."

Sokoloff's office was expansive, occupying an area large enough to park several cars, with a view of downtown and the boulevard that stretched through it. He stood as Jet was shown in, and indicated a round exotic wood table with four chairs.

"Please. I wish I could say it's nice to meet you, but under the circumstances…" he said, offering his hand.

Jet shook it and sat down, placing her backpack beside her on the floor. "I understand." She waited until the woman had departed to continue. "So where are we? You've heard from the kidnappers?"

"That's right. Now they want eight million, or they'll start cutting off fingers and ears and sending them to us. And they want it by tomorrow."

"Can you get the money that quickly?"

He nodded once. "Yes. We've made arrangements to have another shipment flown here in the morning."

"And then what?"

"They said they'll contact us at the same time tomorrow and give us instructions. But they mentioned that we should have a prop plane on the runway, fueled up and ready to go. That leads me to believe they're going to want us to land somewhere remote and leave the money there."

"Or drop it," Jet agreed. "They didn't give you any indication of where?"

He shook his head. "No."

Sokoloff took her through everything he knew, which was a duplication of her earlier effort, but she let him talk, reading his body language and tone. It had occurred to her that the kidnapping could be an inside job, with one of the executives, like Sokoloff, feathering his nest with company funds. But after five minutes with him, she dismissed that thought — he seemed every bit as distraught about the situation as Ahrens.

When he finished, she fired off several questions she knew the answers to, and then asked about Jabori.

"I'm told I'm supposed to meet him here?" she said. "That he's our liaison with the police?"

Sokoloff nodded. "Police and military. After the attack, everyone's involved."

"Great. More bodies to trip over each other."

"Yes. We're singularly unimpressed, if unsurprised, by their performance so far. This morning was a train wreck. There was no excuse. They said that nothing could go wrong, and that our only hope was to allow them to insert a tracking chip with the money." He shook his head in frustration. "Incompetents. We should never have brought them in."

"Whose idea was that?"

He frowned. "It's company policy to involve the police. Also specified in our insurance rider."

"Hmm."

"Yes. Hmm indeed."

"What do you know about Jabori?"

"He was recommended by the embassy. That's about all."

"Was he involved in this morning's fiasco?"

"His company transported the funds to the police."

"Which brings us to the counterfeiting allegation. Could the money have been switched in transit?"

"No. The armored truck has a security camera in the cargo bay. Nobody was back there but the guards, and they never touched the container."

"Then if it was swapped, it had to be the cops," Jet said.

"Which they deny. And since everything was vaporized in the fire, it's their word against the kidnappers'."

"Seems unlikely the kidnappers would invent that, doesn't it?"

"Yes. But what good does it do us to press the police? Then they'll be working against us as well. Miss de Vauvre, Africa is a delicate ecosystem, and things don't operate here the way you might expect. There's a certain ethical...flexibility...that anyone doing business has to understand, or they get steamrollered by the system. It would do us no favors to level unprovable accusations at men with badges and guns."

Jet cocked an eyebrow. "You think they did it?"

His expression darkened. "Of course they did. Which is why this time, the only ones who will be allowed close to the ransom are you and Jabori's armored car staff. That's it."

Jet nodded. "Fine. So when do I meet him?"

"He's down the hall in one of the conference rooms. You'll be introduced as our representative, as we agreed with the embassy." He paused. "I'll admit I was expecting someone…older…to be handling something like this."

"It's a day of surprises all around, isn't it?" Jet said, allowing the hint of a smile to pull at the corners of her mouth.

"Yes, well…let's go find Jabori, shall we?"

"Lead the way."

Sokoloff gave Jet his card, with a private cell number handwritten across the back, and then led her down the corridor to a glass-walled room where a single African man sat at a conference table, sipping a bottle of water, fiddling with his cell phone. He looked up as the door opened and stood when he saw Jet.

"Jabori, this is Claire de Vauvre. Claire, Jabori Attah."

"A pleasure," Jabori said, shaking Jet's hand firmly but not so much so that he was trying to exert dominance.

"Ms. de Vauvre is handling all aspects of this matter for us, Jabori. You're to treat her as though her wishes are my own, and afford her every courtesy," Sokoloff said.

"Of course," Jabori said.

Sokoloff left, and Jet and Jabori sized each other up. Jet set her backpack down on the floor and sat at the head of the table. Jabori waited for her to make the first move, his face a blank.

"So what are we dealing with here?" Jet asked. "Were you involved in this morning's…excitement?"

"No. Not at all. One of my trucks took the money to police headquarters, and then we bowed out. If I'd been in the mix, none of this would have happened."

"Why is that?"

"Because I'm not a greedy moron who thinks he can outsmart a criminal gang that's obviously done this kind of thing before." Jabori paused. "The police tried to pull a fast one but underestimated their opponent, and several dozen good men paid the price. But nobody will get fired or even disciplined. The genius who decided to send in a combat battalion will probably get a medal and a promotion." He shook his head in disgust.

"You have any thoughts about who could have pulled this off?" Jet asked.

"Oh, sure. Plenty. But all of them are untouchable. So what good does it do to speculate?"

"Humor me."

Jabori sat back and his eyes flitted to the ceiling. "Ms. de Vauvre, a number of criminal gangs operate in Nairobi, mostly with impunity due to bribery or extortion. You should be warned – anyone capable of taking on the best the police have and flattening them is also capable of making someone who is asking too many of the wrong kinds of questions disappear. It happens every day. The...veneer of civility is...frail. We like to appear to have entered a new era, but the old ways are still with us, and they're not pretty. Going down that road leads nowhere good."

"You have a particular group in mind?" Jet asked, ignoring his warning.

"I've... There are rumors circulating. Just that, mind you. Nothing definite. But yes, several are rumored to be expecting big scores soon." He shrugged. "Which could mean anything, frankly. I fear that well is dry."

"Which gangs?"

"One is headed by a particularly nasty piece of work named Kimani, and the other by a crime lord named Kimobwa. Adami Kimobwa. But they're both virtually impossible to find unless they want to be. And both are as protected as the British crown jewels."

"Why them?"

Jabori looked away. "People talk, Ms. de Vauvre. It's a favorite pastime. There's no such thing as a secret for very long in Nairobi if you know how to listen."

"You think one of them is behind it, don't you?"

Jabori sighed. "What I think is irrelevant. As I said, they're untouchable. And to try is as certain a death as putting a gun to your head. Many have attempted to remove them over the years. None of their adversaries are around any longer, yet *they* still are." He studied her. "You won't win that battle."

"Perhaps. But there's always a way. We have twenty-four hours. Might as well at least nose around."

"If you don't wish it to be your last twenty-four, I'd advise against it. Instead, have a nice dinner, maybe a cocktail, get to bed early, and wake up to a new day."

Jet's gaze hardened. "I'm afraid I'm not being paid to hide in my room." She tapped a finger on the desk and then checked the time. "If you won't help me, that's fine. I'll see if I can find someone else. And I'll be happy to inform Sokoloff and the embassy of your reluctance to cooperate."

Jabori took another swig of his water before answering. When he did, his voice didn't sound nearly as assured as moments before. "I can see if I can learn anything this evening and call you if I do."

Jet shook her head. "Give me your number. I'll call you. My phone may be charging. I'd hate to miss you."

They both smiled at the thought, and he withdrew a business card from his pocket and set it on the table. "I probably won't have anything until at least ten. And there's a very good chance I don't learn anything at all."

She took the card and stood. "Do your best. This is too high profile now. My employers want answers, and they expect more than excuses and half measures. They want to know who is behind this – and you're either on our team or you're not. Make your choice."

Jabori watched Jet walk from the room and finished his water, his heart rate double what it had been moments before. Something about the woman's demeanor and the look in her jade eyes was more chilling than the thought of rooting out information on the deadliest crime lord in Nairobi.

CHAPTER 12

Highland Plains, Kenya

A column of camouflage-clad gunmen walked along a game trail, with the hostages in the middle of the line. Their progress had been slowed due to a recent cloudburst's obliteration of any solid footing. The mud underfoot sucked at their shoes, Shira's green slacks were stained with red mud from an earlier fall, and Gabriel's and David's trousers were ripped from encounters with sharp branches. All were sweating from the effort of the forced march, their legs trembling after hours of exertion.

Mango and ochre painted the sky as the sun sank like a crimson ember into the trees. The hills in the near distance rose gently above the brush, and a hot breeze dented the tall grass of the plain just beyond. Jaali headed up the procession, an AK-47 slung over one shoulder and a camo army cap pulled low over his brow, two dozen fighters following his lead.

Thatched roofs came into view as they hiked up a rise, and Jaali called to three of his men to accompany him into the village while the rest remained on the trail. They made their way down the winding path as the light leached from the sky, and were met by the village chief and two strapping young men gripping machetes.

"We need some provisions," Jaali said. "Vegetables, fruit, and any eggs you have." He eyed the machetes. "We'll pay."

"We don't have any to spare. There's barely enough for our families. Sorry," the chief said, his distaste for the gangster obvious.

"It wasn't a request. We need the provisions. If you won't sell them to us, we'll take them. Your call."

The chief's face hardened. "I don't know who you think you are, but—"

Jaali moved so fast his arm was a blur. He whipped his pistol from the holster and clubbed the chief in the temple with the butt, dropping him like a sack of rocks. The men with the machetes inched forward, and he trained the weapon on them. "You really want to die over some fruit and a few eggs? They must grow them stupid out here. Go gather up enough to fill two large baskets and we'll give you money. Or escalate this and bleed to death in the mud. Your choice."

The men exchanged a glance, eyed the unwavering aim of the pistol in Jaali's hand, and then the one on the right nodded. They lowered their blades as the chief groaned and felt his bleeding skull, and stepped back. Jaali nudged the chief in the ribs with his boot.

"Get this fool out of my sight before I decide I need target practice."

The chief's helpers lifted him to his feet and backed away from the gunmen, their Kalashnikovs now at the ready. The chief moaned, removed his hand from his head, and stared at the blood running from his fingers down his arm. He seemed about to say something when the larger of the machete wielders whispered to him, and he apparently thought better of it. He stumbled off, supported by the men, and Jaali holstered his weapon.

"Think they'll cause any trouble?" the gunman nearest him asked.

Jaali shook his head. "I doubt even these fools think steel's a match for lead."

The villagers returned after a considerable wait with baskets in hand. Jaali inspected their offering and tossed a few bills at them, and then instructed his men to cart the produce off. As he'd predicted, nobody made a move to stop them, and soon the group was reunited and hiking through the brush again as the night descended around them.

After three more kilometers the gloom was complete, offset by a sliver of moon that glimmered between fast-moving high clouds.

Jaali slowed as the men approached a fork in the trail, and consulted a handheld GPS unit's glowing screen. He twisted to

Gathii, his second-in-command, and called out in a stage whisper, "We should be there soon. It's a half kilometer to the left. This trail probably leads right to the lake's edge."

Gathii sniffed the air and nodded. "Let's hope we can make camp before it rains again."

"A little water never hurt anyone." Jaali made a face. "And you could use a good rinse."

The men picked up their pace, energized now that their destination was in reach. The day had been one of the longest Jaali could remember, between the battle and their escape from the city, all of the egress points clogged with police. Fortunately, Adami's contacts had paid off, and the roadblock leading north on a secondary road had been instructed by the sergeant heading it to take a break minutes before Jaali's van rolled past, its cargo area heavy with fighters and the hostages. The rest of the men had rendezvoused with him later, having fled the city, and Adami's armorer had met and outfitted them before they'd vanished into the brush.

Only two of the fighters involved in the morning's attack had been wounded, and they'd been cared for in a private clinic by a physician with a gambling problem who owed Adami his life. The crime lord had decided after news of the rout hit the airwaves to send all the others who'd participated in the battle with Jaali, lest loose lips lead the cops to Adami. It was a typical problem – jittery from adrenaline and emboldened by success, the fighters would drink to calm their nerves, and the instinct to brag could be overwhelming.

So instead of prostitutes and endless rounds of alcohol, they were rewarded with a fifteen-kilometer slog from where they'd left their vehicles at a farm in which Adami's cousin owned a stake, their backpacks heavy with bottles of Safari Rum. If any minded the duty, they didn't complain; their loyalty to the gangster was total, many having been with him since they'd been children working the slum streets.

They reached their end point, a clearing near a small lake, and Jaali signaled for the group to stop.

"We'll make camp beneath the trees, out of sight. Pitch the tents and set up a perimeter. I want the area contained within the hour." He gestured up at the night sky. "Work by moonlight. I don't want anything that could give our position away."

The men leapt into action, anxious to be done with the long day. Two gunmen watched the hostages while the rest cleared the ground inside the tree line with collapsible spades, and then drove tent stakes to keep their temporary dwellings in place.

Jaali moved to the prisoners and regarded them for several moments. Shira met his eyes.

"Can you take the cuffs off?" she asked. "It's a huge pain to try to go to the bathroom, and your men are…well, it would work better without the bracelets."

Jaali considered the request and, after looking at the surrounding brush, nodded and turned to one of the gunmen.

"Remove them. There's nowhere to go out here, and if they're stupid enough to try, we can hunt them down – or let them get eaten." He looked at Shira. "You can clean up by the lake, but only while it's dark out. During the day, everyone stays out of sight. No exceptions."

"Thank you," she said.

"It's not for any other reason than because I want to conserve my manpower. If my men have to coddle you every time nature calls, with four of you, it's a waste of their energy. There are about a hundred different ways to die if you run off, so I trust that you've got enough self-preservation instincts to stay put until your company pays the ransom and we let you go. If you test me, we'll track you, and you'll wish you'd never been born. That's not an idle threat. I wouldn't risk it unless you have a death wish."

"How long…?" Gabriel asked.

"This isn't twenty questions. Do as you're told, don't make trouble, and you'll go home in one piece. Anything else and it's on you. You've been warned."

Once their wrists were unbound, the executives and Shira rubbed their raw skin and watched the gangsters set up camp. Shira stood and looked to the guards. "I'm going down to the lake."

"Watch for crocodiles," the guard said, and the other laughed.

"And snakes," he added, teeth flashing white in the dark.

When Shira returned, the gunmen were seated a dozen yards away, their assault rifles in their laps. She sat with her back propped against a tree, and Gabriel walked over and sat beside her.

"How are you holding up?" he asked.

"I'm alive. How about you?"

He studied the guards for a moment before answering. "Fine. But we need to figure out a way to escape. We could be out here for weeks, and these animals could turn on us at any point. I'm not so worried about us – it's you who's in the most danger."

Gabriel didn't need to explain why a young, comely female might be in jeopardy in a camp filled with armed men.

"They haven't hurt us so far. I don't think we want to do anything that would set them off," she countered.

He inclined his head at where the tents were set up. The rum had been broken out, and the gunmen who'd finished pitching their tents were passing a bottle around, laughing occasionally after taking long swigs.

"Maybe. Or maybe a few of them get drunk enough to decide they'll still get paid whether you've been raped every night or not."

She frowned in the gloom. "What are you thinking? We're in the middle of nowhere. Plains over there, woodlands and scrub the way we came. Trying to get away would be suicide. We'd never make it."

Gabriel didn't look convinced. "We need weapons."

"They've got machine guns, Gabriel. You're crazy if you think we can take on twenty fighters with rifles. You'd be killed in the first minute."

"So what's your solution? Hope nobody decides to run a train on you, or use one of us for target practice?"

"They want money. If the company sends it, they'll let us go. Why complicate things?"

Gabriel frowned. "All I know is the best defense is a good offense."

"Leave me out of it. I don't want to get slaughtered." She gave a hopeless sigh. "Besides, where are you going to get a weapon, much less four of them?"

He brushed caked mud off his thigh and stood to go into the brush to relieve himself. "I'll think of something."

CHAPTER 13

Dubai, United Arab Emirates

The night was quiet outside a darkened single-story warehouse, the distant sound of traffic a dull roar from the highway. An unremarkable green sedan parked beneath a light at the far end of the parking lot, the only other car the night security guard's weathered sedan. A person stepped from the vehicle and walked slowly across the asphalt.

The figure made its way to a steel door by one of the loading docks and, after verifying he was not being watched, unlocked it with a key hanging from a lanyard around his neck and eased it open. When that attracted no attention from the guard, he slipped through the gap and into the darkened warehouse.

Inside, the man crept along the warehouse floor past stacks of crates and forklifts to a pallet of recent arrivals. He knelt, removed a penlight from his pocket, and used the light to read the address information on the shipping manifest. He looked over the crates on the top of the pile and then stopped at one, biohazard stickers prominent on each side.

The figure made his way to one of the wall racks and quickly located a pry bar, and then returned to the crates and went to work on the one that he'd singled out. He worried the end beneath one corner of the wooden lid and exerted steady pressure to avoid making any sound from a sudden jolt to the nails that sealed it. He cringed at the creak of metal on wood and then grinned when the lid worked free.

He carefully set the top on the cement floor and inspected the inside of the crate. A metal case was nestled in an envelope of foam.

He removed the top piece and was greeted by more biohazard warning stickers. Undeterred, he felt for the clasps on either side of the case and flipped them open.

Four large plastic bottles rested in cavities specially formed to accommodate them. He inspected the lids and removed one that had a small black blemish on the edge. After looking around the warehouse and listening intently, he unscrewed the top and removed a brown paper package the size of a deck of cards. This he slipped into his pocket. He resealed the bottle and, after seating it back in the case, closed the lid and snapped the clasps shut.

The crate took thirty seconds to close again, the nails in the top lining up to their holes thanks to his care in removing the lid. He stepped away, extinguished the lamp, and walked slowly back to the steel door through which he'd entered, the crepe soles of his shoes silent on the hard floor.

Once back in his car, he cranked the engine and pulled out of the lot, secure that the guard on the far side of the building would have noted nothing; he knew the man to be prone to long naps on a job where nothing had happened in the decade he'd been on duty there.

The drive into the city center took fifteen minutes, and after parking, he walked at a hurried clip to one of the storefronts, where the lights were still glowing in the hopes of attracting late customers. He glanced down the street and, seeing no one, pressed a black button at the side of the glass door. A woman looked up from her position behind a glass display case, reached beneath it, and the door buzzed like an angry hornet.

The man entered the store and made straight for the female clerk.

"I'm here for Hamid. He's expecting me."

She nodded and pointed to a door in the rear of the shop. "You remember the way?"

"Of course."

Hamid, a gnome with salt-and-pepper hair and a full beard, was seated at a black desk and smiled as the man walked into his office. "Ah, Khalil, good to see you again. What do you have for me this time?"

"A larger lot. Some exceptional finds in it, I think."

Hamid nodded and sat forward. "Good news. Let's see the goods."

Khalil removed the package and unsealed it. He'd already done so after parking, and had inspected the shipment to confirm everything that had been expected had been delivered. He dumped the uncut diamonds onto a square of black velvet and sat back with a smile of his own.

Hamid removed a loupe from his desk drawer and lifted each stone in a pair of locking jeweler's forceps, turning them slowly to catch the light. After inspecting all nine, he nodded.

"Promising. Do you mind if I use the scope?"

"Take your time."

Hamid carried the stones to a workbench and spent a half hour studying them, taking notes in neat script in a notebook about each stone. When he finished, he toted the velvet square with the diamonds back to his desk and sat slowly in his seat, his expression pensive.

"Five are average quality, nothing exceptional. Three of the remaining four will make nice finished goods in the four-carat range. But the last one...small, but a stunning blue. It could fetch a steep price if it makes it through cutting." He paused. "Did you have a price in mind?"

"I'm hoping you can give me a range."

"Do you have Kimberley documentation for them? Particularly the colored stone?"

Khalil gave Hamid a conspiratorial wink. "I'm afraid that was lost in transit." The Kimberley Process Certification Scheme was a system or certification of origin intended to prevent conflict, or "blood," diamonds, from being trafficked. As with most well-intentioned efforts, it was of questionable effect when big money was involved.

"Ah. Well, in that case, the number I give you will reflect the lack of provenance. Any of the traders I deal with will require some sort of docs, even if they are...lacking veracity."

"I understand. As always."

"The real value's in the colored. The others aren't particularly exciting. But in the interests of our relationship…perhaps…seven hundred?"

Khalil's expression fell. "It is generous, but my boss said not to come back with less than eight. He said the blue alone would fetch at least double that wholesale and, once cut and polished, would quadruple, easily."

Hamid appeared to consider Khalil's words carefully. "There are many steps between it being worth that, and shards on the cutting floor. But it's getting late, and I have a buyer tomorrow who would probably take it off my hands. So seven-fifty for the lot, and no questions asked."

"It pains me to be unable to accept that. I don't want to get fired, or worse. Maybe if I got seven seventy-five, it would be close enough so that he would be understanding."

Hamid regarded Khalil with hooded eyes. "I hate to see you in a rough spot, my friend. Very well. I will give you your number. Is payment by bank transfer tomorrow acceptable, as always?"

"Yes. I will meet you at the bank at ten if you like."

"Perfect."

Hamid scooped the stones back into the brown paper sleeve and handed it to Khalil, who resealed the tape and pocketed the bundle. He rose and offered the diamond trader a small bow.

"Till tomorrow."

Back in the car, Khalil placed a call on his cell phone. To his annoyance, the call went to voicemail. When the tone sounded, he left a brief message.

"All good. I'll be at the theater tomorrow. Probably be a quarter of an hour shy of the curtain, but what can one do? I'll pick up the tickets in the morning."

He hung up and patted the treasure in his pocket. He had just helped triple a quarter-million-dollar investment, with ten percent of the sale price sticking to him. Not a bad haul for a warehouse supervisor with a lucrative sideline of smuggled African stones.

He started the car and grinned at his reflection in the rearview mirror before signaling and pulling onto the street. His car was one of the cheapest in the district among the plethora of Mercedes and BMWs and exotics – which was how he wanted it. Let the peacocks strut, he thought. He would quietly amass a fortune while attracting no attention, and one day would simply disappear, leaving the sandstorms and the arrogance of the money class that called Dubai its home far behind.

But for now, it was home to his apartment for a simple dinner alone and then a good night's sleep before calling in sick to work so he could make his date at the bank – and pocket more than a year's salary tax-free for just a few hours of effort.

CHAPTER 14

Tel Aviv, Israel

Six executives sat around a table in the boardroom at Algernon Pharmaceuticals while the vice president of Research and Development concluded his presentation. Sid Heifetz, a heavyset man in his fifties with a florid complexion and sand-colored hair, pointed at a projection on the wall with a laser pointer and shook his head.

"As you can see, while the preliminary results were promising, the human trials were…disappointing. I'm afraid that at this point, it's back to the drawing board. Enderin X isn't safe for human consumption even at moderate dose ranges, much less at what would be a therapeutic dose."

The men were clearly unhappy with the report. Len Roth, the president, sat forward with a grim expression. "And you don't feel that this is a matter of adjusting the treatment protocol or further limiting the cohort?"

"I'm afraid not. It's…proven to be too unstable once in the bloodstream. The rodent tests didn't suffer from the same drawback, obviously, or we would never have devoted the resources we did to moving it forward."

Roth shook his head. "This obviously isn't the news we were hoping for, Sid."

"Nobody's more disappointed than I. But the results are unequivocal. It's not a solution, due to toxicity and a range of nasty side effects."

Roth pushed the hard copy of the trial results aside as though they had a noxious odor. "Very well. Is there anything you can salvage from the research?"

"We feel that it's a promising direction, and of course everything is documented; but for now, I'm going to err on the side of caution and say that it's unlikely we will get anything useful."

Roth chewed his lower lip as he considered the verdict, and then nodded. "Millions of R&D and two years down the drain. I can't believe we couldn't have seen this coming. The annual results aren't going to be pretty."

The meeting broke up, and Roth asked Sid to join him in his office before he left for the evening. They walked together, footsteps echoing in the empty hall, and Roth inclined his head toward the VP and spoke in a low voice.

"Should I ask how we were able to conduct clinical trials in such an expedited manner?"

Sid's expression was guarded when he answered. "It's probably best if we firewall that. You don't want to know."

"Are we at any risk?

"Negative. We contracted the trials out, so we're one step removed from the field. They'll deal with the fallout – although it's not going to be cheap to make it go away. There were far more–" Sid hesitated "–well…negative consequences…than we could have foreseen, so additional compensation will need to be arranged."

"Dare I ask where the trials were held?"

"It wouldn't be in your best interest to know that either."

Both men were aware that the number one petri dish in the world was Africa, where experimentation with biological and pharmaceutical agents was a thriving cottage industry, as was sourcing black-market organs. But any detail could compromise the company in the event of lawsuits, which while unlikely, given the confidentiality clauses and NDAs the trials typically required, were always a risk. If the president could say with a straight face that he had no idea what the plaintiffs were talking about, it was that deniability that would be the difference between a massive judgment against the company versus the plaintiffs going home empty-handed.

"You're probably right," Roth acknowledged, and slowed slightly.

"You're sure this won't come back to bite us?"

"No chance. We're not exposed."

They reached Roth's office and he opened the door for Sid. "It's been a hell of a week, with the kidnapping in Nairobi and now this. Doesn't seem like we can catch a break lately, does it?"

Sid didn't respond, there being nothing he could say that would be meaningful.

Roth walked to an antique globe and lifted the upper half, which swung open on hidden hinges to reveal a collection of bottles inside. "Scotch?"

Sid nodded. "I could use one."

"Then I'll make it a double for both of us."

Roth poured three fingers of single malt into two tumblers and handed one to Sid, who took it gratefully and sat on a chocolate leather couch by one of the corner office's windows. Roth held his glass aloft in a bittersweet toast, and the men swallowed the smoky liquid in silence. The results of the trials had delivered a body blow to the company's product development and its future profitability.

"So where do we go from here?" Roth asked after a long pause.

"As you know, we have two other potential agents we're working on for the same protocol. We'll switch to the most promising and see if we can pull a rabbit out of the hat. The preliminaries on one of them looks like it might be viable, at least in the initial tests."

Roth nodded. "I don't need to tell you that we can't afford anything like what you just presented. Even in the world's armpits, that sort of thing is bound to be noticed eventually."

Sid studied the Scotch in his glass as though the amber nectar held some secret, and then nodded and swallowed the last of it in a single gulp. He savored the familiar burn in his throat that spread warmth through his chest, and nodded.

"I know."

CHAPTER 15

Nairobi, Kenya

Jet phoned Jabori at ten p.m. sharp. He sounded harried when he answered, and she could hear house music blaring in the background.

"Well?" she asked.

"I've been talking to people for hours. I may have a lead, but I'm waiting to hear from a guy."

"That sounds like you don't have anything. Jabori, don't try to run out the clock. I was serious about what I said earlier," she warned.

"I believe you. But I can't make people talk or know things they don't."

She took a deep breath. "What have you learned?"

"Almost everyone clammed up when I began asking. Only one person had heard anything, and that's who I'm waiting on."

Jet heard someone shout in the background. "Where are you?"

"At a bar."

"What's the address? I'll meet you there."

That took Jabori by surprise. "You wouldn't feel comfortable here. It...it isn't safe."

Jet's tone grew cold. "This isn't about me feeling welcome. It's about getting answers. My BS alarm is going off the more I hear."

He drew a long intake of breath. "Have it your way," he said, and gave her an address.

"How far from downtown?"

"Fifteen minutes, tops."

"I'll be there in sixteen. Watch for me."

"I won't have to. You'll stick out."

Jet slid the H&K into the shoulder holster and pulled on a

windbreaker, and then shrugged it off, stripped off the holster, and worked the pistol into her waistband at the small of her back. She pocketed a spare magazine, slipped the sheathed ceramic blade into her left boot, and inspected herself in the mirror, twisting to confirm that her loose top adequately concealed the gun.

The taxi driver's eyes widened when she gave him the name and address of the bar, and he looked her up and down.

"You sure you have the right address?" he asked.

She opened the back door and sat. "That bad?"

"It's...not for everybody."

Jet smiled at him and pulled the door closed. "I'm not everybody."

He shrugged and put the car in gear. "I can wait outside for a minute just in case you change your mind."

Jet thought about it for a moment. "Deal."

The neighborhood degraded from the genteel area by the embassy to crumbling edifices more typical in a war zone. The driver glanced at Jet every now and again, but she ignored his interest in her, preferring to take in the surroundings. Traffic thinned until it was mostly motorcycles overloaded with entire families on one vehicle, and the air filtering through the vents began to smell of refuse and raw sewage.

Eventually the car groaned to a stop in front of a bar where a half dozen men who looked like day laborers were gathered on the sidewalk, talking and smoking, their frames skeletal beneath shirts that hung off their shoulders like scarecrows. The driver twisted to look at Jet and then the men outside before shaking his head.

"Still time to get out of here," he said.

She gave him a small smile and handed him the fare, along with a considerable tip. "Not on your life. This looks like my kind of place."

She popped the door lock and stepped from the car, closing the door with her bottom as she considered the bar entrance. A neon green shamrock glowed in the dark over the threshold, with the name of the establishment beneath it, half the letters dark from where their lights had burned out.

"Scooters," she whispered to herself, and walked toward the

entrance. The loiterers didn't say anything, which was more worrisome than if they'd made comments. Jet pushed through the door and waited as her eyes adjusted to the darkness, the dim lighting fitting the décor and the run-down look of the patrons.

Thirty stares roamed over her as she stood by the entrance, and she scanned the room for Jabori, her stomach tightening involuntarily at the animosity and tension emanating from the crowd. The handful of working girls by the bar gave her ugly looks, obviously protective of their turf. Jet ignored the glares and spotted Jabori by the pool tables at the rear of the room. He moved toward her with surprising speed and touched her arm as he leaned into her.

"This was a bad idea," he murmured.

"Did you hear from your contact?"

He nodded. "The big man's nowhere to be found, which is expected. But apparently his son is at one of the gang's clubs, shooting off his mouth and buying drinks for his boys."

"What club?"

"Next to a hotel that's a short cab ride away. Assuming we can get one here." He looked over at the bar. "Many won't come to this district. Too dangerous at night."

She nodded. "I don't know. Everyone seems so friendly."

He exerted gentle pressure on her arm. "Let's get you out of here before someone makes a move."

Jet didn't resist and allowed herself to be guided to the exit. A few of the patrons stood with sweating bottles of beer in their hands, watching them leave, their expressions openly hostile. Jabori kept his eyes on the door, and Jet followed his lead, anxious to be quit of the cesspool now that he had the information they'd been waiting for.

The cab was still outside, and Jet smiled at the driver, who looked like he was ready to bolt at a moment's notice. He looked Jabori over and reluctantly reached behind the passenger seat to unlock the rear door. Jabori held it open for Jet and exhaled loudly when he slid beside her.

"Papa Doc's," he said to the driver.

Jabori waited until they were moving, and turned to Jet. "What are you thinking you're going to do when we get there? He's going to be surrounded by his entourage. You won't be able to get within ten meters of him, much less ask him any tough questions."

Jet adjusted her top. "Let me worry about that. Give me all the details you know about him, and tell me what your contact said."

Jabori frowned. "There's nothing more to tell. He's celebrating at a bar his dad owns by one of the big casino hotels. Shooting off his mouth, buying rounds for the house, carrying on. It's not unknown for him to do so, apparently. Too many rap videos or something. He thinks he's on television half the time. The locals have a nickname for him: Lord Yaro. They don't say it to his face – it's not particularly respectful."

"How would you suggest I approach him?"

He appraised her. "He's got a reputation as a lady's man."

She nodded. "Then we'll go back to my hotel. I'll change and then head to the bar."

Jabori shook his head. "Haven't you been listening to anything I've said? This is a fool's errand."

"Maybe. Will they search me?"

Jabori's eyes narrowed. "Why? You...carrying?"

"Will they search me?" she repeated.

"For the bar? No. Maybe the casino."

"Okay, then we'll go in together. You point him out to me and make yourself scarce. I'll do the rest." She leaned forward to address the driver. "Take us back to my hotel."

Jet changed into a short black dress, the scuffed Doc Marten boots she'd worn on the plane lending the outfit an edge, and stuffed the pistol into a small purse before joining Jabori in the lobby, a double application of fragrance signaling her arrival.

The club was considerably more upscale than the previous watering hole. The crowd was young and well dressed, and the air smelled of expensive cologne, perfume, and money. Jabori pointed out a booth at the back of the large room, where six hard-looking young men were lounging with a bottle of imported vodka on the table beside an ice bucket and half full glasses. Jet excused herself and went to the restroom to inspect herself in the mirror, and when she emerged, Jabori was nowhere to be seen.

She walked to the end of the bar nearest Yaro's entourage and ordered a vodka and soda with a lime twist in a tall glass. As she waited for the bartender to bring her drink, she leaned with her back against the bar and watched the dancers on the half-full floor, allowing her eyes to stray to Yaro, who indeed looked like he'd taken his styling cues from MTV. Their eyes met and she smiled, offering a flash of white teeth, and then turned to collect her drink when the bartender set it on the granite countertop.

Jet didn't have to wait long for one of Yaro's men to approach – she'd figured that her exotic looks and obvious foreignness would arouse his interest. A tall man in his early twenties, his gold watch and expensive shirt as subtle as a Humvee, sidled up to her, his head bobbing to the thumping beat.

"How you doing?" he asked, in a pronounced but musical accent.

She cocked her head to meet his eyes. "Good."

"Long way from home?"

"You could say that."

"You in town for long?"

She nodded. "I'm staying at the hotel for a few days. Visiting a friend."

He smirked in what he must have thought was an engaging manner. "My boss wants to buy you a drink."

Jet matched his smirk. "Your boss?"

He gestured to the booth. Jet glanced over and took a small sip of her vodka.

"Are his legs broken?" she asked.

The thug's eyes flashed puzzlement, and then he smiled when he realized what she meant. "That's funny."

She held up her glass. "I already have a drink. Tell your boss that nobody likes middlemen. No offense."

Jet turned back to the bar and pretended interest in the bottles lined up in front of a long mirror. The thug returned to the booth, and she played with the lime, stabbing at it with her straw. A minute later she sensed someone beside her and looked over at Yaro watching her, a glass in hand.

"You having a good time in my place?" he asked.

She turned to face him and offered a small smile. "Your place? You own it?"

"That's right. Among other things." He nodded to her. "My name's Yaro."

Jet pushed her glass to the side. "I'm Isabelle."

His eyebrows rose. "French?"

She nodded. "That's right. Paris."

"What are you doing in Nairobi?"

Her eyes flashed like emeralds in the strobing light from the dance floor. "Right now? Waiting for someone to dance with me."

Jet took his drink from his hand, set it beside hers, and led him onto the dance floor, Yaro's group's eyes glued to them.

Three songs later they returned to the bar, and Yaro pressed closer to her as he reached for his drink. Jet matched the pressure with her hip and thigh, and clinked her glass against his.

"You here by yourself?" he asked, grazing her ear with his lip.

"With my father. He didn't want to leave me alone in Paris. Afraid I'd get into trouble." She winked at him. "I bore easily. I was hoping it would be more exciting here, but up until now it's been a yawn."

"You like to party?"

She grinned. "Depends on what you've got."

"Coke. Straight from Colombia. Uncut."

"Really?" she asked, her expression suddenly more interested.

"You have your own room?" he asked.

She shook her head. "I wish."

"Maybe we should grab a bottle and go to mine? I have a suite in the hotel."

Jet looked impressed. "A suite?"

"That's right. Only the best, you know?"

She pressed closer to him and could feel his excitement against her. "I'm game."

Yaro signaled to his group, and the same man who'd approached her walked over. Yaro said something to him in Swahili and then took Jet's hand. "Come on."

She hesitated. "Just us, right?"

"Yeah. My boys have to watch my back, but inside it's just you and me."

He led her to the table and grabbed the vodka bottle with his free hand, and then escorted her to the exit that opened onto the hotel lobby. Two of Yaro's men trailed at a discreet distance as he led her to the elevators, and Jet smiled when he nuzzled her neck while they waited for one to arrive.

The bodyguards took a second elevator, leaving them to the privacy of their ascent, and Yaro lip-locked Jet the moment the door closed. The ride to the second floor seemed to take an hour, and when the elevator slid open, she pulled away from him, grinning flirtatiously.

"Come on, Isabelle," he said, obviously anxious to get to the room.

"Lead the way," she purred, her face flushed.

The suite was huge, and he tried to kiss her again once they were inside. She pushed him away and looked around the room. "Your guys going to hang outside?"

"That's right," he said, pulling her close, alcohol heavy on his breath.

"You have some coke?" she reminded him, with a playful bat of her eyelashes.

"Yeah. Yeah, that's right," he said, as though only just remembering his offer. He crossed the room to a table by a pair of sliding glass doors, and Jet accompanied him. He set the vodka on the table and fumbled in his pocket, and she opened the sliders and stepped out onto the terrace to look over the grounds. After a few moments, she returned to him and slid the door shut.

"Where's the bathroom?" she asked.

He indicated a doorway. "In there."

Jet walked into the bedroom and found the bathroom. A minute later she was back in the front room, where Yaro was cutting out lines of powder on the glass tabletop.

He looked up as she neared, and his eyes widened at the sight of the H&K in her hand.

"What the—"

Jet clubbed him with the gun, and Yaro fell out of his chair and dropped to the marble floor. He tried to get up and Jet hit him again. He let out a high-pitched whine like a hurt puppy and then groaned and curled into a fetal position before passing out.

When he came to, his hands were lashed to the arms of the chair with the sashes from the robes she'd found in the bathroom, and one of his socks was stuffed in his mouth to silence any attempt to scream. He blinked in pain as he regained consciousness, and Jet pressed the pistol against his temple.

"Stay absolutely still, or I'll blow your head off, understand? You make a peep, you're dead."

He nodded, tears of pain streaming down his face.

"All right. I have some questions for you, Yaro, and I don't have a lot of time. When I remove your gag, you're going to answer them, or I'm going to start breaking things. Fingers, ribs, your jaw, whatever it takes." She regarded him without any emotion. "Did you know one of the most painful injuries you can have is the arch of your foot shattered? It's excruciating, and you never walk normally again. Want me to demonstrate?"

Another head shake. She leaned over and retrieved the knife from her boot, and then unsheathed the blade. "If that doesn't work, I start cutting. Guess what gets hacked off first?" Jet tapped the knife. "It'll take a while for you to bleed out." She looked to him. "Do you believe me, Yaro?"

He nodded.

"All right," she said. "Your gang kidnapped some important people. I need to know where you're keeping them."

A knock at the door interrupted them. She swung around to face it, and a voice called out in Swahili. Jet was turning back to Yaro when he threw himself sideways, tipping the chair over and landing with a crash on the floor. His foot caught the table leg, and the vodka bottle fell and shattered against the marble.

An instant later the door burst open and the bodyguards filled the doorway with their guns pointed into the room. She dove for the floor as she brought her pistol up, and was firing as fast as she could when she landed behind Yaro, using his body for cover.

The bodyguards blasted at Jet. Slugs ricocheted off the floor near her head, and two rounds thumped into Yaro. She squeezed off three more shots in quick succession and knocked one of the shooters back into the hall with a strangled scream. The other fired blind from behind the cover of the wall, and Jet aimed to the right of the opening and stitched the Sheetrock with five rounds.

The shooting stopped, and she leapt to her feet and moved toward the hall, leading with the pistol. A quick look told her both shooters were dead, their sightless eyes staring at the ceiling, their bodies in spreading lakes of blood. She slammed the door closed and made for Yaro, who was struggling for breath, crimson gushing from a chest wound with every attempt. A ruby stain was spreading from another hole in his abdomen.

Jet muttered a curse and ran to the balcony door. She slipped the pistol into her purse, threw the glass door open, and stepped out onto the terrace, painfully aware that she only had seconds before the remainder of Yaro's entourage showed up. She swung her legs over the balcony and lowered her body until her feet were hanging a half story above the lawn, and then released her handhold and dropped to the grass, tucking and rolling when she landed. She was up in an instant and moving through the shadows at a run when the first cries sounded from the room, and had vanished from view by the time the first shots echoed off the walls, rounds striking harmlessly behind her as she disappeared into the Nairobi night.

CHAPTER 16

Tel Aviv, Israel

The director reached for the telephone in the secure room in the basement of Mossad headquarters. The voice that spoke was well known to him – one of the top brass of the American NSA, Leonard Teppit.

"I'm afraid I don't have good news," Teppit began.

"I intuited that when you asked for a voice call," the director replied.

"There was a post to 4Channel with a Wikileaks-style data dump of a bunch of your diplomatic correspondence. We took it down as soon as we were alerted, but there's no telling how many saw it."

The director sighed. "How long was it up?"

"At least…thirty-six hours. It's not positive."

"No. That's a long time. We have to assume everyone and their brother saw it."

"Yes. I wanted to let you know you have a leak."

"Any data on who posted it or from where?"

"We didn't devote any resources to that. But if you like, I can have someone shoot over everything we've got so your guys can follow it down the rabbit hole. Your problem will be that there's no telling where else it was posted, or what private groups it might be circulating in. As you know, once something's out there, you can't put the genie back in the lamp."

"I appreciate that, but we have to do what we can to limit the fallout." The director paused to light a cigarette. "We owe you one."

"A small one. Sorry the damage was done before we could address it."

"It is what it is."

"I'll send it over, along with the communications in the post."

The director hung up, his frown lines deepening as he made his way back to his office. This was the second leak in a matter of weeks, even after they'd changed the communication protocols. Someone had managed to penetrate their secure diplomatic channel and was using it to embarrass the government – and it had to stop. Contrary to what many believed, the business of government was to mislead, to prevaricate, to use deception and stealth in order to achieve its ends. If it was going to be obvious that they were lying every time they moved their lips, his masters would be restricted to the truth – an intolerable state of affairs.

When he reached his office, he stopped at his assistant's desk and growled at him.

"Meeting in twenty minutes in conference room C. I want all the section chiefs there. Make it happen."

CHAPTER 17

Nairobi, Kenya

Jet woke to her hotel phone shrieking like an angry bird, her legs sore from her hard landing the night before and the mad dash from the hotel grounds. Her attempt had almost gotten her killed and had achieved nothing – she knew as little as she had prior to her bungled interrogation attempt, and the kidnappers would be even more on guard now that one of their inner circle had been killed.

She blinked away sleep and checked the time: 5:00 a.m. She could see from the edges of the curtains that it was still dark outside, and she yawned as she reached for the phone.

"Yes?" she said.

"I'm sorry. I think I have the wrong room," Elon said, and hung up.

She rose, unplugged the satellite phone, and dialed the number he'd given her to memorize. He answered on the first ring.

"The café opens at six. I'll meet you there," Elon said, annoyed.

"Don't you sleep?" she asked.

"Just be there," he snapped, and the line went dead.

She stared at the phone for a moment and then switched it off and padded to the bathroom. A long shower later she felt almost human. She donned her cargo pants and long-sleeved top again, making a mental note to launder the shirt in the sink after she was done with her meeting.

A salmon glow was warming the eastern horizon when she reached the café, and she ordered a cup of black coffee from a clerk who looked like she'd just awakened after a nap on the floor. Jet paid and carried the coffee out to one of the sidewalk tables, and sipped it while she waited for Elon, afraid she could guess the topic he wanted to discuss.

When he appeared, he looked like he hadn't slept since she'd last seen him. He passed her without speaking, entered the shop, and emerged carrying a cup of his own, his mouth compressed into a line.

"Let's walk," he said. Jet rose and accompanied him toward the clandestine embassy entrance, but to her surprise, they continued past it without speaking.

"What's the big rush?" she asked when they reached the end of the block.

"Last night, there was a gunfight at one of the more popular casino hotels in town. Two known gang members shot to pieces in the hall outside the most expensive suite in the place. Oh, and best of all, the son of a local gangster died from gunshot wounds on the operating table. But not before he was able to tell his father about a mysterious Caucasian woman who kidnapped him and tortured him. That ring any bells?"

Jet considered his words. "Sounds like it might be a good idea to change my makeup."

"This isn't a joke. You took a risk that might have blown the entire operation. And now the police are going to be subjecting every foreign female to additional scrutiny. You're lucky the CCTV footage isn't particularly high resolution, or you wouldn't stand a chance."

"I didn't kill him," Jet said.

"It doesn't matter. They'll try to hang it on you. This is Africa. They'll do whatever they like, and you won't have any ability to fight it."

"Assuming they determine it's me. I've seen other women who could match that description here. Granted, not a lot, but it's not like I'm the only one." She paused. "Is there an APB out on me?"

"That's what's almost more alarming – no. We picked it up on police radio chatter. But there's nothing official – at least, not yet."

She slowed. "Then what's the big deal?"

Elon took a sip of his coffee and stopped to face her. "The big deal is you've only been in town for a few hours, and you've already aroused the interest of the most powerful crime boss in Nairobi. You were involved in a firefight in a tourist area, and a man's dead. That makes you a problem, not a solution, as far as I can see."

"So…what? You going to order me to leave the country? It's a lovely spot, but say the word and I'm on the next plane out. I'll leave it to you to tell the attaché that his daughter's on her own."

"I've sent a communiqué to headquarters. I'm waiting to hear back. I can't see how they'll keep you in the field now that this has happened."

Jet did her best not to smirk as she imagined the director reading Elon's account and replying with a tersely worded missive to continue providing all possible assistance. She took a swig of her coffee and nodded. "Let me know how that plays. In the meantime, can I go back to sleep? I had a rough night."

"This isn't a game," Elon growled. "We have limited resources here – it's pretty much just me, so it's not like you're operating in Germany or something. I can't send in the cavalry to bail you out if you run into trouble, and this is trouble with a capital T."

"You think I flew halfway around the world to play? Please. I appreciate the heads-up and regret any inconvenience trying to track down the kidnappers has caused, but if you don't have anything else to add, we're done. I don't report to you. You're a facilitation channel, nothing more. I'd advise you to remember that the next time you think about calling me on the carpet and reading me the riot act."

Jet spun and walked away, leaving Elon to stare at her retreating form, mouth agape as she turned the corner, her fading footfalls the only sound on the predawn street.

Back at the hotel, she tossed and turned for several hours but was unable to get back to sleep. Resigned to officially starting her day, she moved to the bathroom and went to work on her hair with the ceramic knife, trimming the length till it was markedly shorter, the razor-sharp edge making short work of it. She studied the result in the mirror – a good start, but not enough.

She next applied eyeliner, accentuating the almond shape of her eyes, and then slathered on enough makeup that she looked like an extra in a music video. She inspected the result and nodded. With a baseball cap slightly askew, she would look like she was in her late teens, as different from the woman in the short black dress from the prior evening as it was possible to get. It wouldn't fool a direct comparison to a close-up from a CCTV camera, but it was good enough for casual scrutiny.

Jet ordered room service and switched on the television. There was a mention of a shooting at the hotel, but the account was vague and attributed it to a dispute between rival criminal gangs, with no details on the number of casualties. She switched to another channel, and it was more of the same – so someone had sanitized what was being reported; the gangster's people, she assumed.

A knock on the door signaled that her breakfast had arrived. When the bellboy left, she powered on her sat phone again, walked to the window so it could acquire a signal, and called Jabori. His voice sounded groggy when he answered.

"Yes?"

"It's me. Today's the big day for the ransom delivery. Did the money arrive?"

"We're supposed to pick it up at the airport in an hour." He hesitated. "How did it go last night?"

Jabori hadn't seen the news yet. "It was a dead end. You were right – it was impossible to get near him." She paused. "I'll be at the company offices in an hour. The call's supposed to come through this afternoon. I want to be ready when it does. Have you got a plane lined up?"

"Yes. It's all handled."

A thought occurred to her. "Do you have access to parachutes?"

"Why?" he asked.

"If they want us to drop the money instead of landing, I want to be prepared." She told him what she wanted, and he grunted.

"Let me write this down. Does it have to be that type?"

"Yes. Any skydiving outfit would have one, I'd think. They aren't uncommon. Or if you have contacts with the military – maybe one could disappear from base?"

"I'll find a way," he said. "Anything else?"

"No. I'll be at the company headquarters all day. Call me there when you have it."

"Will do."

Jet finished her breakfast and then called Ben Sokoloff at Algernon. The operator put her through, and she confirmed that she would be arriving by ten that morning and spending the day there.

"I'll arrange for an office to be made available for you," he said.

"That would be great. What time is the call supposed to come in from the kidnappers to give you the location for the drop?"

"They said sometime after noon. So we're playing a waiting game."

"The funds arrived with no issues?"

"Yes. All we need now is to know what to do with it."

"Okay. I'll see you in a bit."

"Perfect."

CHAPTER 18

Highland Plains, Kenya

Jaali's radio crackled to life, and he adjusted the volume to better hear it. Adami's distinctive voice boomed from the speaker, and he fiddled with the squelch to better make out his words.

"Are you in position?" Adami asked.

"Yes. We're ready whenever you give the word."

"Good. Call me on your satellite phone. Now."

Jaali hurried to his tent, unpacked the phone, and powered it to life. Adami answered immediately, and when he spoke, his tone was dangerously flat.

"Things have changed. Yaro's dead. He said it was someone trying to locate the hostages."

"Dead? God…Adami. I'm so sorry. He was just a kid."

"I know. I'm still trying to figure out exactly what happened."

Jaali thought for a moment. "What does that do for releasing the prisoners?"

"You're not to do so." Adami paused. "Someone's going to pay for Yaro's death. That makes it personal."

Jaali grunted. "I understand. Do you want me to…execute them once we have the money?"

"No. I want to do it. I'll film the beheadings and send the company the damned video. I've left Nairobi for now – it's too hot after the police attack, at least for a few days. I'm staying at my winter place."

Jaali swallowed hard – for Adami to leave Nairobi at such an uncomfortable time of year, things must have been crazy in the capital.

"The ransom drop will still happen today?" Jaali asked.

"Yes. We'll wait until late afternoon so our people can keep an eye on the airports and verify there's no strike force preparing to follow the plane in."

"Have you heard that there might be?"

"No. Which makes last night's attempt with Yaro so much stranger. Everything coming from the Kenyan side is that the police and army are being kept at arm's length now."

"I'll be ready, whatever action you want me to take."

"I'll keep you apprised."

Adami hung up, and Jaali frowned as he looked over at the hostages. The possibility that an unknown variable had been introduced into what should be a straightforward kidnapping troubled him. He couldn't prepare for what he didn't understand, and with Yaro dead, he wasn't sure Adami would make sound decisions.

And there was the question of how whoever had gotten to Yaro had put the pieces together and figured out Adami was behind the kidnapping in the first place. That unknown was the most troubling of all, because it meant that their supposedly foolproof scheme had at least one defect they hadn't foreseen. Which then raised the question, what other flaws did it have that they wouldn't know about until it was too late?

Jaali retraced his steps to his tent, lost in thought. Adami was right about one thing, but perhaps not in the way he thought: Yaro's death changed everything.

Gabriel inched closer to Shira, eyes on the gunmen, who seemed uninterested in them other than to sneak an occasional look at her. She turned to him and offered a smile, noting that he looked far fitter than David and Noam, who appeared to have spent their adult lives seated.

"Morning," she said.

He leaned into her and whispered, "I think I've figured out a way to escape."

She frowned. "I thought we discussed that. You're going to get us all killed."

"I don't believe they're going to let us go."

"Again, why would they keep us? What incentive do they have once they've been paid?"

"I was coming back from the lake, and I overheard the main guy talking to someone on the phone, in Swahili, which I speak. He was asking whether he should kill us after the drop."

Her intake of breath was audible. "He what?"

"You heard me."

Shira ran trembling fingers through her hair. "And what was the answer?"

"I don't know. I wasn't on the call."

"Then that might have been the field guy asking a question and being told not to."

Gabriel was quiet for a moment as they both considered the guards by the row of tents. "You want to bet your life on that possibility? Not me."

"So you'll risk everyone's necks on the off chance you can successfully get away from twenty-something heavily armed gunmen, in the middle of the African nowhere…?"

He scowled and wiped away a rivulet of sweat trickling from his hairline down his cheek. "What choice do we have? You want to wait to get killed?"

"You don't know that's what they plan to do. I keep telling you, they have no reason to do anything but let us go. If they get paid and they kill us, it ruins the model, doesn't it? Who's ever going to pay another ransom if the hostages get butchered? Nobody. So they'd be effectively ending the easiest money they ever made. And Gabriel? This obviously isn't the first time they've done this, so I'm going to guess that kidnapping is how they make their living." She shook her head. "I don't see them throwing that away for nothing."

"And if you're wrong?"

She looked away. "Did you manage to get a weapon?"

He nodded. "I sharpened a branch on a stone. Made a spear."

Shira laughed. "You're seriously thinking you can go *Lord of the Flies* against an AK and come out on the winning end? You're nuts."

"You'd be surprised what you can do if you put your mind to it."

"I'll pass on the suicide run."

Gabriel grimaced. "For it to work, I need you to create a distraction."

"For it to work, you need more than twenty gunmen to simultaneously go blind, and a helicopter to land by the lake and fly us to freedom."

He gave Shira a long, appraising look. "I thought you'd be willing to help. You seem smart."

"Too smart to take a flyer on a sharpened stick against hundreds of high-velocity rounds. No thanks."

Shira rose and walked away, leaving Gabriel to consider her departure with a sour expression. He knew what he'd heard, and while what she'd said about the kidnappers' motivations was doubtless true, he knew that in a highly charged situation, things could turn ugly quickly, and the only way to ensure survival was to be clear of the camp before they did.

CHAPTER 19

Nairobi, Kenya

Jet looked up when Sokoloff entered the office she was using, his face animated.

"The call came in. Didn't stay on it long enough to trace. But they instructed us to get the money to the airport. Once it's loaded on the plane, they'll call and tell us to take off and give us a direction."

"No drop point?"

He shook his head. "No. He said he would relay the information once we're in the air."

"How will they know when the money's loaded?"

"They gave us three hours."

Jet checked the time. That would put takeoff in the late afternoon. "So, by five? What time does it get dark?"

"Six-ish, this time of year."

She thought for a moment. "They're not making this easy, are they?"

"No. Did you expect them to?"

"Hardly."

"Did the bank agree to send someone to check the bills?" Jet had suggested spot-checking some of the banknotes before they were loaded onto the plane, to avoid a repeat of the previous debacle. Sokoloff had suggested doing so at Jabori's building, and Jet had agreed.

"Yes. They'll meet Jabori in half an hour."

She rose and shouldered her backpack. "Sounds like I better get over to his place. I don't want to let the money out of my sight from the time it leaves his facility."

Sokoloff offered his hand, and Jet shook it. "Good luck, and thanks for shepherding this," he said.

"No problem."

Jet took a taxi to Jabori's warehouse, where she was happy to see six armed guards with submachine guns in hand manning the gate. All looked hardened and were taking their job seriously, which made sense – eight million dollars was a fortune, and there was a reasonable probability that if word had leaked of its whereabouts, there could be an attack.

She showed her passport at the checkpoint and waved to Jabori, who was standing by a steel roll-up door. He didn't wave back, so she crossed the gravel yard to him.

"Getting close to the big event," she said. "You ready?"

He gave Jet a hard look. "I saw the news about a gunfight at the hotel last night."

Her expression didn't change. "Don't worry. I'm fine."

"Word on the street is that Yaro's dead."

Jet nodded. "His men shot him when they were trying to kill me."

Jabori absorbed that, as well as the calm way Jet had spoken about it. "Did you learn anything?"

"No. It was a waste of time."

"You realize that Adami isn't going to rest until he tracks you down and kills you, right?"

"He'll have to stand in a long line." She held his stare. "Did you get the gear?"

He shook his head in wonder. "You're really something else."

"Is that a yes? We don't have a lot of time."

Jabori exhaled and looked away. "Yes. It's inside," he said, motioning toward the door.

Jet followed him into the warehouse, where three identical armored vans were parked at the far end, near a four-meter-square concrete bunker with a bank-vault door. Beside the first van, a parachute harness and backpack lay on the concrete, and next to them the distinctive shape of a black ram-air elliptical parachute.

Jabori stopped by the parachute. "I figured you would want to pack it yourself."

"You figured right," Jet said, and knelt, set her backpack next to her, and inspected the chute with expert fingers. Jabori watched her for a moment and then moved to the van and walked slowly around it, checking the tires.

A voice called from the entrance, and Jabori went to meet his men, who were escorting a woman in a business suit with a briefcase in one hand. Jabori introduced himself to her and accompanied her to the bunker, where he placed his finger on a scanner by the side of the door and then heaved the thick steel slab open.

"In here," he said, and the woman followed him into the vault. Jet finished her inspection and folded the chute carefully, packing it into the knapsack before carrying it to the vault and setting it by the door. She watched as the woman held a selection of bills to the light and checked the security ribbon, watermarks, and optically variable ink. After ten minutes she'd verified twenty of the banknotes selected at random and declared them genuine. Jabori dialed Sokoloff's cell phone number and, when Sokoloff answered, put the woman on the call so she could report her findings.

When she'd finished speaking to Sokoloff, the woman departed. Jabori repacked the bills in the bundles from which they'd come and spoke to Jet in the doorway. "We'll put a tracking chip in each of the rucksacks, stitched into the ribbing, but they'll find them. They did the last time."

Jet nodded. "We expect them to. But looking for them should slow them down, which will buy me time."

"Time for what? You're seriously thinking of parachuting into the unknown to follow the money?"

"It's what I get paid to do."

"There could be a dozen of them. Or more."

"I'm not going to try to rescue the hostages. Just verify that they're safe and get released."

"Then why do you need the MP5 and the grenades?" Jabori asked. In addition to a night vision monocle, he'd sourced six hand grenades and an H&K MP5 submachine gun at her request – a small, relatively light weapon that could spray lead up to two hundred meters with acceptable accuracy.

She gave him a dark look. "In case they aren't."

Her mission had been so loosely defined by the director that she had no specific objective other than to ensure that the hostages made it out alive. She had no idea what she was going up against and wasn't planning on trying to break them out, more to track them, and if necessary, call in the military through Elon. Still, she wanted to be prepared to go on the offensive if things looked ugly, while still being able to travel light. Between the gun, six spare magazines, and the grenades and satellite phone, she could take on a battalion yet still be able to cover a lot of ground.

"Chute check out?" he asked.

She nodded. "It'll do." Jet motioned to the stacks of hundred-dollar bills. "I'll ride with the money to the airport."

"Fair enough. We're going to have all three vans leave at the same time, so on the off chance anyone's watching our movements, they won't know which is transporting the money."

"You think that's a danger?"

"I'm not taking any chances. I'm responsible for it until it's on the plane. A group that's organized enough to pull off that kidnapping, not to mention an assault against the police like yesterday's, is capable of anything."

Jet regarded Jabori with new respect. "Prudent."

"I don't plan to add another disaster to my résumé if I can help it."

"Nobody's blaming you."

"Any time your name is associated with a train wreck, even if you had nothing to do with it, you're tarnished. Nobody cares about the details. But I'm not going to have problems on my watch. If this comes apart, it'll be after you're in the air." He paused. "Which, by the way, seems crazy to me."

"Your opinion's noted," Jet said. "Where's the gear?"

"In the first van. I checked it myself. All there."

"I'll have a look."

Everything was in order, and Jet packed the night vision monocle, submachine gun, and magazines into her backpack, which was empty except for her pistol, a portable GPS unit, several liter bottles of water, and her satellite phone; her passports and most of her money were safely stowed in the hotel room safe. When everything was in the pack, she estimated it weighed at least fifty pounds, which would be tiring to haul for long distances, but no worse than she'd managed on other missions.

The ride to the airport was thankfully uneventful, and when the guards swung the van doors open, she stepped onto the tarmac with the parachute knapsack in one hand and her backpack in the other. The plane was a Cessna 208B Caravan, a single-turbine aircraft that had been outfitted for skydiving, with an ample rear area equipped with a pair of bench seats and a sliding back door, so it was perfect for dropping the two heavy duffels of money. Four of Jabori's men carted the duffels to the plane and stowed them under Jet's watchful eye, and Jabori introduced Jet to the pilot – a crusty local named Felix, with two days of stubble on his gaunt face.

"Just you and the bags?" he asked.

"That's right," Jet replied.

Felix looked up at the cloudless sky, which was already beginning to darken as the sun completed its arc across the sky. "Where we off to?"

"You'll know as soon as I do," she answered, and called Sokoloff on her satellite phone.

"We're loaded and on the runway," she said when he answered. "I need a flight plan for the pilot."

"I'll have one shortly. They're due to call in about five minutes. Give me your number."

Jet did and signed off. She returned to the plane, where Felix was talking in hushed tones with Jabori, whose gaze was roving over the nearby buildings. The guards were alert, their weapons out in the open, ready in case there was a last minute attempt to grab the cash while it was on the runway. Felix looked up at her expectantly, and she shook her head.

"How long does it take you to get into the air?" she asked.

Felix laughed. "About as long as it takes to taxi to the other end of the runway."

"You have a full tank?"

"That was the deal, wasn't it?" he shot back. "It's going to be dusk pretty soon."

"I know."

Her phone rang and she answered. Sokoloff gave her a compass heading and instructed her to leave her phone on once they were in the air. She hung up and gave Felix the numbers, and within minutes they were accelerating down the runway, the engine a roar in the cabin, the palms on either side of the tarmac swaying in a gentle breeze.

Twenty minutes later, Jet heard her sat phone screech. She raised it to her ear, and Sokoloff's voice gave her the GPS coordinates.

"You're to proceed to that location. Make one pass. There will be a signal from the ground. You're to drop the bags from no more than five hundred feet and then ascend and return to Nairobi."

She repeated the coordinates and hung up, and then worked her way forward to Felix and gave him the instructions. He entered the coordinates into the plane's GPS and nodded to her.

"That's pretty remote. We're about fifteen minutes out," he said, and checked the time. "It'll be pretty dark by then."

"They probably want to avoid being tracked by a high-altitude plane. They timed it so the sun would be down by the time we're over their location."

"I'll let you know when we're close."

Jet moved back to where her parachute and backpack sat beside the twin duffels containing the ransom. The plane hit an updraft of warm air rising from the trees below and lurched sickeningly to the left before straightening out. Jet waited until Felix had stabilized the aircraft and then entered the GPS coordinates into her handheld. She strapped the backpack containing the weapons and night vision gear to her chest. She hadn't bothered with a portable receiver for the locator chips – she understood that the kidnappers would find them and discard them, so they were purely to reassure them that they'd eliminated anything that could track them, and to delay their departure sufficiently so Jet could pick up their trail.

Minutes dragged by, and then Felix called to her. "We'll be on top of it within sixty seconds."

"Do one pass, circle around, and I'll toss the duffels."

Felix nodded and returned to the controls, shedding altitude as they neared their destination. Jet stared at the brush below, details difficult to make out in the fading light. Felix called out again as he cut their airspeed back further.

"Should be any second."

"You see anything?"

"No."

"Neither do–" Jet stopped as a white light strobed beneath them, blinking on and off until the plane had flown well past it. "You get that?"

"Yes. So now we'll do a gentle bank and drop down farther, and then it's showtime?"

"Correct."

Jet twisted the rear door handle and slid it open. Hot wind buffeted her and she gripped the bench seat for dear life as Felix began his turn. When he'd completed his course reversal, he called out over the roar of the turbine. "Twenty seconds."

"Okay."

Jet heaved the first duffel along the floor, the ninety pounds of bills unwieldy in the vibrating cabin, and when it was adjacent to the door, did the same with the second. She lowered herself onto the floor, back against the side of the bench seat, and rested the soles of her hiking boots against the bags.

"Now!" Felix yelled, and she gave the duffels a push, using all the strength in her legs. The first bag dropped into the darkness, but the second stopped short. She swore and lay flat on the floor and thrust with her legs again. After an agonizing moment her effort was rewarded, and the second bag tumbled from the fuselage.

Jet called to Felix, "Get some altitude. I saw on the handheld there are a couple of lakes about half a kilometer to the west. I'll bail there."

"That's forty-five seconds away," he cautioned.

"I only need twenty."

The plane's nose lifted, and she struggled to slip the parachute knapsack's straps over her shoulders and fasten the harnesses. She'd just locked them into place when Felix's voice rose above the din of the motor.

"We'll be over water in ten seconds."

"Altitude?"

"Twelve hundred feet."

She nodded to herself, checked her watch a final time, and called to Felix. "Safe travels, Felix. Head back to base," she said, and threw herself into the black of night.

CHAPTER 20

Wind tore at her clothes like greedy hands, and her eyes instantly began to tear from the wind. The rush of air was a roar in her ears as she counted three seconds and then pulled the rip cord. The ram-air elliptical unfurled above her with a crisp snap, and then the harness straps bit into her chest and upper thighs and her acceleration abruptly slowed.

Her hands felt for the handles that would allow her to steer her descent, and she blinked away the burn in her eyes. She heard the Cessna continuing on its way to Nairobi, and then peered down and saw the moon's reflection silvering water a hundred meters south of her. Jet pulled on the right cord and directed her descent toward a clearing near the lake edge, the lighter color of tall grass faint but obvious next to the surface.

Moments later she slowed further as the landscape rushed up to meet her, and then she was on the ground, instantly unsnapping the harnesses as the chute drifted toward the lake before coming to rest in a pile nearby. She shrugged out of the straps, quickly gathered the chute cords, and stuffed them back into the knapsack as she pulled the fabric square toward her.

A half minute later she'd jammed the chute halfway into the bag and carried it to the tree line, where she pushed it into dense brush where it wouldn't be seen during the day. She paused and got her bearings, and then slipped the backpack from her chest, withdrew the submachine gun and the handheld GPS, and reversed the straps and cinched the bag onto her back.

When the GPS had acquired a signal, Jet called up the waypoint she'd set in the plane. The lakes were graphically rendered on the map, her position a blinking cursor beside the smallest one. She zoomed in and saw that she was three-quarters of a kilometer from the drop point.

Jet chambered a round in the submachine gun and, after pulling the night vision monocle over her head, set off on a course that she estimated would take her to the drop zone after about thirty minutes of hard hiking, assuming the terrain was relatively flat. She saw that the area the kidnappers had chosen was high plain near where heavy underbrush and wooded area encroached onto the flatland, which made sense – they would want to be able to disappear into the trees with the ransom once it was in their hands, but not risk it snagging in branches far above their heads. She zoomed out on the map and looked for any outpost of civilization, but didn't see any, not even a small town. It looked like the nearest road was at least twenty kilometers away. The area was desolate, emptiness stretching for hundreds of kilometers in all directions.

She set off at a rapid clip, but soon was forced to slow as the grass gave way to more treacherous brush. Jet revised her travel estimate and settled into a moderate pace that skirted the outcroppings of rock and dense bushes. Ten minutes into her march she came across a game trail that led more or less in the direction she was going, and she followed it, eyes scanning the ground ahead, the gun in her hands giving her little comfort when she considered the plethora of threats that called Kenya home. Lions, all types of big cats, jackals, rhinoceros, elephant, Cape buffalo, not to mention an impressive array of snakes and the plentiful crocodiles that abounded anywhere water was found. While the kidnappers were the immediate concern, she'd researched enough to know that the wilds of Kenya held greater dangers than the human predators that were her quarry.

The night vision gear Jabori had sourced offered her some reassurance, but she had serious misgivings with every step farther into the brush and was already second-guessing her instinct to follow the money. She couldn't be sure that the kidnappers would have the hostages in the same place as the drop, but she figured that they would be keeping them somewhere remote, and the chances were good they'd have them close by – if for no other reason than because that was how she would have done it if she'd been in the kidnapping game.

This type of operation was Jet's least favorite, with no set plan, no strategy, and no objective other than to follow the money and hope for a break. If the Kenyans hadn't blown the prior exchange, she would have already been on a plane home; but now she was having to wing it and rely on her tradecraft and survival skills rather than research and planning – a good way to wind up dead, she knew. But she'd promised Ahrens she would do what she could to see his daughter back safely, and hiding in the hotel room wouldn't do that, so here she was slogging through the African brush with no idea what she was getting into.

Jet paused periodically to listen for any movement ahead, but heard nothing outside the thudding of her pulse in her ears and the occasional calls of night creatures in the trees. She was keenly aware that it was feeding time for many of the Highland Plain's denizens, and for some of the larger ones, she would make a tempting main course. When she didn't hear voices or the sound of boots, her fingers tightened on the grip of the MP5 and she pressed on, confident that even after an hour, between locating and jettisoning the tracking chips and presumably verifying all the money was there, she wouldn't be far behind.

When she reached the drop point, she swept the area with the submachine gun, watching for any sign of life. After five minutes of crouching motionless in the grass, she advanced toward the trees, confident that she could intuit the direction the kidnappers had gone. The empty duffels glowed in her monocle ahead of her; they'd been discarded near the brush, the seams sliced open where the tracking chips had been inserted, and she nodded to herself – they'd had to have used a scanning device to locate them with such precision, which confirmed that she wasn't dealing with amateurs likely to make stupid mistakes.

Jet scanned the underbrush by the tree line, looking for a clue to where the kidnappers might have disappeared. A hundred and eighty pounds of hundred-dollar bills was a considerable amount of weight to cart any sort of distance in the dark, requiring, she would think, some sort of trail to make the passage easier. Jet didn't have to search for long and quickly spotted a gap in the bushes where branches had been broken and the grass around it trampled flat. A closer look confirmed boot prints in the spongy ground beneath the trees, leading off into the gloom, as easy to follow as she could have wished for. She checked the time, retrieved her sat phone from the backpack, and placed a whispered call to Elon to alert him that she was in pursuit of the kidnappers, and then hung up and shut the power off, now completely on her own. What transpired from here was a wild card even she didn't dare attempt to predict.

CHAPTER 21

Tel Aviv, Israel

The director groaned. His back pain was flaring up again, and whatever position he sat in sent agony shooting down his leg and through the base of his spine. Days like this he was reminded that he wasn't getting any younger, and the toll of the years of stress and a sedentary lifestyle demanded to be paid, regardless of what else was going on.

He opened a bottle in his desk and popped a Celebrex, secure that the anti-inflammatory would work its magic and reduce the misery his sacroiliac was causing, and washed it down with the dregs of a cold cup of coffee on his desk. It was another late night in the office, his third packet of cigarettes of the day sitting beside an overflowing ashtray. The report on the ministry leak that had arrived in his inbox was spread out before him – nine pages of nothing, as far as he could tell.

The analysts had run system checks on the most obvious culprits but had detected no hacking, with the caveat that a sufficiently skilled actor wouldn't have left any traces. Because of the breadth of the communication network that had been breached, they were unable to say whether it had been a cyber-attack or a mole who had physically accessed the system and downloaded the data. After two read-throughs, the only thing the director had gleaned was that the comm network wasn't secure and that they could expect more leaks, even after issuing new passwords to everyone with access – over a thousand users.

The only good news seemed to be that the level of information that was exchanged using the channel was classified, but not critical to national security. The recommendation of the report was to limit communications to trivia until they could figure out where the leak was coming from, and either apprehend the mole or patch the problem so it couldn't be accessed further.

The director pushed the report aside and frowned. Tomorrow morning, first thing, he was to give a briefing to the ministry and advise the members of the Mossad's progress, which he now understood was nine pages of nil. He wasn't looking forward to making that presentation but couldn't wriggle out of it, barring a direct attack on Jerusalem by the country's collective foes.

He stubbed out his fifty-eighth cigarette of the day and debated heading home to an empty row house where he barely spent any time. He'd almost convinced himself of the merits of a relatively early evening when his desk phone rang insistently.

"Yes?" he answered.

"There's been another leak on 4Channel. Revealing diplomatic chatter between the Saudis and our people that's pretty embarrassing in light of recent pronouncements from both sides."

"How long until you can expunge it?"

"Unknown. My next call is to ask the Americans for some assistance. They're better at this sort of thing than we are."

"Anyone pick up on it yet, or did we get lucky?"

The silence on the line told the director everything he needed to know. He reached for his cigarettes and tapped one from the nearly empty pack. "I see," he said, and lit it with a flick of his lighter.

"We'll do our best to contain it."

"Send me everything you have. I don't suppose you have any idea how it was obtained, do you?"

"Negative. But we're hoping that with the NSA's help, we can trace it. These might have been part of the same data dump as the earlier one. Everything's dated last week."

The director exhaled a long stream of yellow-gray smoke. "The gift that keeps on giving."

"I thought you'd want to know. I'll send the material shortly."

"I'll be waiting."

The director hung up and stood, ignoring the pain radiating from his back with the persistence of a rotting tooth, and walked stiffly to the coffee maker. He dumped out the old grounds, scooped two fresh helpings into a new filter, and switched it on.

"So much for the early night," he muttered, coils of smoke from the cigarette in his mouth snaking toward the ceiling, where the air-conditioning dispersed it before it could mar the paint. The machine began hissing and popping, and his computer pinged at him, signaling that he'd received a message. He hesitated in front of the coffee maker, suddenly overcome by a fatigue deep in his bones, and then returned to his desk, dreading what he would find when he opened his mail and the implications it held for the next morning's meeting.

CHAPTER 22

Highland Plains, Kenya

Jet stood in a grove of trees, listening while she caught her breath. The trail she'd been following now veered toward the edge of the wooded area and potentially left her dangerously exposed if the kidnappers had thought to leave lookouts. She doubted it, but her survival depended on her being right, not guessing, so she was playing it safe and moving cautiously rather than pushing herself to greater speed.

She was preparing to venture farther when she heard the snap of a twig from what she estimated to be no more than thirty meters away. She froze and angled her head to better hear; the rustle of the treetops in the breeze off the plains made it difficult to discern whether the sound had been caused by an animal or humans.

Jet didn't have long to wait. Another crack sounded, this time closer, and she ducked behind a tree and then crept to another farther off the trail, her heart rate measured even after the nearly two hours of tracking. She flipped the fire-selection switch from the safe position to automatic and forced herself to breathe normally, the submachine gun at the ready.

After a seemingly unending wait, three men came into view, moving along the trail in her direction. She could just make out the rifles in their hands, and relaxed slightly – bolt-action hunting rifles, not assault rifles. Felix had mentioned that the area they were making the drop was infested with poachers, and Jet presumed the trio were on the hunt for rhino or elephant, not two-legged prey.

Still, any gunfire would put the kidnappers on alert, so she held still, watching through the monocle as the reed-thin men trudged toward her, their postures loose and their strides barely more than an amble, indicating they had no idea she was there.

She was congratulating herself on averting a crisis when the lead man paused only footsteps from her position and turned to his companions. He muttered something, and one of the others laughed softly. He adjusted his rifle sling and set his pack on the trail, and then made his way toward where Jet was crouched with the barrel of the MP5 trained on his chest.

He stopped no more than a dozen feet from her, pulled down his shorts, and relieved himself while Jet held her breath, finger hovering over the trigger. Thirty seconds later he returned to where the others stood, and mumbled something unintelligible, which was greeted with snickers.

The poachers continued along the track, and Jet remained in her hiding place until they disappeared from view. She gave it another few minutes, forcing herself to be patient, and when she didn't hear anything more, cautiously worked her way to the trail, the MP5 safety engaged again, leading with the submachine gun's ugly snout.

CHAPTER 23

Democratic Republic of the Congo, Africa

Dr. Lindsey Stafford rocked in the passenger seat of a military-issue Land Rover Defender, Malek, her driver, mute by her side. The man hadn't spoken a word since he'd greeted her with a nod at the airstrip and loaded up the back of the vehicle with her medical kit, hazmat suit, and various metal cases with test equipment, all bearing the logo of the U.S. Centers for Disease Control.

She'd flown halfway around the world from her comfortable office in Atlanta after word had reached the agency of the outbreak of a new disease with unusual symptoms and a high mortality rate. Stafford was there as one of the center's ranking field physicians, chartered with cataloging the spread, interviewing villagers in afflicted areas, and establishing the epidemiology of the outbreak so that it could be identified and added to the myriad viruses that circulated in the area.

No stranger to sub-Saharan Africa, Stafford was a veteran of two prior Ebola outbreaks as well as a Ugandan flare-up of Marburg virus – both among the deadliest afflictions in the world, the latter with a ninety-percent fatality rate, making it one of the most feared hemorrhagic fevers on earth. She'd seen suffering on an epic scale, whole extended families wasting away from Ebola, and had been part of the media circus that had greeted the latest outbreak because of her camera-ready looks and her gentle demeanor; a perfect representative of Western compassion, broadcast in regular rotation on the news networks.

With a support staff soon to arrive, she'd debated waiting a few days until her team was on the ground, but had decided on the flight over to go into the field upon her arrival and begin work. She knew better than anyone the importance of timing in short-circuiting any sort of contagion, especially given the questionable hygienic practices in the more rural areas, where caring for the dead by relatives and handling them without precaution ensured that easily contained pathogens spread like wildfire.

Adding to her burden was the innate distrust many of the villages had for Western care workers. Rumors that they were witches, or were deliberately infecting people in order to carry out some form of population control, abounded and had their genesis in fast-circulating stories from negative reactions to widespread vaccination campaigns. Stafford's friendly smile and genuine compassion enabled her to sidestep much of the apprehension the locals displayed when a non-African physician appeared on the scene, and she hoped that by going alone into the first villages that had reported casualties, she could earn the trust of the villagers and get to the bottom of the outbreak in short order.

Malek downshifted as he turned off the main road, and the dodgy pavement was replaced by rutted washboard with pools of standing water from a predawn rain. The engine strained as the wheels lost grip in the slick mud, and beads of sweat appeared on Malek's forehead as he worked the gear shifter to gain traction.

After ten minutes of increasingly uncomfortable jostling, Stafford looked over at Malek. "How much farther?"

"Maybe three, four kilometers," he replied.

Stafford braced herself against the door as the SUV lurched around a bend and skidded to a stop. An army truck was blocking the road, and a pair of soldiers with assault rifles stood by its grill. Malek frowned and set the emergency brake as one of the gunmen approached while the other watched from the truck.

"Sorry. Road closed," the soldier said.

"We have authorization from the high command to pass," Malek said, and withdrew a signed document from his shirt pocket.

The soldier took the document back to the truck, and a hushed discussion ensued. The other soldier, who had remained by the vehicle, reached into the cabin and withdrew a radio, and raised it to his lips as he walked around to the truck bed with the clearance form.

Stafford frowned as they waited in the building heat, the air-conditioning in the military vehicle nearly nonexistent, the requisite Freon charge to keep the system cool obviously a disposable luxury. Eventually the first soldier returned with the document in hand and thrust it through the window at Malek.

"Sorry. Have to go back. Nobody's allowed past this point," he said, his expression stony.

Stafford leaned forward. "We have permission from General Okadigbo. There must be some mistake. You should call him."

"My orders are that nobody is allowed for any reason. Now you have to clear the road," the soldier said, one hand on the rifle strap, his eyes slits.

"We're on a medical expedition with the full support of your government. We need to get through," Stafford explained patiently, the smile never leaving her face.

"Maybe, but my orders are clear. I can't do anything for you."

Stafford's smile vanished. "What's your name and rank? General Okadigbo will be very interested to hear how his invited guests are treated by his men."

The soldier's gaze hardened, and he stepped away from the window with a darting look at his companion. "Turn the car around and leave. Now. I'm not going to argue with you."

Stafford was about to protest, but Malek nodded and touched her arm, his sidelong glance an obvious warning. He depressed the clutch and grunted, and then the SUV was backing away from the soldiers, edging toward the shoulder so he could execute a three-point turn.

"What's going on here, Malek? We have every right to go to the village," she demanded.

"The one by the truck had positioned himself like he was ready to start shooting if we didn't get moving. I don't know why, but they're not going to let us through."

"But they can't block us from going!"

"There's just you and me, and two men with guns who look ready to use them. You should fight this battle with the general, not out here. People have been known to disappear without a trace. You don't want to be one of them. I don't."

"But…why would they do that?"

Malek finished backing up and shifted gears to pull forward. "Nothing has to make sense. The man decides to shoot us, he just pulls the trigger. Nobody ever finds out who did it or why. Your organization makes some noise, there's outrage, but then eventually it fades away…and we're still dead." He paused. "I'm not paid enough to risk that."

Stafford had no rebuttal, so she switched her approach. "Who would want to block us from going to the village?"

Malek shrugged. "Does it matter? A local warlord. Smugglers. Whatever."

"I want to speak with the general when we get back to town."

He nodded and goosed the gas. The engine growled and the tires spun in the muck, and then they were bouncing along in the ruts left from their arrival, the soldiers in the rearview mirror, both now with weapons in hand, watching them depart. Stafford swallowed hard at the sight and only began breathing again once they were around the bend and picking up speed, Malek obviously as anxious as she.

She blotted her face with a bandanna and sat back, her first few hours on the ground very different than what she'd imagined, or what she was accustomed to from her prior visits.

She didn't understand what had just happened, but whatever it was, the knot in her stomach signaled that there might be more to her mission than identifying a disease.

The expression on the soldier's face, the dead eyes, and the almost mocking way he refused to allow them access to the village gave her serious pause. It was bad enough working in primitive conditions out in the middle of nowhere. If she had to worry about being shot by her own side…well, that wasn't in her job description.

"We'll see what he has to say," she muttered.

Malek kept his eyes on the road, coaxing the SUV along the track noticeably faster than on the trip out, the fear radiating off his body palpable in the cabin's stifling confines.

CHAPTER 24

Highland Plains, Kenya

Shira jolted awake from the sensed presence of someone near her and was opening her mouth to cry out when a strong hand clamped over it in the darkness, and Gabriel's voice whispered in her ear.

"Quiet. It's me."

She frowned in the darkness as he removed his hand, and rolled toward him. A peek over his shoulder revealed a few of the guards gathered around a fire pit, where the remains of a cooking fire were smoldering. The sheet of metal they'd mounted on branches over the flames to shield against the unlikely event of a satellite spotting it had been removed hours earlier when the orange glow faded to a few embers.

"What?" she whispered back, her annoyance clear even with the muted tone.

"We're going to make a break for it, but we need your help."

"*We?*"

"I've talked to the others and told them what I heard: they're going to kill us."

Her frown deepened. "We've been through this."

"No. I'm talking about tonight. After the men arrived with the ransom, the leader guy told one of the senior gunmen that the plan was to take us to some village by a river, where the gang boss was going to have us killed."

"That makes zero sense, Gabriel."

"You keep saying that, but I know what I heard. They don't know I speak Swahili, obviously. But they're going to do it, and this is our last chance."

"So you plan to fight two dozen men with your stick? Please."

"Better than dying tomorrow."

"You mean accelerating it is better than waiting to see you're wrong? How do you figure?"

His expression hardened. "I'm not wrong, Shira. And we need your help."

She sighed. "What do you want me to do?"

"Create a diversion so we can slip off. Once we're clear, you can duck out when they see we're gone."

Shira snorted and looked at him incredulously. "Sounds like I sacrifice myself so you can make a break. What am I missing?"

"They won't be expecting you to try to get away right when they discover that we have."

"That's the stupidest idea I've ever heard. If you think it'll work, why don't you create the diversion and we'll run off?"

Gabriel glared at her in the dark. "If you're not going to help, then we have to take our chances and slip off one by one. We're far likelier to get caught that way."

"It's pitch black out. We're in the middle of nowhere. That's why they let us go to the bathroom by ourselves." Shira paused. "You honestly think we have any chance of not being caught anyway?" She shook her head. "You're out of your mind."

Gabriel's jaw clenched and he edged away from her. "What part of 'they plan to kill us' do you not understand?"

"Why don't you just go to the lake like you're going to pee, and keep walking?"

"I want more of a lead than that."

She exhaled in frustration. "Then good luck. I'm going back to sleep," she said, and after another look at the guards, rolled over on her side.

Gabriel bit his lower lip and inched back to where David and Noam were pretending to sleep. When he was close enough for them to hear, he whispered to David, "She won't help."

He nodded in the dark. "So now what?"

Gabriel thought for a moment. "I'm going to dog-crawl into the bushes. If they don't miss me, you two follow in a couple of minutes."

"And leave her to them?" Noam asked.

"Hey, it's her choice."

Gabriel didn't wait for them to object. He eyed the fire pit and then began inching toward the brush line ten feet away. When he reached it, he pulled himself into the bushes and disappeared from view.

David and Noam were startled by Shira's sneeze. They looked over at her, and then one of the guards was walking toward them, AK-47 in hand. When he reached them, he peered around the sleeping area and straightened, his eyes alert, and called out to his companions. Moments later the other two guards came running, and three heads poked out of tents, awakened by the yelling.

The first guard leveled his assault rifle at the hostages, and Jaali approached, bare chested, his face puffy from sleep. He glowered at the hostages and then drew his pistol and pointed it at Noam's head.

"Where's your friend?" he demanded.

"I...I don't know. Maybe relieving himself?"

Jaali shifted his aim to David. "And you?"

David rubbed his face and squinted at him. "I just woke up. How would I know?"

Jaali cocked the hammer and pointed the weapon at Shira. "I want answers."

"I have no idea where he is. Where could he go? There's no place to go to," she said.

Jaali's expression was stony as he regarded her for several beats, and then he turned to bark orders at his men. They scrambled to obey, and Jaali's second-in-command, who'd remained behind when Jaali and his team had gone to collect the ransom, made his way to where Jaali stood, pistol gripped tightly by his side. They had a hurried conversation, and then another one of the kidnappers arrived with a satchel. He handed it to Jaali, who withdrew four black aluminum flashlights and distributed them with terse instructions.

The second-in-command and three of the gunmen twisted the

lamps to life and moved to the brush line. Seconds later, one of them called out in triumph and pointed to tracks in the moist ground, where Gabriel's shoes and knees had left indentations. Jaali joined them and snapped at the men, who lunged into the dense foliage, guns in hand.

Gabriel heard the outcry back at the camp and abandoned any pretense of trying to make his way through the brush silently. The branch he'd sharpened and retrieved once he'd made it out of sight now felt foolish as the reality of pursuit by heavily armed guerilla fighters set in. He peered ahead in the darkness and barely made out a trail in the faint moonlight that filtered through the branches of the trees.

Flashlight beams flickered behind him, and he took off at a run. The dress loafers he'd worn to the dinner didn't provide much traction on moist leaves and mud. He nearly went down a few moments later and barely caught himself against a tree trunk before pushing off and scrambling deeper into the foliage, the trail barely more than a faint thinning of the brush ahead.

The kidnappers weren't making any attempt to be quiet as they crashed through the bushes, and Gabriel cursed between clenched teeth at how little of a head start he'd gotten. He'd hoped to go unnoticed for at least an hour if he took off on his own, but now...now he'd be lucky if he wasn't shot in the back before he could make it to the lake.

Gunshots rang out behind him, and bullets shredded the leaves to his right. He ducked lower and pushed himself to his limit as the shooting stopped and an angry voice rang out, scolding the shooter and ordering him to save ammo.

Gabriel veered left at a particularly thick clump of bushes, pushed a hanging vine out of the way, and continued in the direction of the water, although he couldn't be sure – his plan had assumed time to get his bearings and maintain a steady course, not zigzagging through the wilds like a hare with hounds on its tail. He paused and heard the gunmen pounding through the brush toward him, an occasional flare of light through the leaves all the evidence he needed that they were gaining on him.

His breath was coming in rasps as he altered direction again, and then his foot caught on a root and he went down, the wind knocked out of him when he slammed onto the ground with a grunt. He fought to regain his footing and nearly jumped when a voice whispered to him from the spread of a nearby tree.

"Get over here and grab the straps. Hurry. They're almost on top of you."

CHAPTER 25

Jet gripped her backpack as Gabriel scrambled up the tree trunk, pulling himself higher using the straps until he could reach the lower branches and use them to leverage himself toward her. Once he was able to climb on his own, she scrambled up until she was three meters above the lower branches, her back propped against the trunk and the MP5 pointed toward the ground. He made it to the area just beneath her, and she hissed a warning to him.

"Stay absolutely still and don't make a sound."

He froze in place, and the pounding of boots along the trail reached them from where he'd stood only moments before. Jet's NV monocle remained fixed on the area beneath the tree, her finger hovering over the submachine gun trigger, fire selector on full auto.

A flashlight beam played over the bushes near the trunk and then continued bouncing farther along the trail. Two gunmen trotted by only a few feet from the tree, weapons at the ready, their breathing audible to Jet and Gabriel high in the branches. They vanished into the brush, and then two more kidnappers followed close behind, their pace matching the lead men's urgency. Jet tracked them with the gun barrel, and then they too disappeared, leaving Jet and Gabriel motionless high above the ground.

A minute dragged by, and then another, and when the men didn't appear, Jet flipped the firing selector back to the safe position and leaned forward.

"That looks like everyone," she murmured so softly it could have been the wind. "We need to get down and backtrack before they figure out you've outfoxed them."

He nodded and studied the monocle headset and the gun. "Who are you?"

"A friendly. Which one are you?"

"Gabriel Ross."

"Only you made a break for it?"

He nodded in the darkness.

She shifted her position. "Climb down and keep quiet until I signal. Once we're on the ground, I'll lead. Don't make any noise or we're dead."

Gabriel lowered himself slowly, taking care to avoid a mishap that would send him tumbling fifteen feet. When he was on the ground, Jet swiftly followed, the MP5 hanging by its sling from her shoulder. She dropped catlike onto the mushy terrain and pointed to her right. Gabriel followed her to a forked smaller game path, and then they were jogging away from the lake, skirting the edge of the tree line as the scrub rose to meet the plain.

They stopped twice, and Jet held her fingers to her lips both times to remind Gabriel not to speak. He obeyed her hand signals, which she assumed he would based on the background file she'd read – Gabriel was a former IDF commando, albeit over a decade and a half out of practice, gone slightly to seed from a comfortable corporate life behind a desk. Still, at least enough of the training remained so he hadn't done anything stupid, ceding the lead to Jet and allowing her to direct them to safety.

When the trees gave way to tall grass, Jet led him to an outcropping of rock and crouched behind them, scanning her surroundings with the monocle. Gabriel joined her and waited until she'd finished, and then raised an eyebrow in silent inquiry.

"Okay," she said, her voice quiet. "We're in the clear. They'll lose the trail at the fork unless they have infrared. Do they?"

"No," he whispered. "I didn't see any."

"That's the first bit of luck so far." She regarded him and flipped the monocle out of her field of vision. "Are the others okay?"

He nodded. "For now."

"The ransom arrive with no problems?"

Another nod. "They were counting it until an hour or so ago." He paused. "But it doesn't matter. They're planning to kill everyone tomorrow."

Jet didn't blink. "Why?"

"I don't know. I overheard their leader talking to someone, and then he told one of the guards that they were going to take us to their boss's camp and execute us. It's outside by a village on a big river half a day from here."

"Why go to all that trouble? Why not kill you here? Unlikely anyone would ever find the bodies."

"Again, I didn't hear the other side of the conversation. But that was what he said."

Jet mulled over the new information for several long beats. "How's the girl? Shira?"

"She's fine. Everyone is. I mean, as fine as you'd expect after a forced march for half a day and sleeping in the dirt."

She checked the time. "Four hours till sunup."

"We have to go back for them or they're dead," Gabriel said.

"So you say."

"I know what I heard."

"Doesn't make a lot of sense, does it? The kidnappers got paid. Why bring that kind of grief down on their heads?"

He frowned. "You sound like Shira."

"Because it isn't rational. What possible reason would they have for guaranteeing nobody would ever pay them again?"

"I have no idea. Maybe the gang leader's nuts. You ever consider that?"

Her expression didn't change. "How many gunmen are there? I counted nineteen, but some had already gone to sleep by the time I made it here."

"Where did you come from?"

"Heaven." She paused. "How many?"

"Twenty-five, including the leader."

"What did they do with the money?"

"He's got four men guarding it." Gabriel thought for a moment. "Why? Is this all about the ransom?"

"They'll prioritize keeping that safe over anything else. If you're correct and they plan to kill everyone tomorrow, we can't change that. But if they think someone's trying to steal their cash, they'll react differently than if they're on the alert for an escape attempt." Jet paused. "Are the three of them in good enough shape to run?"

"Sure. But…how are you planning to take on twenty-two armed thugs and come out alive?"

A hint of a smile played across her features. "I probably have a better chance than you did with a spear."

Color rose in Gabriel's face. "It was a last resort. Defense."

"Whatever. But if you're right, we need to create some sort of distraction so they think they're under attack. Or rather, that the money's in jeopardy. Given a choice between saving that or watching the hostages, what would you do?"

"What kind of distraction?"

She thought for a few moments. "How rusty are you?"

"What do you mean?"

"I know your military history. Think you can mount a convincing offense if you have the right gear?"

He looked at her submachine gun. "I can shoot, but that thing's not going to be enough. If twenty-something AKs open up on my position, it's game over before it starts."

She nodded. "I figured that out. But that's not the only trick I've got up my sleeve."

He studied her face. "What are you thinking?"

This time the smile was icy, sending a mild shiver up his spine in spite of the heat.

"It'll have to be timed perfectly," she began, and explained to Gabriel what she had in mind.

CHAPTER 26

The search party had returned empty-handed to the kidnapper encampment an hour earlier, the gangsters unaware that they were being watched by their quarry from the opposite side of the brush. Jaali's dressing-down of the leader for his failure had been audible from Jet and Gabriel's vantage point, the rage in his voice clear from fifty meters away. Now the men had gone to sleep, the exception a pair guarding Jaali's tent and the ransom inside, and another two watching the prisoners from the fire pit.

Jet's eyes had adjusted after removing the monocle. The crescent moon's rise into the heavens was now complete, bathing the area in a spectral glow. She was belly down on the ground behind the cover of thick vegetation, Gabriel lying beside her, watching the tents with single-minded intensity. She'd called Elon on the sat phone a half hour earlier, waking him from a sound sleep, and reported the position of the camp, but he'd told her that there was nothing he could offer her except good wishes – the Kenyans had proven too unreliable to trust with the location in case there was a leak, at which point they'd know that they were being observed and any chance of surprising them would be forfeited.

Gabriel shifted next to her. "Well?" he whispered. "What do you think?"

She checked her watch. "We have to make our move before they have a chance to wake up. The confusion will work to our advantage." She hesitated, something about the set of his jaw giving her pause. "You okay with this?"

"Should be like shooting fish in a barrel, right?"

Lines creased her forehead. "It's never that easy. You should know that."

"It was meant to ease the tension. I understand what we're up against. But the grenades change everything."

"Don't run through them too quickly, and choose your targets carefully. We have limited ammo. It'll be tempting to just spray the area after the first blast, but you need to maintain discipline so I can get them out before the kidnappers know what hit them."

He nodded. "I got it."

She slid the MP5 to Gabriel and passed him the backpack after removing two grenades and her pistol. She'd already pocketed the extra magazines and was under no illusions that if she was forced into a firefight, the little nine millimeter was a popgun compared to the withering firepower of AKs on continuous fire. Her plan depended on stealth, and if she was right about the kidnappers' priorities, they were unlikely to expend too much effort moving out of the camp to hunt Jet down, justifiably wary of walking into a killing field.

If she was wrong, she wouldn't live till dawn.

They had synchronized their watches earlier. After a final glance at hers, Jet leaned into Gabriel. "Eight minutes."

"Good luck," he said, and slipped away into the darkness with the monocle, submachine gun, and her backpack with the grenades and sat phone.

She waited until the sound of him moving through the brush had subsided, and then circled around the encampment until she was halfway between where the hostages were sleeping and the tent Gabriel had identified as that of the leader, which contained the ransom. She chambered a round in the pistol and slid it back into the shoulder holster, and retrieved one of the grenades and hefted its weight in the palm of her hand.

Jet estimated that the command tent was fifty feet from her hiding place, which was at the limit of her effective ability to hurl the grenade with any hope for accuracy. She eyed her watch while forcing her heart rate slower, adrenaline accelerating it in advance of the onslaught. When the eighth minute had ticked by, she rose, pulled the pin on the first grenade, and lobbed it toward the tent.

The detonation was deafening and sent a shower of earth and rock into the air. The grenade had fallen short of the tent but landed close enough to the fire pit to knock the guards aside like rag dolls. The flash from the blast would have blinded her, but she'd closed her eyes for the explosion and was already in motion when the first screamed orders rang through the camp.

Jet zigzagged toward the prisoners and, when she was at the brush line, pulled the pin on her second grenade and threw it as hard as she could toward the clustered tents as gunmen poured from them. She ducked down and waited for the eruption and, when it came, made for the hostages, who were visibly in shock from the sudden attack.

She ducked as she ran, and when she reached where Shira, David, and Noam were sitting up, staring wide-eyed at the blast craters and carnage from the grenades, hissed a warning at them.

"On your feet. Follow me," she ordered.

They looked at her uncomprehendingly, and she drew her pistol and peered at where the kidnappers were struggling to form a defensive perimeter around the command tent. "Hurry. We need to move before they figure out what's happening."

David pushed himself to his feet, but Noam didn't move, and neither did Shira. She stared at Jet. "Who are you?"

"I'm rescuing you. Get up and follow me."

A yell carried from the camp, and Jet winced, waiting for Gabriel's gunfire to draw the guards' attention from her. He was to start picking them off to buy her time to move the hostages to safety, but the expected diversion never came, and another yell confirmed that some of the kidnappers had turned their attention to her position.

"Come on..." she whispered to herself, waiting for the next grenade to shatter the night.

Moments went by, and nothing, and then another cry from the kidnappers and the sound of running boots told her she was in trouble. She made out two gunmen making their way toward her and threw herself on the ground, clear of the prisoners so they wouldn't be hit, and opened fire with the pistol. Her shots missed their mark, and then a volley of answering fire blew divots of muddy earth from around her. The shooting paused, and an authoritative voice called out in English.

"Drop the gun or the next shot's between your eyes."

Jet delayed as though thinking, waiting for her chance – a grenade blast behind the gunmen all she'd need to be able to put them down – but it never happened. The voice called out again.

"Last warning," he said, and a shot rang out, the muzzle flash orange in the darkness. A round snapped by her ear and tore a chunk of dirt loose a foot from her head, sending a spray of earth onto her hair.

Jet set her pistol down by her shoulder, moving slowly and deliberately. "Okay. Don't shoot," she said, praying that Gabriel would put a bullet through the leader's skull before he made it any closer.

Boots approached, and a trio of sweating gunmen materialized out of the gloom, their Kalashnikovs pointed at her. The man in the middle lowered his rifle when he saw her and leaned toward the shooter on his right.

"She moves, kill her," he ordered, and then strode back toward the command tent, the still of the night returning after the deafening explosions, the only sound now the moans of the wounded and the leader barking orders.

Jet's breath was hot against the ground as the gunmen edged nearer, and then a rifle butt slammed into her head, sending a starburst of pain shrieking through her synapses before the world went black.

CHAPTER 27

"She's coming to."

Jet's breath caught in her throat and she coughed. A lance of agony radiated from the back of her skull through her eyes and down her spine, and when her eyes flitted open, her vision was blurred.

Shira was looking down at her in concern, David and Noam standing behind her, their faces tight with fear. Jet looked beyond Shira to where a kidnapper was glaring at her from the shadows, the barrel of his AK-47 glinting in the faint moonlight. Jet blinked and tried to control the wave of nausea that threatened to overpower her, and closed her eyes, fighting the accompanying dizziness with every beat of her heart.

"Here," Shira said. "Drink some water."

Jet opened her eyes to find Shira kneeling beside her with a scarred canteen. She debated the wisdom of shaking her head but decided against it as the dull ache in her brain reminded her she probably had a concussion. Shira pressed the cool neck of the canteen against Jet's lips.

"Don't worry. It's been boiled," she said.

Jet took a cautious sip and swallowed the metallic gulp. She exhaled through her mouth and coughed again, triggering another wave of disequilibrium, and closed her eyes, willing the sick feeling in the pit of her stomach away.

"I can't believe you tried to break us out by yourself. Crazy," David said, speaking softly.

Jet didn't reply, preferring to focus her resources on damage assessment. Nothing hurt besides her head, although she could feel that her wrists had been bound behind her back with some sort of rope.

"Are you okay?" Shira asked.

"Not really," Jet managed. "Is my head bleeding?"

"Only a little. I blotted it so it would clot. But you've got a pretty bad bump on the top."

"I'm not surprised."

Jet's mind was churning over the obvious betrayal by Gabriel, who had done none of the things they'd agreed upon to enable her to free his companions. The plan had been for him to rain destruction down on the kidnappers while she guided the prisoners to freedom, and then they would rendezvous at the boulders and Jet would call in a helicopter via Elon to fly them out. Instead, he'd left her hanging out to dry, and now she was in jeopardy while he was somewhere out in the brush, presumably safe since he hadn't participated in the attack.

Of course, something could have happened to him, she supposed. A predator could have attacked, or he could have tripped and hit his head and be bleeding out...but she suspected not. He'd simply chickened out at the last second and decided that risking his neck to rescue his friends wasn't worth it.

Even if it meant leaving Jet, who'd saved his bacon, to be killed by the kidnappers along with his friends and Shira.

She suppressed the rage that bubbled up in her chest and ignored the murderous thoughts that ran through her mind. She'd been clubbed like a baby seal and hog-tied, with a gunman only footsteps away. Thoughts of Gabriel would have to wait. For now, she needed to survive the current ordeal to address his treachery.

As if reading Jet's mind, Jaali emerged from the command tent and stalked over to where she lay.

"Who are you?" he asked in a tone as menacing as a cobra's hiss.

"Security. For the drug company," Jet said after several seconds.

"You're dead. There won't be any ransom. You killed six of my men and wounded three more. One of them probably won't make it."

Jet didn't respond. There was nothing to say.

"I contacted my boss. He's taken an interest in you. I described you to him, and he said you sound exactly like the woman who killed his son."

Jet's expression didn't change. "I didn't kill him."

Jaali stared holes through her. "Doesn't matter. He holds you responsible. That's all that counts." He turned to where his men were tending to the fallen, and called to them. "Pack up the camp. I want to be out of here before dawn."

"Where are we going?" Shira asked.

"Your friend here killed Adami's son. Figure it out," Jaali snarled, and walked away, leaving the prisoners in shocked silence. Eventually David sat heavily on the damp ground.

"Gabriel said they were going to shoot us," he said. "I thought he was out of his mind, but now…"

Shira's gaze followed Jaali to his tent, and when it returned to Jet, her eyes looked frightened. "Is it true? What he said about Adami's son?"

"I didn't kill anyone," Jet repeated.

"If he thinks you did, we're all in danger because of it," Shira said.

Jet studied the younger woman. "You seem sure of that."

"Isn't it obvious? If he isn't going to let us go, it's because he wants revenge. That's the only thing that makes sense. Which means we…it means we can't depend on them to release us, even though they got the ransom."

Jet closed her eyes again, her headache intensifying. "Then we have a problem, don't we?"

"That's all you can say?" Shira demanded. "We're all dead because of…because of you, and that's the best you've got?"

Jet sighed wearily. "You're not dead. And if you will be, it's because they kidnapped you, not because I tried to rescue you. Seems like you have this upside down." She paused. "But save your energy. It isn't over till it's over."

"What does that mean?" Noam asked, his voice tight. "Is help on its way?"

Jet opened her eyes and took in each of them before her gaze settled on Shira. "If we're going to get out of this, it's going to be on our own."

David shook his head. "You really are nuts."

"There were twenty-five of them," Jet whispered. "Now there's sixteen, with three more wounded, which will slow them down. I'd say your odds just went way up."

"Still impossible odds," he muttered.

"Nothing's impossible," she said. "Just keep your eyes open. If I see an opportunity, you won't get any warning."

"You're half dead and tied up. You're talking about opportunities? You're really certifiable," David fired back.

"So what's your solution? Wait to die?" Jet snapped, and then closed her eyes. "Leave me alone for a while. My head's splitting, and I need to think."

David grunted and shook his head again. "We're on our way to be murdered by some psycho, and she wants to think—"

"This isn't helping," Shira said angrily.

"We should have listened to Gabriel," Noam said. "He got away. Maybe we could have, too."

Shira stood and tossed the canteen on the ground. "Or been shot trying."

"Sounds like that would be better than what we're facing," David said, a note of panic to his voice. "Who the hell is this Adami, anyway?"

Nobody answered, each lost in their own thoughts, the activity at the tents as the men broke camp a stark reminder that their march wasn't over, and any hopes they might have harbored of being allowed to go free were as likely as a winged unicorn swooping in and whisking them to safety.

Noam looked at the guard and then at Shira. "I'm not going to wait to be tortured to death," he said quietly.

Shira's eyes widened. "Noam, you need to stay calm. Seriously."

Jaali emerged from his tent and moved to the fire pit, where his second-in-command was fashioning a tourniquet around one of the wounded men's legs. Hearing Jaali's voice, the guard looked over to where his boss was advising his subordinate on how he wanted the money safeguarded, taking his eyes off them. Noam took several steps toward the tree line, his face frozen in a rictus of fear. Shira shook her head in warning, but he didn't register it. Instead, he broke into a run and tore for the tree line.

Jaali looked up at Noam and drew his pistol with quiet calm. After sighting on him, he squeezed off three rounds. One of them caught Noam in the shoulder and spun him around, and he went down with a cry of agony. He was scrambling in the mud, still trying to get away, as Jaali approached with his handgun, a look of annoyance his only reaction. Noam slipped on the muddy grass, now slicker from his blood, and Jaali shook his head and fired again, drilling a hole through the back of his skull.

He holstered the weapon and threw Shira and David a warning glare, and then returned to the fire pit as though nothing had happened, leaving them staring at their dead companion with gaping mouths.

"We move in fifteen minutes," Jaali warned in Swahili. "No time to bury the dead. Leave them for the buzzards. I want to be clear of here by daybreak."

CHAPTER 28

Manchester, England

The dawn sky was a bleak gray as two sedans rolled to the curb in front of a red brick two-story building whose industrial history was obvious from its utilitarian lines. Converted into lofts following a frenzy of urban development that had gripped the nation a decade earlier, the run-down neighborhood where it was situated had enjoyed a renaissance funded by borrowed money seeking a return.

Four men in cheap, shapeless suits exited the vehicles and made for the front entrance. One of them tried the front door, and when it didn't open, signaled to the man behind him, who knelt and went to work on the lock with a set of picks. A minute later the bolt sprang open with a snap, and the men pushed through it and into the darkened lobby.

A row of mailboxes ran along the far wall beside a stairway that led to the second level, and the men mounted the stairs in silence, the rubber soles of their oxfords silent on the wooden steps. At the second-floor landing they paused, and the lead man motioned down the hall on the left, where a string of doors stretched to a window at the end of the corridor.

They stopped at the second-to-last loft, and the lead man checked the number on the door before nodding to the others. He stood to one side as his men framed the entryway and depressed the doorbell next to it.

After fifteen seconds with no response, he pushed the button again and, when there was no evidence of movement inside, inclined his head at the man on his right. The cheap lock proved no match for the picks, and moments later the lead man swung the door open, a

Browning Hi Power pistol in his hand.

Two of the men remained in the hall while the other pair entered the loft, walking softly, weapons drawn. The lead man pointed at a wooden stairway that led up to a platform above, supported by a pair of steel girders that served as columns. The other nodded in understanding, and they mounted the stairs, leading with their pistols.

A king-size bed occupied the far end of the platform with two motionless forms beneath the blankets. The man with the Browning glanced at a poster of Che Guevara over the headboard, fist raised in defiance, iconic beard and beret depicted in black with the rest of the image in gray, and signaled to his companion to move to the opposite side of the bed. They moved in tandem until they were beside it and trained their guns on the sleeping form of a young man with longish hair and a goatee, one arm wrapped around a girl whose delicate features and high cheekbones would have been at home on a Milan runway.

"Morning, Mr. Ender," the lead man said conversationally, the Browning steady in his hand.

The sleeper's eyes popped open, and he gazed down the barrel of the gun in dazed confusion.

"What the bloody–" he exclaimed, and then the girl stirred before crying out in alarm.

The lead man held a finger to his lips and motioned with the Browning to the girl. "Go ahead and put your clothes on and get out of here. Our business isn't with you," he said quietly.

"Andrew…" she said, reaching for her lover, whose face radiated shock and fear.

"All my money's in my wallet," Andrew said, eyeing the gun.

"Go on, luv. Get out of here. We need a word with Andrew here," the lead man said, and the girl pulled away.

"Who are you?" Andrew demanded. "What do you want?"

"You've been a rather naughty boy, Andrew. Don't make this worse than it has to be. Have your friend here go home or out for a coffee. You're coming with us."

The girl slid from beneath the covers, clad only in a thong, one arm covering her breasts, her caramel skin flawless as only youth could be, and moved to where a pair of jeans and a bohemian top hung on the back of a chair. She hurriedly tossed on the clothes, turning her back to the bed in an effort to preserve any modesty, and then slid on a pair of sandals and reached for her purse.

"You can leave that here, luv. The door will be open. Come back in ten minutes and get it at your leisure," the lead man said, his eyes still locked with Andrew's.

The girl nodded and edged along the wall to the stairs. She threw Andrew a final frightened glance and then descended them two at a time before rushing to the loft's open front door and disappearing through it.

The leader cleared his throat. "Now then, Andrew. Put on some clothes, and let's get some coffee and have a chat, shall we?"

"I haven't done anything. Who are you? What gives you the right—"

The lead man sighed and slipped his weapon back into his shoulder holster, and then removed a wallet from his inside jacket pocket and flipped it open. "MI5. We need your assistance with a problem. Now be a good lad and get dressed. Sooner we can clear everything up, the sooner we can go on with our lives."

"MI5? I haven't done anything. What do you want with me?" Andrew asked, frown lines etched into his brow.

"We'll discuss it at headquarters. I'm just the welcoming committee. Tasked with bringing you in."

Andrew's face twisted in anger. "You bloody broke into my flat, and—"

The leader held up his hand. "Just stop, Andrew. Don't make this harder than it has to be. You've been up to no good, and we know everything. Under the terrorism act, we can hold you for weeks without a hearing if we like, so I'd shut my gob and do as we say, or it's going to go badly. Now, for the last time – get dressed, or we'll drag you naked into headquarters. Doesn't matter much to me either way."

Andrew threw off the covers and stood, his boxer underwear

bunched around his thighs. He moved to where a pair of corduroy pants hung over the railing and pulled them on. "I want a lawyer," he said, and indicated a rough-hewn wooden armoire. "Shirts are in there."

The lead man nodded and fixed Andrew with a hard stare. "Easy, now. Wouldn't make any fast moves while choosing one, or my friend here might overreact. Be a shame — a lot of unnecessary paperwork if he shoots you."

"I said I want a lawyer."

"All in good time, young Andrew. Now get your shirt and we'll be on our way. We can discuss your barrister options on the way to headquarters."

CHAPTER 29

Tel Aviv, Israel

The director leaned forward to answer the telephone that was ringing on his desk.

"Yes?"

"We caught our first break in the ministry leaks."

The director grunted. "About time."

"Agreed. We were able to trace the latest info dump to an anarchist organization in the UK. One of its cyber leaders is based in Manchester, and his IP showed up as an upload site. We put word out to the Brits, and they hauled him in this morning and are sweating him."

"That's positive. But have we learned anything about how they're getting the information?"

"So far, they've been told a story about the dark web and retrieving leaked documents from offshore sites. We're working on obtaining the location, but the prisoner believes the servers are located in Russia or Latvia."

The director digested the news. "It's the Russians?"

"Not necessarily. I mean, it could be, but it's more likely that that's just where the servers are located. And there's always the possibility that it's some sort of spoofing scheme made to look like it's a Russian server, but with the true location on the other side of the world."

"What's the plan, then? Doesn't seem like that much progress," the director said.

"Once we identify the servers and confirm they're not spoofed, we can look at searching them to see who's been uploading files to them. The logs will likely have that information."

"Can we hack them?"

"Unknown at this time. But we're working on it. We should know more shortly."

The director nodded to himself. "Good. Keep me informed, and do whatever you need to do. Call if you require clearance for additional resources."

"I appreciate it."

The director disconnected and reached for his tepid cup of coffee. He took a long pull and then lit his sixth cigarette of the morning and blew smoke at the air vent on the wall above his desk. The ministry had been frantic over their network being compromised, and the tone of their emails and phone calls had escalated as their embarrassment deepened. With all the other matters on his desk, the leak was a distraction he didn't need, and if he could bring the matter to a successful conclusion within hours, he could focus on more important issues – like rumors of a terrorist cell attempting to purchase nuclear material from the Ukraine, and a suspected plan to target Israeli tourists in several countries in Asia, coinciding with another fruitless round of talks over Palestine.

He made a note on his blotter to check on the MI5 interrogation later in the day and turned to a report on increasing Iranian arms shipments to Hezbollah and the possibility of a major push by the Iranians in Lebanon.

"Never a dull moment," he muttered as he opened the file, smoke spiraling from another forgotten cigarette in his ashtray.

CHAPTER 30

Highland Plains, Kenya

Gabriel was streaming sweat as he followed a game trail through the trees, the handheld GPS serving as a rough guide as he pushed southwest. According to the digital map, he was still thirty kilometers from the nearest road, in an area known for poachers and drug runners and myriad criminal elements. The methamphetamine trade in that part of Africa was a lucrative enterprise, and the news was routinely filled with accounts of farmers or hunters stumbling across mass graves or the remains of clandestine laboratories destroyed during territorial squabbles.

The shade from the wooded area canopy had worked against him when the sun had come up; instead of cooling things off, the moisture was held in the ground, which created an effect not unlike a pressure cooker as it converted to steam. The humidity was unbearable even if the heat was mitigated, and the last two hours had been among the most miserable of his life.

He had no plan other than to try to reach the highway and flag down help. The mystery woman's arms cache ensured a certain measure of security, but even so, he paused every ten minutes to listen for the sounds of pursuit. His decision to make a run for it instead of helping her had been simple self-preservation – there had been no chance, as he saw it, that her scheme would work, and to play the role she'd assigned him would have been suicidal.

And Gabriel was many things, but anxious to shed his mortal coil in an African backwater wasn't one of them.

At his current rate of progress, he would reach the highway by the end of the day, best case, although according to the GPS terrain map, the heavy foliage would become rolling plains several hours before he arrived at the road, so he might make better time. The big risk he was now worried about was dehydration – he'd consumed the last of the woman's water stock a half hour earlier, and at the rate he was sweating, he would run out of energy before making it to the highway.

His feet were blistered in his dress shoes, the skin rubbed raw from many miles of hiking, and it was all he could do to ignore the pain and continue at a reasonable pace, as each step sent a lance of fire through the soles. But bad as that was, passing out from dehydration would be worse, and he periodically imagined his unconscious form being eaten by fire ants or jungle cats or any of the other creatures that would view him as their next meal.

Gabriel stumbled and almost face-planted before regaining his footing. He shook his head to clear it and glared back at the uneven spot on the trail where he'd tripped. His thoughts were increasingly wandering as the heat of the day built, a sign of incipient delirium caused by exertion and lack of food and water. He tried to remember what he'd read about loss of salt through perspiration, and how long the body could continue before it shut down in order to preserve its resources, but nothing came to mind. The near fall served as a warning that he couldn't push himself to the limit without the effort taking its toll, and he slowed to a moderate pace, the light-headedness that had been haunting him for the last leg another sign that he was in trouble.

He paused to catch his breath at a bend in the trail, his legs aching like he'd run a double marathon. He decided to sit beneath the spread of a tall tree and rest for a few minutes, suddenly drained by the exhaustion of the sleepless night and the prior days of stress. He slipped off the backpack and set it by his side, and then removed the empty water bottle, unscrewed the top, and held it to his lips while tapping on the bottom in an effort to eke out a few precious remaining drops.

He barely got enough to moisten his tongue.

When he screwed the top back on and returned the container to the pack, a wave of despair washed over him – after everything he'd endured, if he died of thirst in the tropics, it would be beyond ludicrous.

He closed his burning eyes and leaned his head back against the tree, a vision of a cool waterfall tormenting him in his imagination. His breathing slowed as his limbs grew heavy, and then his chin drooped forward onto his chest and he began to snore softly.

Gabriel's head jolted back and his eyes snapped open to find himself staring down the barrels of a half dozen AK-47s gripped by camouflage-clad Africans with dead eyes. One in the center of the group, a soiled red bandanna tied around his head, grinned menacingly, revealing unevenly spaced yellow teeth.

"Take his gun and search him," he commanded the others in Swahili. He peered down the sights of his rifle at Gabriel as two of the gunmen stepped forward. "Don't move," he ordered in accented English.

Gabriel's stomach sank as the men took the MP5 from him and rummaged through the backpack, their eyes widening when they came across the grenades and sat phone. The bandanna-topped man motioned for them to bring the weapons to him, and after inspecting them, he grinned again and nodded to Gabriel.

"What you doing out here with this, big man?" he asked in English.

Gabriel debated how to answer. He didn't want to take the chance that these thugs would turn him over to the kidnappers for a reward, but his brain wasn't firing correctly, and his thoughts seemed to be floating in a thick fog.

"I…I'm hunting," he said, and regretted the lie the moment it left his lips.

The gunman laughed. "With a machine gun and grenades? Come on, man. You think we stupid? What, you a cop or something?"

Gabriel shook his head. "No." There was no response he could think of that would be worse than silence.

"Then what?"

"I…I'm tracking poachers."

The man's grin faded. "I don't think so. Not with grenades. No, I think you're out here looking for drug labs, isn't that right? Who you with? CIA? DEA? Who?"

When Gabriel didn't answer, the gunman turned to the others, his weapon still trained on Gabriel, and growled in Swahili, "Bring him to the camp. I'll call the boss and see what he wants to do with him."

One of the fighters prodded Gabriel with his rifle, and Gabriel struggled to his feet. The gunman took in his filthy shoes and laughed in genuine amusement. "You dressed for the wrong dance, big man."

"Tell me about it," Gabriel muttered, and then limped forward in response to being jabbed in the back with an AK.

Ten minutes later, they emerged from the underbrush into a small clearing with camouflage netting strung from the branches of the surrounding trees, masking the ground from any aerial surveillance. A collection of vats and drums were piled at one end, and Gabriel swallowed dryly at the sight. It was a drug-manufacturing plant, which meant that he was unlikely to make it out alive. The irony of being captured by another criminal gang, and possibly ransomed twice, sickened him, and he leaned to the side and dry heaved, his eyes watering in spite of his dehydration.

The gunman with the bandanna watched him impassively. Gabriel rested with his hands on his knees, trying to catch his breath.

"Please. Water," he begged.

"You in a bad way, big man. Bad, bad way," the gunman said, and snapped instructions to his men to watch Gabriel while he radioed his boss, Jomo.

Gabriel did a double take at the name and straightened slowly. "Jomo? Jomo Makori? That's your boss?"

The gunman frowned at Gabriel's question. "You know of him?"

"You could say that."

"How?"

"That's between me and him," Gabriel said, an edge to his voice. "Go ahead and call him. Tell him you came across Angel." Gabriel paused. "And get me some water in the meantime. You'll wish you had after I talk to him."

The gunman looked unsure and called to one of the men by the drums and instructed him to bring a canteen. The man complied, and Gabriel drank from it greedily while the gunman watched him drain it, his expression now openly curious.

"Watch him," the gunman warned the others, and marched to one of the tents. He emerged moments later holding a satellite phone and moved to the far edge of the camp to make his call.

When he returned, his expression had softened.

"We're to meet him in a few hours. He's going to helicopter to the nearest village and come here. Do you want some food? More water?" The gunman looked Gabriel over. "Maybe some new pants and some boots? We can probably find something that fits."

Gabriel nodded. "All those would be good," he said in Swahili. "What's your name?"

The gunman's eyes widened at Gabriel's use of his native tongue rather than the English they'd been using to that point. "Meja."

"When will he get here?" Gabriel asked.

"Maybe in two or three hours."

Gabriel looked around the camp. "Do you have a field shower set up? I could use one."

"Yes."

"And I'll want my weapons back."

Meja looked away. "Jomo didn't say anything about that."

Gabriel grunted. "You can take my shoes and match the size while I'm washing up. I'll want to rest for a while before we leave, so if you have a tent and a cot I can use, that would be good," he said, and then swatted a mosquito that had landed on the side of his neck. He looked at the bloody smear on his hand and shook his head. "And some insect repellent so this godforsaken hellhole isn't the death of me."

CHAPTER 31

Jaali led the surviving kidnappers along the edge of the woods, preferring to avoid the game trails in favor of the more circuitous but easier to navigate grassy area. The prisoners brought up the rear with two gunmen prodding them along, Jaali's group at the front busy hauling the rucksacks with the ransom.

They'd been marching for hours with only a few rest breaks, and the sun was high in the sky when Jaali called another respite. Everyone sat in the shade of the trees, the hostages silent as Jaali spoke with his men to advise them on the next stage of the trek.

Shira leaned toward Jet and whispered to her when Jaali had finished speaking.

"He says we're going to meet Adami's group at a river. We'll load onto some boats, and they'll be waiting ten kilometers downstream at a village on the water."

"You speak Swahili?" Jet asked.

Shira nodded. "I take lessons at a café in Nairobi – Lorelai's, near the embassy. The owner's a nice lady who teaches foreigners the basics." Shira paused. "What I wouldn't do for a cup of coffee right now. I haven't slept for days."

Jet looked over at the kidnappers. "Did he say how long until we get to the river?"

"Not specifically, but he said we wouldn't have to walk much farther." Shira looked at Jet's wrists, now bound in front of her so she could balance better while walking. "That's starting to look ugly. It's rubbing your skin raw."

Jet shrugged. "Least of my worries."

"You really believe they're going to kill us, don't you?"

"Question is why you don't. They shot your friend like a dog."

Shira didn't say anything. She eyed David, who had been withdrawn and sullen since the shooting. "I do now. But what can we do?"

"The river may be our last opportunity. Follow my lead if I do anything."

"Like what?"

"Nothing specific," Jet said, and looked away, tired of the interaction and the woman's naïve chatter.

One of Jaali's gunmen came over and handed them a plastic water jug, the outside of it crusted with mud. David drank a few swallows, grimaced, and passed it to Shira, who did the same and then held it to Jet's lips so she could drink. Jaali called out to the men, and everyone rose. The one who'd given them water retrieved the bottle from Shira and carried it back to the front of the procession, and after consulting a map, Jaali led the group into the rainforest, leaving the relatively easy terrain of the Highland Plains behind.

They followed a track deeper into the brush, and Shira whispered to Jet as they stumbled along the muddy route.

"This looks like a poaching trail. Kenya's got a real problem with them. They kill tons of elephants and smuggle the ivory to China." She hesitated. "There's so much corruption here. Half the officials who are supposed to be stopping it are involved."

Jet exhaled. "Par for the course."

A pause, and Shira whispered to her again. "The drug company sent you? Why didn't they send more than one person?"

"I wasn't supposed to be trying to rescue you. Just making sure the money made it."

"It surprises me they paid. Probably didn't want a PR problem," Shira said, obviously worried and releasing tension by prattling on about nothing.

"Maybe," Jet agreed, her unfriendly demeanor making it clear she didn't want to talk. She was running scenarios in her head, trying to figure out a way for them to escape without being killed. The throbbing in her temples had receded to a dull ache now, and the dizzy spells had subsided to the point she felt reasonably capable again, although she was still acting as though she were incapacitated, depending on Shira to help her with her balance.

Rustles and chirps sounded from overhead as they pushed farther into the brush, the birds and monkeys that called the treetops home sounding cries of alarm as the column filed below. Nobody said a word as the heat increased from unbearable to stifling, and soon everyone's clothes were soaked through, the heat of the plain nothing compared to the humid inferno they were traversing.

After what seemed like an eternity, Jet cocked her head at the sound of rushing water nearby. Jaali called out from the head of the line, and the men visibly relaxed as the trees gave way to the banks of a wide river. The muddy sluice streamed by at a fair clip, an occasional branch carried by the current offering a clue of its speed.

An old man in filthy cargo shorts and a faded blue T-shirt greeted Jaali. They conversed for a few minutes before the man led them farther down the bank to where five wooden traditional Swahili boats had been pulled halfway out of the river and tethered to stakes driven into the gravel slope. David and Shira exchanged a worried look, and then Jet caught Shira's eye. She moved to Jet and steadied her, and Jet murmured under her breath, "If they put us all in the same boat, that's our chance."

Shira whispered back, "What do you mean?"

"Can you swim?"

Shira's sharp inhalation was audible. "In that?"

"Can you swim?" Jet repeated.

"Um…yes…but…"

"Can David? Ask him."

Shira squeezed Jet's arm and moved to where David stood. She returned a moment later.

"He says he can, but not well."

"Once we're out on the water, here's what we need to do," Jet said, and then relayed her improvised plan in low tones. When she was done, Shira looked crestfallen.

"What if they don't put us in the same boat?"

"Then do what you can in yours." Jet paused. "When I'm going to make a move, I'll pretend to have a coughing fit right before so you can get ready. Tell David."

Down at the bank, Jaali clasped the old man's shoulder and shook his hand, and then called to his men, who approached with the ransom. The guard assigned to keeping an eye on the hostages motioned with his AK, and they made their way to the boats.

Jaali pointed at one of them. "You go in that one," he said in English to Shira.

"All of us?" she asked. Jet cringed inwardly, hoping that her question hadn't triggered his suspicion.

He looked around. "I don't see any other boats, do you?"

The old man helped the kidnappers push the boats into the water, and held the nearest one steady for the women as they climbed aboard the narrow hull. His eyebrows rose when he helped Jet, noting her bound wrists without comment. The kidnappers loaded their wounded into two of the other boats, and Jaali directed them to put the ransom into the lead craft once he was seated in the rear, his AK replaced by a wooden paddle.

Jaali's boat was the first to navigate into the current, a pair of his men rowing while he steered from the stern, using his paddle as a crude rudder. The others followed behind him, pushed out into the rush by the old man.

Two gunmen climbed into the craft with the hostages and used their oars to move it into the river. One of the kidnappers paddled from the bow while the other steered them toward the current, and then they were paddling in unison, balancing their strokes on either side of the hull so it stayed on a straight track.

Jet was sitting in front of Shira and David. As the boat worked its way down the river, she studied the shore, noting the hulking shapes of crocodiles basking on the red clay banks. The river made a gentle turn to the west and narrowed as it cut through densely overgrown brush on either side before widening, the current slowing as the channel expanded.

Jet worked her bound wrists against the wooden bench seat between her legs, its rough edge useless to cut the rope, but sufficient to fray the line. After ten minutes of steady effort, she felt the first strands give and the pressure on her wrists loosened slightly. She continued, staring straight ahead as the kidnappers concentrated on keeping up with the other boats.

Another bend, and as the lead skiffs disappeared around it, Shira gasped behind Jet and pointed at the bank. "Look! Hippos."

A dozen of the huge creatures floated in the shallows by the shore, and two babies waddled along the bank behind their mothers.

"They look like gentle giants, but they're really dangerous," Shira said. "They kill more people every year than any other animal in Africa."

Jet scanned the bank, confirming that the seemingly ever-present crocodiles were steering clear of the hippos. When she didn't see any of the familiar reptilian shapes near them, Jet coughed three times, and then again in rapid succession before heaving herself to the right, knocking the narrow boat off balance.

Weight and momentum did the rest, and Shira and David were thrown to the right. The kidnapper in the stern cried out as the hull leaned dangerously and then capsized, dumping everyone into the river with a chaotic splash.

CHAPTER 32

Gabriel woke from a restive sleep to the distinctive beating of helicopter blades from the south. The muggy heat had been only somewhat relieved by the bucket shower he'd taken, and his bare chest was slick with sweat inside the tent. He groaned softly and forced his eyes open, and after a couple of deep breaths, sat up, the astringent smell of bug spray strong on his skin.

Meja had scavenged a pair of serviceable boots only a half size too large, and had given him two pairs of socks and a pair of army-issue camouflage pants with a torn knee. An olive tank top that smelled of the industrial soap the men used to clean their garments rounded out the ensemble, and Gabriel pulled the clothes on before inspecting his ravaged feet.

He slipped on the first pair of socks, wincing as the nerves of his blistered and torn skin radiated fire from the coarse fabric's touch, and then donned the second pair and forced on the boots, grimacing at the pain.

Out in the afternoon air he felt marginally better than before he'd rested, but still disoriented and fatigued by his ordeal. Meja spotted him from where he was sitting at a collapsible table and rose to join him, leaving three of his men to their card game.

"I heard a chopper," Gabriel said.

"Yes. Shouldn't be long now," Meja answered, checking the time on a cheap black plastic watch.

Gabriel blinked as a sliver of sunlight filtered through the trees and hit his face. "How far is the village?"

"Maybe...half an hour. You want some more water? Or tea? Coffee? We have some brewing."

"Coffee would be great."

Gabriel accompanied Meja to a fire pit, where a dented metal pot sat in a bed of embers. Meja pulled another bandanna from his pocket and used it to grip the handle, and then poured two tin cups to the brim with rich dark roast. Gabriel took one, noting a slight tremor in his hand, and sipped the hot drink, ignoring the burn on his tongue. Meja sipped his and then set the cup down on the ground and returned the pot to the embers.

"Want anything else?" he asked.

"No. Just my stuff."

"Talk to Jomo," Meja said, and walked away, leaving Gabriel to wait for the warlord's arrival.

Gabriel was on his second cup of coffee when a trio of gunmen appeared, accompanied by a heavyset African man who could have been a twin of Idi Amin, his khaki pants and shirt spotless and pressed, his safari hat almost comedic atop a massive head. He spotted Gabriel and strode over to him. Gabriel smiled at the sight of the man, and set his cup down on the flat stones of the fire pit before straightening to greet him.

"Jomo!" Gabriel said with a grin.

The warlord's hand lashed out like a striking snake and slapped Gabriel across the face, knocking his head to the side.

"What the hell is going on, Angel?" he growled. "You owe me half a million dollars, and you disappear, don't return my calls? I should shoot you and be done with it."

Gabriel's hand flew to his cheek, and he swore under his breath. "I was kidnapped, Jomo. Hard to return calls in the wilds." He paused and his eyes narrowed. "What do you mean I owe you half a million? What happened?"

"Your partner, Antoine, dropped off the radar in Kisangani. He never made his flight – I checked. They found pieces of him in a dumpster yesterday."

Gabriel blanched and swallowed hard. "Antoine's dead?"

"You heard me. And the stones are gone. Which means you owe me for them. He was your boy. He screwed up; it's your problem, not mine."

Jomo knew Gabriel as Angel, his conduit for diamond smuggling into Israel, Dubai, and Amsterdam. The business relationship had worked out well – Gabriel could pack blood diamonds in biohazard containers along with other samples, ensuring they wouldn't be inspected by customs personnel, who weren't anxious to be exposed to an African death plague. One of his ring of accomplices could then retrieve the stones, sell them for a hefty profit, and Gabriel would pay the warlord, pocketing the difference. It had been a profitable sideline for all involved, but if Antoine was dead…

Jomo interrupted his thoughts. "So where's my money, Angel?"

Gabriel cleared his throat. "I just escaped from a gang of kidnappers, Jomo. It's not like I carry a half mil around in my wallet."

"I want my money," Jomo growled. "No excuses."

"What happened with Antoine? Something must have gone wrong with your people in Kisangani. He was too careful to have slipped up."

Jomo frowned. "So you say. Again, I'm not interested in stories. I want the money for the stones. Period."

Gabriel looked over at where Meja was watching the exchange with interest. He returned his gaze to Jomo. "It'll take a few shipments, but I'll make good on it. You know me."

Jomo shook his head. "I'm not feeling much trust for you anymore, Angel. Only a few people knew Antoine was going to Kisangani for another delivery – you, me, and him. I know I didn't hijack my own shipment, which leaves you." He paused. "Make it look like a robbery, you pocket a half million, and you don't have to pay me or your partner. Maybe you had a fight with him? Disagreement? Doesn't matter. Nobody screws me, Angel. Nobody."

"You forgot your contact down there. He knew, too."

"We've been doing business for years together. He wouldn't dare." Jomo stepped back. "Which leaves us where we started. You owe me. I had to pay him for the stones. So that means you need to come up with half a million."

"How am I supposed to do that, Jomo? Be reasonable. I told you I can work it off."

"Or vanish on the next plane out and I never see you again. Not a chance. You're not going anywhere until I get paid."

"I can't do anything in the middle of nowhere."

The warlord scowled. "Not my problem."

Gabriel's eyes narrowed and he lowered his voice. "I know where I can get you your money. More than I owe you. But I'll need your help."

"I'm not interested in playing some game."

"This is real. I told you I was kidnapped. My company paid them a ransom. They have it in cash." He paused. "I know where they're taking it."

"Who are these kidnappers?"

"I don't know. Maybe a rival gang. They seem organized, and they're well equipped."

"Where are they?"

"They have a camp. But they'll be gone by now."

"Then what good does that do you?"

"I told you. I know where they're taking the money. Or at least, roughly where. I'll need to look at a map, but there may be a way to intercept them."

Jomo studied Gabriel's drawn face. "What are you proposing?"

"Give me ten men with weapons and I'll figure out a way to get the money. We'll split it. Millions, Jomo. Millions of dollars, ours for the taking."

The big man shook his head. "Sounds like a fairy tale."

"Look at me, Jomo. You think I want to be here? I'm telling you – there's millions in hundred-dollar bills – I watched them count it. We hit them, take them by surprise, and the money's ours. Untraceable. A fortune for both of us."

Jomo considered the offer, and his beady eyes drilled into Gabriel's as he nodded slowly. "If this is a trick, I'll order my men to shoot you in the stomach and leave you for the bugs."

"It's no trick. Look, Jomo, my feet are trashed, I'm exhausted, and I've been through hell. But I'm willing to push myself to get you your money. Only I can't do it alone. That's the only way I can pay you back while I'm in Kenya." His voice softened. "The money's waiting for us. All we have to do is take it."

Jomo regarded him, his expression blank, and then he smiled, revealing a gleaming set of pearl white teeth. "Even you aren't stupid enough to lie to me with ten armed men looking for an excuse to shoot you." He paused. "You say they're taking the money somewhere by a river? Where, exactly?"

Gabriel tried not to let his relief show. "Let me worry about that." He looked Jomo up and down. "Do we have a deal?"

Jomo nodded. "You better know what you're doing."

Gabriel returned the warlord's nod but not his grin, his expression dead serious. "I owe these scum for what they put me through. They planned to kill me, Jomo. So you could say it's personal." He leaned to the side and spit the sour taste of burnt coffee into the dirt. "The money's a bonus. But the truth is I'd pay to do it."

Jomo smiled again. "How much are we talking?"

"Six million," Gabriel lied. "Three each. That should settle our account, don't you think?"

"Take as many men as you need. But don't come back without the money."

"I won't."

CHAPTER 33

Jet's lungs burned as she floated in the warm river water, contorting in the current until her hands reached her boot. She'd had the advantage of knowing when she was going to be submerged, and had hyperventilated in the seconds before capsizing the boat, ridding her system of as much CO_2 as possible so she could stay beneath the surface as long as necessary.

It had been years since her training had involved remaining submerged for minutes in an Olympic-sized pool on the Mossad grounds, but she'd never forgotten the lesson, and it was paying dividends now as she felt for the ceramic knife. Her fingers found the slim handle and she drew it slowly, careful not to slice her leg open, and then she turned the blade using her boot top for leverage until the handle was pointing away from her and the razor-sharp edge was resting on the bindings.

She could see the boat's hull above her, and she kicked, slowly propelling herself toward it. When she reached it, her head emerged in the upside-down hull, and she gulped air before raising her arms above her and using the hull to push the blade against the cord.

The work she'd done earlier fraying the line on the seat resulted in the blade slicing through the remaining strands with minimal resistance. She gripped the knife with her right hand to keep it from dropping into the depths and snapped her wrists apart, the rope drifting away as it released its hold on her. She breathed rapidly and treaded water for a moment, and then dove away from the hull.

Splashing from nearby drew her attention and she swam toward a male torso – one of the kidnappers, she could tell from his boots and pants. She remained below the surface and drew near him, and then plunged the blade into his abdomen, slicing laterally before kicking away. The water quickly turned crimson from blood, and she rose toward the sunlight at the surface to get her bearings.

Her face broke through the water and she lay on her back, floating, conserving her energy while she looked around. She spotted Shira fifteen yards away, with splashing David nearby. The surviving guard was farther downriver, treading water as he stared in her direction. Jet's eyes followed the direction of his gaze, and her breath caught in her throat at the sight of long dark shapes moving into the water on the far shore – their greenish brown bulk impossible to mistake as anything but crocodiles.

"Shira! Over here!" Jet called, waving a hand.

Shira began swimming toward her while David struggled behind her, obviously not as capable in the water as the younger woman. Jet returned her attention to the crocodiles on the shore, but only saw their trails in the rust-colored mud.

Shira was halfway to Jet when the swimming kidnapper seemed to rise out of the water a foot and a half, his mouth open in a silent scream, and then vanished beneath the surface, the only trace of his position a flicked tip of a reptilian tail as a big crocodile claimed him for its own. Jet yelled again to Shira and began swimming toward the bank on her right, where the hippos were still enjoying their bath, oblivious to the drama playing out in the middle of the river.

"Follow me, and swim fast!"

Jet didn't wait to see whether Shira and David had heard her, and concentrated on driving herself through the water as rapidly as she could. She remained submerged for long stretches and was approaching where the hippos were soaking when her head broke the surface. She gasped for air and looked behind her, and then automatic rifle fire exploded from down the river. Geysers of water sprayed around where Shira and David had been, and peppered the capsized boat hull, likely for want of a better target. One of the other skiffs had come back around the bend to see where they'd disappeared to, and the gunmen were now emptying their rifles in frustration.

Shira's voice called out from Jet's left. "Stay away from the hippos."

Her warning was answered by gunfire a few seconds later, and Jet ducked below the surface again and swam farther downriver, steering well clear of the big animals. Her hope was that the blood from the guard she'd stabbed and the body of the second guard would keep the crocodiles occupied long enough for them to make it to safety onshore, but she didn't know a lot about their habits, so it had been an instinctive act rather than an informed one.

The bank rose up to meet her, and Jet pulled herself through the water until she saw the shadow of a tree above her on the surface. She dragged herself out of the river and was relieved to find that the tree's branches afforded her cover – the kidnappers couldn't see her, although she could still make them out through the leaves, their rickety boat drifting in the current.

Jet scanned the surface for signs of Shira and David and, when she didn't see anything, looked over at the hippos to make sure none of them had taken an interest in her. More gunfire echoed off the water, and then she spotted Shira breaststroking fifteen yards away.

"Shira. Over here! Under the tree!" she yelled, hoping the shooting had deafened the gunmen.

Shira seemed to hear, because she dove again and didn't reappear until she splashed to the surface directly in front of Jet, where the tree's branches bowed down to the water.

Jet offered her hand in help, and Shira crawled onto the bank. Jet pulled her to her feet, and they stood looking out at the river, both dripping.

"Where's David?" Jet whispered.

"I don't know. He was right behind me when I started swimming. But..."

"Then either the crocs or the shooters must have gotten him."

Shira's face fell. "Oh, God..."

"We have to get out of here. They'll search for us, at least until they get tired or the sun starts going down. The only good news is that they're not likely to go near the hippos, so they won't pick up our trail unless we have extremely bad luck."

Shira nodded. "True. Hippos are really territorial. They'll bite a man in half and charge without provocation. Turn over boats, too. Nobody who knows Africa will go near them." Shira paused. "You don't think we should wait for David, just in case?"

"Every minute we're here reduces our own chances of staying alive. If he was going to make it to shore, he would have by now. I'm sorry, but we have to go."

Shira pushed her sopping hair out of her face and tried to finger comb it back. "Go where? I have no idea where we are."

"There are bound to be villages near a river, right? I seem to recall a few on the GPS after I flew in."

Jet looked at the water again and pointed to another of the kidnappers' boats that was paddling toward the first. "Time to go."

Shira nodded. "You're right. Lead the way."

Jet threw a final glance at the hippos and then turned to make her way up the bank and into the brush, her ears still ringing from the echo of the gunfire.

CHAPTER 34

Democratic Republic of the Congo, Africa

Dr. Lindsey Stafford bolted awake in her bed, the mosquito netting hanging from the poles that framed it gray in the darkness. Something had pulled her out of a deep sleep, and she squinted to see what had done so.

The sound of clothes rustling nearby and the scrape of a sole on the dirt floor of the room froze her blood in her veins. She'd been waiting for the general to get back to her since calling and being informed that he was unavailable – out in the field attending to military matters, she'd been assured when she had pressed – and had arranged to stay in a guest hut in a large village on the road to the city.

She hadn't devoted any bandwidth to worrying about being attacked or raped; but now, in the dead of night, the possibility was immediate and very real. Malek was sleeping in the SUV fifty meters away, but it might as well have been on Mars for all the good it would do her. She decided to confront her fears and sat up in bed, her backpack beside her.

"I have a gun," she said in Swahili, her voice calm. "I'm not afraid to use it." She repeated herself in French and waited for answering movement. It was a bold strategy, but an intruder wouldn't know whether she was telling the truth or not, and her poise in the face of danger might be interpreted by a would-be assailant as the assurance that a firearm would bring.

"Please. Don't shoot," a female voice answered in Swahili.

Stafford pushed the netting out of the way. She could just make

174

out the diminutive form of a native woman standing by the hut door, the moonlight from the window bathing the interior in a dim glow.

"What are you doing in my room?" Stafford asked, her hand still on her backpack as though she was prepared to draw a weapon from it.

"I...I'm sorry. I didn't know what else to do. I heard about you from my cousin – you're a doctor, right?"

"What if I am?"

"It's my husband. He's sick. Very sick. But the soldiers won't let anyone through...he's going to die if he doesn't get help, just like the others."

"What others?"

"In my village. Nine have died so far, and four more are sick. My husband is one of them."

Stafford frowned. "Where's your village?"

"Maybe two hours away. I rode a bike, though, so only half an hour for me."

Stafford thought about the woman's story and made a decision. "What's wrong with your husband? You say he's sick..."

"He's as weak as a child. Can't get up. Diarrhea. Vomiting. Shakes like a leaf, like he's got a fever, but he isn't hot. And he has a rash." She hesitated. "Just like the others."

"The others...did they get sick together? Are they all in the same families?" Stafford was trying to figure out how contagious the mystery illness was.

"No. I'm fine. So are some of the other wives and husbands. It isn't catching, I don't think. Our mayor says it's from drinking bad water, but I'm always careful. My husband hasn't drunk any bad water."

"Do you know why the soldiers aren't letting anyone pass?"

"No. They just say nobody in or out."

"Has that ever happened before?"

The woman shook her head. "No."

Stafford's voice softened. "What's your name?"

"Nel."

"Nel, I'm Dr. Stafford. If you think you can get me to the village without being stopped by the soldiers, I'll come see your husband. But no promises – I don't know what I'm dealing with until I examine him."

"I think I can. My cousin has a bike you can borrow. I already asked."

"Give me a moment to get dressed. I'll be out in a minute," Stafford said.

"Thank you," Nel whispered. "Thank you so much."

"One minute, and then I'll come with you."

Nel slipped out the door, and Stafford hastily threw on her cargo pants and a long-sleeved shirt. She pulled on her boots and slipped the straps of her backpack over her shoulders, and checked the time – eleven o'clock, the sun having set five hours earlier. The idea of following a stranger into the jungle in the wee hours might have given some pause, but Stafford was an African veteran, and she knew that things worked differently on the continent. Nel was clearly distraught and had risked arrest by the military to beg her for help. Since the general was stonewalling for reasons unknown, the only way Stafford was going to learn what she was up against was going outside official channels – so far, following the rules had gotten her nowhere, and when Malek had reported earlier that there had been a problem with the entry visas for the rest of her team, she'd understood that she was being blocked at a high level and was unlikely to be successful in overcoming the obstacles being placed in her path.

She exited the hut and walked to where Nel was waiting with a relic of a bicycle. Stafford looked her over in the moonlight and saw that she was really just a girl, barely out of her teens, her legs two sticks jutting from a hand-sewn shift.

"Where's your cousin live?"

"Not far. This way," Nel whispered.

"I need to stop at my truck to get some supplies," Stafford warned. "It's over there," she said, pointing at the silhouette of the Land Rover – the only motor vehicle on the dirt street.

"Okay."

Malek was snoring when she reached the SUV, the windows all down and his seat reclined almost flat. She leaned through the window and whispered to him, "Malek, wake up. I need to get some stuff out of the back."

Malek stiffened and his eyes opened. He stared at her in groggy confusion, and then awareness crept into his gaze.

"What? Why? What happened?" he asked.

"I have a patient I need to see. I want to be able to pull some blood, swab his mouth, and protect myself from infection."

"A patient? Where are we going? The soldiers…"

Stafford shook her head. "Don't worry about that. It's just me. You stay here with the gear."

His eyes narrowed. "You're going somewhere alone? At this hour? It's not safe."

"I'll be done getting my gear in a second. You can go back to sleep once I'm gone." Stafford whispered the name of the village. "If I'm not back by dawn, something went wrong. Notify my headquarters and they'll take appropriate action."

Malek's tone hardened. "I can't let you go off on your own in the middle of the night, Doctor. Your people would kill–"

"I'm not a child, Malek. I'll be fine. Go back to sleep, and in all likelihood I'll be back by the time you wake up." She paused. "You wouldn't be willing to lend me your gun, would you?"

Malek had an old Mauser pistol in a hip holster that he'd worn the entire time they'd been together.

He undid his belt and pulled it and the holster free, and handed her the rig. "If you're caught with a gun, it'll be bad for you. I have a permit as a driver, for safety. But you're a foreigner…"

"Then I'll have to be careful not to get caught. I'll see you in the morning. Thank you, Malek."

Stafford rounded the rear fender and opened the cargo door, and quickly removed the items she needed and stuffed them into her backpack. She debated putting the gun in with them, but then reasoned that if she needed it, she probably wouldn't have the luxury of digging through her things for it. Stafford strapped on the belt, adjusted the holster, and pulled her shirt out of her pants so it covered the bulge, and then stepped away from the SUV with a wave to Malek.

Nel's cousin's bicycle was barely more than rust and rubber, and guiding it down a muddy road took some getting used to for a physician who hadn't ridden in twenty years. Once well away from the hamlet where Stafford had set up base, Nel led Stafford onto a trail that ran through the jungle, toward a river that was a major artery for the region.

The moon was high in the midnight sky when they reached Nel's village, and Nel indicated to Stafford to stay quiet until they had reached her dwelling. Outside the hut, she leaned her bike against a wall fashioned from branches, and Stafford did the same.

Nel's husband was in bad shape – a cursory inspection was enough to confirm the young woman's account. Stafford did a hurried examination and then asked Nel's permission to draw blood and take specimens. Nel agreed and, once Stafford was done, faced off with her, her youthful expression lined by stress and worry.

"What do you think?" Nel asked.

"It doesn't look like anything we've encountered from drinking bad water, I can tell you that much. The rash on his back, for example – that's an oddity. As are the symptoms of fever, yet with no temperature." Stafford paused. "Is he taking anything? Maybe some sort of herbal remedy? Or a potion of some kind?"

Nel moved to a wooden chest, opened it, and extracted a plastic pill bottle with a lot number printed on a blank label. "Just this. It's for malaria. Everyone was given some."

Stafford took the bottle from her and opened it. She shook out a few capsules and scowled. "How long ago did he start taking them?"

"About two weeks ago. There are only a few pills left."

"What about you? Did you take them, too?"

She shook her head. "No. I've already had malaria. It wouldn't do me any good."

Stafford studied the bottle. "Who gave them to you?"

"A man who came with the doctor from the vaccination clinic. Our mayor said it was safe to take."

"Who was this man? Did he give you a name?"

"No. I mean, the mayor handles all that for us. And he was brought by the vaccination clinic. Why? You think it's the pills that are making everyone sick?"

Stafford did her best to remain composed. "I don't know what to think. But I want to take this back to get it analyzed. It's probably nothing, but I don't want to make any assumptions without all the facts."

"What about my husband? Can you give him a shot or something? Some drugs?"

"Nel, I don't have all the answers. But I promise as soon as I know what we're dealing with, I'll return and help you."

"So you can't do anything for him?" she asked, her words damning.

Stafford shook her head. "Not yet. But I'll rush the results. Once we understand the problem, we can look for a solution."

"All the others died within three days of getting sick. This is the second night he's been like this."

Stafford swallowed sour bile that rose in her throat. "I'm sorry, Nel. I'll work as fast as I can."

The ride back to Stafford's hut seemed to take forever, not the least because of Nel's wordless condemnation of her inability to help her husband. Stafford tried not to let it get to her, but the pained look in the young woman's eyes had touched her to her core. If her husband's condition deteriorated like the others, he wouldn't last till nightfall of the next day, and they both knew it.

When they reached Stafford's village, Nel waved and rode off into the night, leaving Stafford to return the bicycle and do whatever she had to do. She wheeled the archaic conveyance to the Land Rover, unpacked her bag, and paused with the pill bottle in her hand. After a long moment of thought, she slipped the bottle into her shirt pocket along with the blood sample and the swabs, and after returning the bicycle to Nel's cousin, made her way to her hut, Malek's pistol still strapped to her hip, her expression determined and her eyes clear in spite of the hour.

CHAPTER 35

Highland Plains, Kenya

Mbogo, Adami's top lieutenant, stood in the shade of an overhang crafted from dried fronds, watching the river that Jaali would be coming down at any moment. He checked his watch for the fifth time in the last hour and refrained from any further pacing in the dirt – his new boots were already filthy enough. His subordinate was sitting out of the sun on a log that served as a bench by the side of the thatched building, smoking a cigarette, his relaxed demeanor the opposite of his boss's. Two SUVs and a pair of vans were parked beneath some trees near the water's edge, their sides splattered with dried mud from the trip there, and Mbogo gazed at them wistfully, wishing he were sitting in air-conditioned comfort instead of slow roasting on the banks of a desolate river.

Adami emerged from the building wearing oversized camouflage fatigues that could have doubled as a tent and glared at Mbogo as though he'd insulted him. "I thought you said they would be here by mid-afternoon."

"That's what Jaali told me. It must be taking them longer than he thought because of the rain this morning."

"It's hotter than the surface of the sun," Adami snapped.

Mbogo nodded, there being nothing productive to say that wouldn't anger the gangster more. He was framing a response when Adami's satellite phone rang.

The crime lord answered immediately, and Jaali's distinctive voice came over the speaker.

"We'll be there in ten minutes. There's been a wrinkle."

"A wrinkle?" Adami demanded. "What?"

"The hostages. We lost them."

Adami digested the information with his mouth hanging open. "Lost them? What the hell are you talking about?"

"Their boat capsized. We know the two women survived, but the rest didn't make it. We lost a couple of good men, too."

"How?"

"Crocodiles."

"How do you know the women made it?"

"We spotted them in the water. But we decided that it was more important to get back with the ransom than to try to pick up their trail on land. We wouldn't have made it to your position before dark, and that area of the river was teeming with crocs. It would have been a long shot to find where they landed and track them."

"So you let them go?"

"There wasn't much choice. But I'd be surprised if the crocodiles didn't get them."

Adami bit back his anger and nodded to himself. "I'll see you when you get here."

He hung up and cursed. He didn't particularly care whether the hostages lived or died, but the woman had become somewhat of an obsession for him. The area upriver was as wild as any on earth, and the chances of a pair of women living till nightfall were slim, but that didn't satisfy Adami – he hadn't trekked all the way from the shade of his winter camp to go back empty-handed.

He turned to Mbogo. "He lost the hostages and the woman. But I want them. I don't care what he has to do. He needs to find them and bring them to me, do you understand?"

Mbogo knew that Adami was blowing off steam telling him, but nodded as though he would take responsibility for supervising Jaali. It would further solidify his position as being superior to Jaali in Adami's eyes, which was critical for his aspirations.

He frowned. "I do. We can have him return to where they were last seen and see if he can find them."

"He should have stayed there and hunted them down."

Mbogo wasn't about to defend Jaali, and nodded assent. "You're right. I don't know what he could have been thinking. Probably about keeping the ransom safe."

"I don't care. My order was clear – I intend to deal with the woman myself." Adami shook his head and glared toward the river. "Incompetent idiot. He had her in his hands and managed to lose her."

Mbogo fought the urge to smile at Adami's reaction. There was no love lost between Mbogo and Jaali, and now that Yaro was out of the picture, Mbogo was the next in line to the throne. But Jaali was a serious contender, a capable enforcer with a quick wit, which meant that for Mbogo, he was a potential threat that would need to be neutralized. Adami ordering him back into the wilds of Kenya was a good way to keep him out of the loop for at least a little while. Mbogo could work on eliminating him permanently if he made it back alive.

Adami paced in front of the building for a few seconds, but the heat was too much, and he threw another dark look at Mbogo before heading back inside.

"Tell me the second you see them on the river," he ordered, and stormed back into the building, where he and eighteen of his men were lounging in the shade, the relative cool making the oppressive humidity slightly more bearable.

Mbogo turned to his subordinate and licked his lips. "Won't be long till they get here." He paused and eyed the doorway to make sure that Adami was out of earshot. "Wouldn't want to be Jaali right now."

The subordinate stubbed out his cigarette and nodded once. "That's for damn sure."

CHAPTER 36

St. Petersburg, Russian Federation

An old woman with a kerchief tied over her hair and sunglasses in a style ten years out of date pulled a cart laden with groceries along the sidewalk in an industrial area on the outskirts of town. She walked with the slow deliberation of someone whose every bone ached, her sensible lace-up shoes, heels rounded from use, brushing along the pavement. Her posture signaled fatigue and defeat, her shoulders stooped and her head hanging forward like a plow horse at the end of a demanding day.

She rounded the corner and continued to trudge along the cracked walkway. The building on her right that occupied half the block was a Soviet-era bunker with all of the architectural charm of a brick. Rows of grimy windows stretched the length of the two-story edifice, the structure's dank gray finish heightening the ponderous bluntness of the lines. The parking lot in front was empty because of the weekend, and a half dozen seagulls from the nearby Gulf of Finland were taking advantage of the solitude, squabbling over bits of refuse with noisy abandon.

The woman stopped near the service driveway and adjusted her overcoat. An observer would have noticed nothing to arouse suspicion as she muttered to herself. Nobody would have guessed that she was speaking into a micro-transmitter secreted in the lining of her collar; the idea of a geriatric babushka doing anything but trying to make it home before nightfall would have been ludicrous.

"Lot looks clear. No sign of the watchman," she said.

"He's probably inside," a voice answered in her earbud.

"Not dark enough to see whether there's a light on, but the

blueprints show the security desk as being by the front lobby."

"Then we should be clear."

She glanced at a CCTV camera mounted above the service entrance. "One cam. I'll hit it on your order."

"Make your move. We're on our way."

The woman tottered into the parking lot as though she'd lost her way. Once out of the camera's field of view, she abandoned her grocery basket and sprinted to the side of the building, where she edged along until she was at the limit of the camera's range. She removed a miniature can of flat black spray paint and pressed herself against the wall, and was nearing the camera when a black delivery van rolled to a stop at the curb.

She covered the remaining ten meters in a matter of seconds and emptied the can at the camera lens, standing on her tiptoes. Three men climbed out of the rear of the van and jogged to where she was waiting.

"All done," she said.

"Wait out here. You know what to do if the guard comes to investigate."

"Of course."

She returned to her character's shambling gait and made her way back to her grocery cart. When she reached it, she dropped the paint can in one of the sacks of produce, adjusted the vegetables in it so the container was hidden, and wheeled the basket back to the corner, her hand in her pocket clutching an aerosol-propelled dart gun that could penetrate two layers of clothing at up to four meters, its projectile loaded with enough nerve agent to drop a lumberjack and knock him out cold for several hours.

The hope was she wouldn't have to use it; the research division had assured them that the guard was likely slumbering – she knew his name, birthdate, history, home address, and habits, and in addition to being in his late fifties and in poor health, he was a drinker, as were many Russians of a certain age. The chances that he wasn't passed out on a weekend when his replacement wouldn't arrive until midnight were slim, but nevertheless she was prepared to take him if he showed his face while the operation was in progress.

The men gathered at the service entry, and one of them pressed a length of thermite rope around the lock, wedged three inches of det cord into the gummy rope, and inserted a small radio-controlled detonator cap. They stepped away and turned from the door, and after a moderately loud pop and a white-hot flare from the lock, returned to the entrance and tried the handle.

The door swung open, leaving a trail of molten metal where the thermite had cut through the bolt. Two of them hurried down the hall while the third stayed by the entrance, a more traditional, longer-range dart pistol in hand. They'd been instructed not to leave any casualties if they could help it, and the tranquilizer darts had been a compromise, although each member of the team also had a small 9mm pistol of Russian manufacture in the event the mission went sideways.

The pair worked their way down the corridor, their black knit caps serving as balaclavas now that they were unrolled over their faces. Their timeline was too short to bother with the half dozen security cameras that would film their entry and egress. However, their situation analyst had assured them that the cameras didn't feed live to security, which only monitored the two exterior cams and one in the lobby – these were purely for internal monitoring to prevent employee pilferage, their images stored on one of the servers in the vault where they were headed.

The building was home to a number of businesses involved in mining crypto-currencies, as well as to hundreds of private servers that required segregated operation in climate-controlled privacy.

They arrived at what the blueprint they'd memorized identified as vault six, and used another length of thermite rope and det cord to cut through the lock. Once inside, they quickly moved to the rack on the closest wall, where their target sat along with three other computers, each connected to its own private internet port for high-speed access.

An in-person incursion had been the only option – the server's firewall had been deemed unhackable in the time frame they had to work within, so the team had been deployed from Moscow, where they lived; all except the operative known as Rudolph, who was the technician of the group.

Rudolph knelt in front of the server, studied it for several seconds, and chuckled. "Piece of cake."

"How long?"

Rudolph removed a small leather wallet filled with tools that he spread out on the ground. "A minute, maybe less."

He was good to his word, and ninety seconds later, the server, numbered V13, was out of commission, and with it one of HonestyInternational's hosting resources.

They were back outside in a blink and moving to the van, the hard disk heavy in Rudolph's pocket. His earbud crackled and the woman's voice purred in his ear.

"That everything?"

"Yes. You can get going. See you back at base."

"Enjoy the drive, and good luck."

"You too."

CHAPTER 37

Democratic Republic of the Congo, Africa

Malek braked to a stop at the gate of the dirt airstrip, where Stafford's prop plane was scheduled to arrive any minute. He nodded to the armed guard, who approached the driver's side to check his identification. The man looked over his driver's license, glanced at Stafford, and then returned to the barrier that blocked the approach to the airstrip and raised it.

Two military vehicles and a police truck were sitting by the corrugated tin shack that served as the airstrip's terminal, customs clearance, and air traffic control. Malek drove to where four men in uniform were waiting, and threw Stafford a worried look.

"That's odd," he said, twisting the ignition off. The motor died with a shudder, and Stafford and Malek climbed from the SUV and walked around to the rear cargo door. He helped her with her bag; the hazmat suit and the medical kit would remain with him until she returned – which she might not, based on the lack of cooperation she'd received since her arrival. The general had yet to return her calls, and she'd finally lost patience late that morning and taken matters into her own hands. She'd called her headquarters and arranged for a plane to fly her to a larger airport for an international flight, and was scheduled to travel to Paris, where she would be allowed to use the facilities at the Pasteur Institute to analyze her samples.

The officials stood in the shade and waited for her to approach. One in a police uniform gave her an insincere smile and indicated a metal table by the door.

"Customs. We'll need to check your things," he said.

She held his stare. "I'm not leaving the country on this flight. I'm headed to Kinshasa International Airport."

"Sorry. But orders. It's to curtail smuggling," the man explained, his tone adamant.

"I'm a guest of your government. A physician. Hardly a smuggler."

"That may be, but we have to check every traveler's luggage."

She sighed and placed her backpack and bag on the table. "What do people smuggle?"

He moved to the table. "Ivory. Drugs. Rhino horn. Weapons."

"All I have are some blood samples in a biohazard container."

He opened her backpack and upended it onto the table, spilling the contents across the metal top. He sorted through her things, pausing at the biocontainer and setting it to the side. When he had gone through everything, he did the same with her travel bag, taking obvious pleasure in handling her underthings.

The roar of an engine overhead approached, and a four-seater Cessna scarcely larger than the SUV dropped from the sky and touched down on the dirt runway in a cloud of russet dust. The aircraft decelerated to the end of the strip and then pivoted and taxied toward the shack.

The officer stopped when he came to the plastic pill container Nel had given her.

"And what is this?"

"Oh. Those are part of the samples," she said, raising her voice to be heard over the plane.

"Drugs?"

"I don't know. I need to have them tested."

He unscrewed the top and peered inside at the four remaining tablets, and his eyes narrowed. "You don't know what these are?"

"No. That's why we need to test them."

He slipped the bottle into his pocket and tapped the top of the biocontainer. "You can't take either these or the pills with you. I'll have to have our experts verify that they aren't anything prohibited."

Stafford's face fell. "But that's the entire reason I'm here. To take samples and identify the disease that's killing your villagers." She withdrew the general's permission document from her shirt pocket and unfolded it. "Your government approved it."

The man didn't even glance at the document. "Then they should have no problem passing these items along. You say you're headed to Kinshasa? If they clear them, we can have them sent on the next flight."

Her expression darkened. "This is outrageous. You have no right to confiscate these. I told you – they're samples."

He nodded, but his face remained set. "So you say. I don't know anything about that. I'm just doing my job. And that is to stop any contraband from leaving. That could be contraband. I can't take the chance."

"Then there's no reason for me to get on the plane. I'll wait for your expert. When will he be here?"

"No way of knowing. I'll radio once I get back to the station," he said, disinterested in her outrage.

Stafford made a visible effort to compose herself. "Officer, I need those samples to do my job and to stop the spread of a new plague. You have the paperwork there, which authorizes me to do whatever I need. What I need is to get those to a testing facility before the blood isn't useable."

"I heard you the first time. Now you need to listen good. I don't know what you're doing here or what your story is, and it's not my problem to figure it out. I'm not stopping you from leaving, but those items aren't going with you. So you can get on the plane, or you can wait until our customs process is finished, which could take hours…or days. Doesn't matter to me which you do."

Stafford's jaw clenched. "I want a receipt for both the pills and the container."

He patted his pockets and gave her an unpleasant grin. "I don't have any receipts with me."

"You can write it on a piece of paper."

He looked to the military men, who were smiling at the exchange, and shrugged. "No pen or paper, either."

She exhaled in frustration and threw her belongings back in the bag as the men watched in amusement. When the table was cleared, she gave them a dirty look and stalked to the plane, her anger more than obvious. The pilot greeted her, and she handed him her bags and then waved at Malek, who was chatting with the officer. Malek waved back, and Stafford climbed up into the seat next to the pilot and strapped in as he rounded the prop and slid into his harness.

Two minutes later they were airborne and climbing into a dusk sky. Stafford resisted patting her back pocket, where she'd secreted the pills Nel had given her in a ziplock baggie along with a small vial of blood in anticipation of the locals pulling something at the airport. She'd substituted Nel's pills with four of her vitamins, and the ruse had worked. She wasn't out of the woods yet, she knew, but the likelihood that they would have someone at the international airport to do an even more thorough search was unlikely.

She sat back as the plane bounced through rough air and gazed out the window at the jungle below.

Whatever was going on, she would get to the bottom of it. They'd badly underestimated her. As had Malek, who had obviously tipped them off.

"How long?" she yelled at the pilot over the drone of the engine.

"Forty-five minutes, maybe a little more," he said.

She nodded and closed her eyes. The most arduous leg of her trip was over, but the next hours would determine whether the journey had been a waste or not.

CHAPTER 38

Highland Plains, Kenya

Gabriel and Jomo's men had been in position for half a day on the dirt road from the river village to the township he'd overheard Jaali discussing, but there had been no sign of Jaali's group. Gabriel had dispatched a man to the little hamlet to verify that they hadn't arrived before Gabriel had organized the ambush, and the man had returned an hour earlier to report that nobody had seen anything – the procession hadn't gotten there yet.

The trip had been grueling, with the river crossing the most arduous part, there being a dearth of boats on that desolate stretch. They'd eventually found a fishing camp and convinced the fishermen at gunpoint to ferry them across, but had lost valuable time in their search, heightening Gabriel's anxiety and frustration.

He'd been dozing since the scout's return, trying to catch up on his sleep deficit. The men sat silent in their hiding places. The wooded area they'd chosen was perfect for an ambush – the only road to the town snaked through it, and the brush was dense enough to hide a small army. Whenever Jaali showed himself, the fight would be over quickly, and Gabriel would be four and a half million dollars richer after paying off the diamond debt – enough for him to bow out of the game for good and enjoy the good life somewhere civilized. With what he'd already managed to put away, he could envision a big boat and a harem of willing companions someplace where trade winds cooled blue water and the beer was always cold. Perhaps the Caribbean, he thought absently, drifting in and out of sleep.

A whispered warning from his left woke him to alertness in

seconds. "Someone's coming up the road. But...they're in vehicles."

"What?" Gabriel blurted.

"You can hear the engines." The gunman paused. "What do you want to do?"

Gabriel's mind turned over the possibilities. "Where would they have gotten vehicles?"

"Could be they were waiting for them on this side of the river."

"Hold your fire until we can confirm it's them and not some safari group."

The man nodded and passed the word over his handheld radio. Gabriel chambered a round in his rifle and waited for the trucks to come into view, the sound of their engines straining along the road growing louder by the moment. He squinted in the gloaming as the first vehicle rolled into view – an SUV with two men standing on the running boards on each side, gripping the roof railings one-handed, AK-47s pointed at the brush. Next came a pair of vans, their side doors open and windows down, packed with armed men.

"That's no safari," Gabriel murmured to the gunman at his side. "Open fire when they're in range. Start with grenades to disable the vehicles."

The gunman relayed the order on the radio and slipped it into his breast pocket. Gabriel shifted his rifle into position and fought to slow his heart rate, the adrenaline that had flooded his bloodstream at the appearance of the motorcade fighting against him. He hadn't bargained on attacking a motorized convoy. The ten men he'd brought were hardened fighters, and Gabriel had figured they could cut down Jaali's exhausted troops before they knew what hit them. But this was a large force, and the men looked alert and wary, giving Gabriel a moment of doubt about the viability of his plan.

He considered calling off the ambush and radioing Jomo for reinforcements, but dismissed the idea. It would reflect badly on Gabriel that he'd walked into something he hadn't foreseen, and the warlord might be reluctant to mount a frontal assault on Adami's stronghold, ransom or not. Worse, it could be that now that Adami's men had collected the money, they planned to continue straight through to some other destination, and all of Gabriel's assumptions had been incorrect.

Either eventuality didn't bode well for Gabriel's survival, so whether wise or not, he was committed to attacking the convoy.

When the lead SUV was in grenade-tossing range, Gabriel gave the nod to the radio operator, pulled the pin on one of the orbs, and flung it at the SUV. The grenade's arc fell just short of the road, Gabriel's aim off from having to avoid the branches overhead, and the blast shook the vehicle from near the shoulder, peppering the side of it with shrapnel but failing to disable it.

The men on the explosion side fell to the road, their bloody torsos shredded, but the big vehicle sped up, its flattened tires disintegrating as the rims cut grooves in the dirt. Then all hell broke loose, and Gabriel's men were firing at the road, their rounds punching into the remaining SUV and the vans before he could lob another grenade.

The vans stopped and reversed as the gunmen inside returned fire through the open doors, and bullets snapped by Gabriel's head. He ducked down and tried to focus his aim at the lead SUV, which had careened off the road ahead and was now stationary, with its doors open and its gunmen firing at Gabriel's force. One of Adami's shooters flew backward with a scream, his chest blown apart by an AK burst, but three more instantly loosed volleys at Jomo's gunman, their concentrated fire silencing him for good.

"There's too many," the radioman warned over the bark of his rifle. Gabriel ignored him. There was no option now but to fight it out, and they still had the high ground even if outnumbered three to one. Gabriel hurled another grenade at the road, and this one made it onto the dirt, blowing a crater a yard and a half wide but doing little damage to the vehicles other than shattering one of the van's windshields.

He'd obviously revealed too much of himself to Adami's force when he'd stood to throw the grenade because the brush around him shredded from incoming fire. Gabriel flung himself flat against the ground, eyes clenched as rounds whistled through the leaves only inches away. Chunks of bark flew from the tree behind him, and for a moment he thought he'd been hit when several of them struck him in the back.

A lull in the shooting told him that the gunmen were changing magazines, and he looked over to his radioman. "Tell them to fall back," he yelled, his ears still ringing from the gunfire. Only when the man didn't move did Gabriel take a second look and see that the top of his skull was blown off, layering the back of his olive green shirt with bone shards and brains.

Panic rose in Gabriel's throat, and he dog-crawled backward, his thoughts now on self-preservation rather than leading the attack. More rounds sizzled through the greenery around him as the gunmen renewed their onslaught, and he paused, lying in a depression that offered partial cover. He waited, his pulse thudding in his ears, and when the shooting stopped again, continued backing away from the road. Once he was clear of direct sightline, he twisted around so he could move faster and began crawling for all he was worth.

That choice rewarded him with the burn of a slug searing through his calf muscle, and he rolled onto his back, dropping his rifle and clutching his wounded leg. Blood oozed from the entry and exit holes, and his hand came away smeared with red when he felt for his belt buckle with trembling fingers, the pain so excruciating he nearly blacked out. He managed to get the belt free and cinched it around his knee, maintaining pressure on it until the bleeding slowed to a trickle.

He probed his shin with his free hand and was relieved to feel that the bullet hadn't hit bone. If it had, his tibia or fibula would have shattered, eliminating any thought of escape. As it was, evading Adami's men would be difficult but not impossible – assuming he could choke down the blinding agony that radiated up his leg and get clear of the killing field the brush had become.

The intensity of the shooting from the road diminished as Adami's men mopped up the remainder of Jomo's force, back shooting the few who attempted to scramble away into the brush. When the gunfire stopped, Gabriel's ears were ringing so badly he could barely hear, and the appearance of two of Adami's men, AKs pointed at his head, took him by surprise.

"Don't shoot," he begged in Swahili, raising his hands over his head, completely exposed as he lay on the ground. One of the men called out over his shoulder to the SUV while the other trained his weapon on Gabriel.

"Got a live one here. A white man. You want I should shoot him?"

"White?" a baritone voice answered back. "No. Bring him down here so I can have a look at him."

"Half his leg's blown off. Want to send someone to help?"

A pair of men emerged from the brush a minute later and hauled Gabriel to his feet. The accompanying pain was so severe he lost consciousness, as well as control of his bladder. When he came to, he was lying on the road, flies buzzing around his leg wound, with a man the size of a small mountain staring down at him.

"Who are you?" Adami asked, his voice quiet. "Who are you, and what are you doing here? Mercenary?"

Gabriel attempted to think up a convincing lie, but the blood loss and shock had slowed his wits. He tried to speak, but only managed an incoherent croak. Adami took in the stain on his pants and grimaced in disgust.

"Last chance. Who are you?" the gangster demanded, an edge in his tone this time.

"I...they made me...go with...them. Ambush."

"Made you? What are you talking about? Who are you?" Adami demanded.

"I recognize him," a gunman from the vans called to Adami. "He's one of the prisoners we took from the dinner."

Adami scowled at Gabriel with new animosity. "One of the hostages? Really..."

"They...made me...tell them where...you were going..."

"Tell who? Who's helping you?"

"A drug...lord. Jomo. He...after...the ransom..."

"Jomo?" Adami's eyes narrowed to slits. "Jomo put you up to this?" Adami hesitated. "Or is it the other way around? How did he know about the money? Of course. You told him. To save your skin. Isn't that right?"

Gabriel tried to answer, but his vision blurred, and then the world swam as his consciousness receded and he was out again.

This time when he regained consciousness, the pain in his leg was joined by searing agony from both sides of his rib cage, where Adami had kicked him mercilessly before ordering his men to toss him into the van. Every bounce of the vehicle over the road felt like a thousand needles stabbing into his kidneys and liver, and each breath brought new misery. Any hope he'd had of making it out of his predicament alive vanished as he came fully alert, although a faint glimmer remained – they hadn't killed him yet, which meant they wanted something. Maybe to ransom him?

The van coasted to a stop in front of a Kenyan country house, a colonial relic that was a symbol of repression by British and German settlers, now fallen to disuse, its wood siding curled and its paint stripped away by the relentless baking of the sun. Adami appeared at the side door of the van and instructed his men to drag Gabriel to a pole by the gate, and to lash his wrists to it so the heat could broil him alive.

"No," Gabriel begged. "Please. I can…help you…" he croaked.

"Help me?" Adami boomed. "Good. I want help."

"Anything."

"Who is the woman Jaali captured?"

Gabriel debated lying, but the time for that had passed. "Works…for…Alger…non."

"She works for the drug company?" He looked over at Mbogo, who was watching with his arms folded across his chest. "I knew it." He prodded Gabriel, his broad face hard. "Is she Israeli? She has to be."

"Don't…know…" Gabriel grimaced. "Maybe." He coughed once, and the agony was so profound he nearly blacked out again.

"You want me to spare your life, tell me everything you know about her."

"I…can help…catch…her…"

"You keep telling me you can help. How?"

"She…she…if you…grab…Shira…"

Understanding flashed in Adami's eyes. "Ah, I see. She's involved because of the girl? Probably Israeli intelligence, then. That would explain how capable she is," Adami said. He glared at Gabriel. "So Jomo, and this woman. Is there anything else?"

"I…I'll help you…with…her…"

Adami laughed, the sound ugly, like a steel crate dragged across rough pavement. He glanced at Mbogo again and motioned to Gabriel. "Leave him here. Our friend here deserves to see the miracle of our country firsthand."

Gabriel tried to shake his head and groaned in pain at the attempt. "No…"

"The hyenas and jackals are probably the worst, although the fire ants will eat you slowly. Maybe you'll be especially lucky and your last impression will be a cheetah or leopard. No matter. Nothing wounded makes it through an African night. Kenya is unforgiving of interlopers like you, my friend." He stared at Gabriel with a cold smile. "I'll attend to the woman and Jomo myself. You will feed the worms and will beg for a swift death."

CHAPTER 39

Shira followed close behind Jet as she wended her way around thickets of dense vegetation, the ground firmer after the heat of the day had baked the moisture from it. They'd been hiking for hours, and the terrain had slowly changed from brush to long stretches of tall grass interspersed by forest.

Jet looked up at the plum-colored sky and slowed as they approached another seemingly impenetrable area of trees and underbrush. She checked her watch and stopped at an outcropping of rock.

"Let's rest for a few minutes before we continue," she said, and Shira nodded.

"At least it's not as hot as earlier."

"That's about the only thing going for us right now," Jet agreed.

"So what do we do next? It'll be dark soon."

"I think we keep going until we're too tired or can't see anymore."

"There are a lot of natural hazards. It probably isn't smart to try to continue at night."

"No question." Jet paused. "We just need to find a village."

Heat lightning crackled over the mountains, and Shira studied the clouds that hung over the peaks. "Looks like a storm."

"If there's no village nearby, we should probably try to find some shelter," Jet said.

"Like what? This is mostly plains."

"The trees might give us at least some cover. Better than nothing."

Shira looked off into the distance. "I still can't believe they're all dead."

Jet hadn't told her about Gabriel's betrayal. "But we're not," she said. "That's the important thing, for now."

"Assuming we get out of this alive, you mean."

"So far we're in one piece." Jet sat on the ground and rolled her head slowly, loosening the kinks that had collected in her neck.

Shira joined her with a heavy sigh. "Sure is different than I thought it would be. I signed up for hosting a dinner."

Jet managed a smile. "Why that kind of job?"

Shira's face clouded. "It was about the only thing my father would let me do. I wanted to take a position with a humanitarian aid group, but he wouldn't hear of it. Too much chance of falling on the wrong side of authority, he said. Didn't want to rock the diplomatic boat with his daughter working with unfortunates and maybe forming opinions that ran counter to the accepted narrative."

Jet appraised her. "You sound bitter."

"Oh, it's not his fault. I mean, I get it. He has to be careful, and there's so much corruption here…he didn't want me to get involved in any of the relief efforts. Some of them are controversial with the locals. Especially with the government officials who siphon off most of the money earmarked for their people. They don't want any of that getting reported." She paused. "I mean, I understand that all governments are imperfect. But the level of crookery here is…it's like the Wild West, you know?"

"I just keep my head down and try to do my job," Jet countered.

Shira looked away. "I've heard stories you wouldn't believe. Atrocities that would be front-page news if they happened anywhere else in the world. But nobody seems to care. It's like Africa is a different planet, where anything goes. Same as ever. It's got a long history of being abused by everyone. Nothing new about that."

"You sound passionate about it. What would happen if you defied your father?"

"Oh, it's not like that – it's not that I'm afraid. It's that I don't want to mess up his career – it's all he's got, besides me. He explained the issue, and I completely understand. He has to play a part, and he can't afford for me to become a liability." She sat in silence for several seconds. "It's just hard to watch all the injustice and stay on the sidelines. Whole areas starve every year because their governors stole the food and sold it elsewhere. Medical supplies intended for hard-hit areas somehow wind up being rerouted and marketed for ten cents on the dollar. And the drug companies…Africa is like an unregulated lab."

Jet frowned. "Funny that you wound up hosting dinners for one of them."

Shira matched her expression. "The irony's not lost on me." She sighed. "I still can't believe they only sent you. No offense. I mean, what you did back in the boat and at the camp…but…"

"Is it because I'm a woman?"

"Um, that's part of it. But actually it's more that they sent you in here alone."

"Again, I was only supposed to make sure the kidnappers got the money, not start a war," Jet said.

Shira studied Jet's face. "That must be odd. Doing this for a living."

Jet smiled. "I was going to say the same thing about being a hostess for people you despise."

"Oh, I don't have a problem with them as individuals or anything. They were all really nice. It's more…ideologically. You meet enough people who have been really harmed by these companies, and you see the world differently. I worked for a charity the first months I was here, to learn the language some and get acclimated, and the victims I met, the stories I heard…really terrible stuff." She shifted to a more comfortable position and stretched her arms over her head. "Many of the problems Africa faces are because the countries' leaders are a bunch of crooks that steal everything that isn't bolted down, and they sell their populations out instead of protecting them."

Jet sighed. "Don't most countries work the same way?"

Shira frowned. "Maybe. But that doesn't make it right."

Jet cocked her head, and her expression grew serious. "Do you smell that?"

Shira sniffed the air. "What?"

Jet pushed to her feet and looked to the east. "Smoke."

Shira rose too. "A village?"

"Maybe. Let's see if we can figure out where it's coming from."

Jet led the way from the grove, following her nose. Fifteen minutes later they drew near to another cluster of trees, this one spanning a larger area, and Jet touched Shira's arm.

"It's coming from in there."

"So not a village."

"No. Probably poachers."

"That's bad. They're almost as dangerous as the kidnappers."

Jet nodded. "Maybe. But if they have weapons, it might solve one of our problems."

"How?"

Jet pointed at the darkening sky. "Once it's night, I'll find their fire and see what we're dealing with. They won't be expecting anyone out in the middle of nowhere."

"You're going to take them on? How?"

She shook her head. "Not take them on – see if I can steal a weapon. We need to eat, or we're not going to be able to keep going. A gun would help bag something edible."

Shira looked at her like she was crazy. "Are you serious?"

"You need to stay hidden. I'll be back. Don't move no matter what you hear, understand?"

"What are you going to do?"

Jet's expression darkened. "Make it up as I go along."

Shira sat by one of the tree trunks at the edge of the wooded area, her demeanor making clear her disapproval for Jet's decision to go off on an adventure and leave her helpless and alone. Jet didn't react, and crept into the brush, her footsteps silent in the grass.

She spotted the source of the smoke near the other side of the trees – three tents, new by their appearance, grouped around a cooking fire, with a fourth larger tent that was weathered and sun-faded set apart from the rest.

A trio of Caucasian men, well fed and wearing expensive safari garb, were passing a bottle around the fire and smoking cigarettes as a pair of Kenyans cleaned up an area where they'd dined. The hunters were bantering in American-accented English, joking about the coming hunt. She listened for a few minutes and then crept away from the camp, retracing her trail to where Shira was waiting, now enshrouded in darkness.

"So?" Shira whispered.

"It's a bow-hunting party. Not poachers. American."

"They do a fair number of those. More and more popular since the backlash against trophy hunting with guns."

"They're putting away a fair amount of alcohol. I'm going back to see if I can snag one of their bows. Silent."

"You know how to shoot one?"

Jet smiled in the gloom. "I'll try my best. Hang out here until I return. Then we'll see about hunting down dinner."

"I don't think I can eat raw meat. I'm starving, but…it would make me sick."

"One problem at a time."

The hunters were still drinking when Jet returned to her vantage point, but the locals had called it a night and were nowhere to be seen. The bottle emptied as it made the rounds among the men, and one by one they staggered to their tents, obviously the worse for their bout with what appeared to be single malt Scotch. She gave it a half hour after the last of the Americans had gone to bed, and then sneaked into the camp, moving through the shadows like a phantom.

The bows were leaning up against a fallen tree near the service tent, and Jet selected the most expensive one, along with a quiver of arrows. She looked around the camp and spotted a pack of Marlboros by the fire pit. She worked her way to the circle of stones and pocketed the lighter, and after a moment's thought, the cigarettes, and then jogged toward the brush and vanished into the darkness.

Shira hadn't moved, and when Jet materialized beside her, she almost screamed.

"You startled me," she complained, and then eyed the bow. "You got it!"

Jet held her finger to her lips. "Let's get moving," she whispered. "We still need to find dinner."

"I was thinking…there must be a village or a road nearby if they're on foot. We should look for a trail once it's light out," Shira whispered back.

Jet nodded. "Good idea. But for now, keep your eyes peeled for anything we can eat."

An hour later, at another stretch of wooded area and heavy brush, Jet held out her arm to stop Shira and froze, listening intently. They heard snorting and rustling from the trees, and Jet signaled to Shira to stay put as she drew an arrow from the quiver and notched it.

She took cautious steps, grateful for what light the moon was offering, and spotted several dark forms scuttling along a trail ten yards ahead of her. Jet raised the bow and drew the bowstring, and after following the last in the clump of animals with the razor-sharp hunting point, loosed the shaft with a twanging snap.

The arrow flew true, skewering the last warthog through the neck. The animal shrieked and went down as the rest of the boars scattered, and Jet had another arrow ready as she approached the wounded animal. She fired at its skull from close range, putting it out of its misery, and waited until the sound of the rest of the passel of hogs had receded before she knelt by the fallen warthog and cut steaks with her blade.

The moon was high by the time Jet and Shira had found a suitable area to make a small fire and cook the steaks. They ate in silence, the meal their first in over twenty-four hours, and when they were finished with the meat, Jet tromped through the embers in her boots and kicked dirt over them.

"I'll keep watch for the first couple of hours," Jet said. "Get some rest."

"I…I've never shot a bow, so I'm not sure how much good I'm going to do keeping watch when it's my turn."

Jet gave a small smile. "You don't need to be able to shoot. If you see anything, just wake me up. But for now, don't worry about it. Get some sleep and I'll wake you when it's your turn."

CHAPTER 40

Berlin, Germany

Heinrich Mueller looked up from his computer monitor as Laurel Weiss entered the lab and approached his work area. Mueller was one of the Mossad's top computer techs and had been handed the assignment of searching the Russian hard disk for clues as to the identity of whoever had uploaded the classified ministry documents. Weiss, a tall woman with ebony hair pulled back in a severe ponytail, was in charge of field operations for the section, and because of geographical proximity, the job had fallen into her lap.

"Anything?" she asked.

Mueller returned to the monitor, giving a slight frown at the odor of nicotine that wafted from Weiss's clothing. He reached for his coffee mug but after a moment's hesitation pushed it aside, remembering that he hadn't filled it since draining his fifth cup of the day.

"Yes," he said. "I've cracked the encryption, and I've isolated the log files. Right now I'm verifying the IP addresses of the uploads. I should have something shortly."

"What's shortly?"

Mueller's frown deepened. "That's hard to pinpoint. But sometime today." Mueller had been called in before dawn, and his voice was hoarse with fatigue.

Weiss stepped closer to him with her hands folded in front of her. "I'm receiving a lot of pressure on this, Heinrich. I'm not trying to tell you how to do your job, but…"

"Then don't. It's like making a baby. It takes as long as it takes."

Weiss appeared to be ready to say something else, but then

thought better of it and nodded. "I'll go back to twiddling my thumbs, then. You know where to find me."

Mueller tapped a command on his keyboard. "I'll let you know as soon as I have something concrete."

"Have you at least narrowed it down to a region of the world? A country?"

Mueller let out an annoyed exhalation and swiveled toward Weiss. "Yes. That's what I'm verifying. But it appears the posts originated in Africa."

"Africa?" Weiss repeated.

Mueller nodded. "Assuming that the poster didn't use a proxy redirect. But those leave fingerprints, which is what I'm running searches for right now. There's no point in announcing I have the area when later it will turn out that it was faked. We both know that all the clandestine agencies have the ability to spoof each other, as well as any country they choose."

Weiss's expression hardened. "You think this is a state actor?"

"It could be. I don't rule anything out until I've run all the tests. It could also be some twelve-year-old in his parents' basement using a proxy mask. Anything's possible."

"But you'll be able to tell definitively?"

"If I'm allowed to work without interruption, yes." His voice softened. "Sorry. I didn't mean to bite your head off. It's just that I wasn't expecting to spend my birthday hammering at the keys."

Weiss's eyebrows arched. "It's your birthday? I…I didn't know."

"Not your fault. But believe me, I've got every incentive in the world to get this cracked so I can go home."

Weiss nodded. "Well, happy birthday."

"Thanks," Mueller said morosely, and returned his attention to the screen.

Less than an hour later it was Weiss's turn to look up from her workstation at Mueller, who was standing in the doorway of her office.

"I've got it," he said.

She rose and approached him. "You don't sound too excited."

"I've got it isolated to a city, but I can't narrow it down any further without access to the phone company's database so I can pin the IP to a physical address."

"Where did the post originate?"

"Nairobi, Kenya."

"You're positive?"

He nodded. "Absolutely. And there are no artifacts that would indicate that it was bounced, so that's where they were uploaded."

Weiss thought for a moment. "We need to send this to headquarters. They've got hackers who can get into anything."

"I figured. But that's all I can do from here with just the hard disk. Hacking's not my thing."

She offered a tired smile of congratulations. "Good job, Heinrich."

"Thanks. I'll shoot you my notes with the backup along with the report. You can forward that to Tel Aviv, and then it's in their hands."

CHAPTER 41

Highland Plains, Kenya

Jet awoke to Shira shaking her shoulder. She sat up and looked at the younger woman, and blinked away the grogginess.

Shira whispered in the predawn, "I heard something."

"What?" Jet asked.

"Dogs."

Jet was on her feet in an instant. She scooped up the bow and looked around. "How far away?"

"I don't know. But I heard a bark." She swallowed, the fear in her eyes real. "Nothing in the wild out here barks that I know of."

"Which direction?"

"Back where we came from."

Jet nodded. She hadn't considered the possibility that the kidnappers would be so tenacious. But if they'd gotten tracking dogs at a village, which was the likely explanation, she'd badly underestimated them.

"Follow me."

"What are we going to do?" Shira asked.

"We're dead if they catch sight of us once it's light out. So we need to put as much distance between us and them as possible before the sun's up."

"But if they have dogs, won't they just keep coming?"

"Maybe. As long as we've got a decent head start and we stay low in the grass, we have a chance."

"Against automatic rifles?"

"They can only shoot us if they see us. Now move. We're going to have to run for a while."

Jet took off to the southwest, running as fast as her legs would carry her. Shira struggled to keep up, and after a quarter hour Jet could hear her breath coming out in wheezes. Jet slowed to a trot and waited for her to catch up, and then twisted to whisper to her, "The sun will be up in a few minutes. Any lead we're going to get has to be now."

"I...I don't know how much farther I can...go..."

"Do the best you can," Jet countered, and picked up her pace again, driving herself hard, but keeping her speed to one she could sustain for hours if need be. Jet had the benefit of years of training, not to mention a workout regimen that would have been daunting for a triathlete. It was obvious that despite her youth, Shira wasn't in anywhere near the same shape. But Jet's ace in the hole was that after tracking them through the night, their pursuers would be exhausted and moving at a sluggish pace. Unlike Jet and Shira, they weren't running for their lives, and human nature would have them plodding along rather than sprinting.

Amber and titian painted the eastern horizon when they reached a watering hole surrounded by scraggly trees. Wildebeest scattered as they neared the water, galloping away at the unexpected sight of humans in their domain. Jet watched with bow in hand as Shira drank her fill, and then knelt to quench her thirst when the younger woman had finished.

A distant plume of smoke in the direction they'd been heading caught her eye, and Jet rose, pointing at it. "Signs of life."

"You think...?"

"Don't get your hopes up. But it looks like it's about an hour away if we make decent time."

"My legs are killing me."

"I know. But you don't want to give your muscles a chance to stiffen up."

"Can't we rest a few minutes?"

Jet shook her head. "Not now. If they catch sight of us, it's game over. We have to keep moving."

Shira moaned in protest, but nodded. "You're like the Terminator or something. I don't have that kind of stamina."

"Find it in you. Choice B is they catch us."

"I know."

Jet took off at a jog, and Shira reluctantly followed in her footsteps. A pair of curious buzzards wheeled in the dawn sky, the only other living things in the vicinity now that the wildebeest had fled. To the west, Mount Kilimanjaro's peak jutted in the distance, ringed by clouds glowing pink in the morning light. Soon Jet was running with a fluid gait, a second smoke spire near the first urging her forward, the likelihood they were nearing civilization increasing with every step.

A half hour later they could see the outlines of buildings shimmering in the distance like a mirage. Jet slowed to an easier pace as they approached, and the scattering of huts on the outskirts gave way to cinderblock buildings with sun-bleached façades. Locals stared at the unlikely apparition of two women covered in red dust walking into town from the plains, Jet sporting a hunting bow, and then averted their eyes, as though looking at them for too long might cause them harm.

"Now what?" Shira asked.

"We stick out like sore thumbs. We need to find someone to buy the bow so we can get some clothes and pay for bus fare to Nairobi."

"Most towns will have street markets – stalls the locals set up to trade whatever they've got to sell."

"Then here's a chance to practice your Swahili. Ask the first person who doesn't look like they'll run away when you open your mouth."

Shira got her chance at the next intersection, a dusty junction where a spindly old man was seated in the shade, a rail-thin dog by his side. Shira greeted the man with a smile and spoke in friendly tones, and he responded in kind, rolling his eyes as though considering a great truth before answering. Jet waited for Shira to translate, her eyes roaming over the street.

"He says down that way is a market, and there's a store next to it that buys and sells things, but the owner is a thief and will try to steal your bow for next to nothing."

"Sounds promising. Did he have any advice?"

"To try the street vendors first. Maybe somebody will recognize its value. He says it's a fine bow, and if he were a younger and richer man, he would gladly buy it."

Jet managed a smile and they set off down the road, no cars in sight, only a few bicycles and gaunt men and women, those with baskets on their heads moving with surprising speed given their cargo. The sidewalk market was quiet, with only a few vendors there at the early hour. A swarm of flies buzzed around pools of mystery fluid in the dirt rut that served as a gutter.

Shira made inquiries at each stall, and a few asked to inspect the bow, but nobody had any interest in buying it. After thanking the last merchant, they made their way to the shop the old man had described, and found it closed. Shira asked a woman who was walking by, her robe and headdress signaling her faith, what time it opened, and she flashed a shy smile and said something that sounded to Jet's ear like a guess before hurrying away.

"Well?" Jet asked.

"She said maybe in a few minutes. Which could mean anything. It's cultural. That's the same as saying she didn't know, which would have been impolite."

"If we had any money, I'd say let's get something to eat, but first things first."

Time crawled by and the heat rose. Eventually a portly man in his fifties ambled down the sidewalk and approached the iron bars that shuttered the store. They waited until he'd unlocked the barrier, swung it to the side, and disappeared inside before mounting the steps and looking through the open doorway.

The man was seated behind a glass display case, which he was wiping with a rag. He looked up at them and offered Jet a smile that reminded her of an eel. He said something in Swahili, and Jet nudged Shira into action. She stepped forward and indicated the bow that Jet was holding. The man grimaced like she had spit in his face, and then held out a hand. Jet offered him the bow, and he inspected it carefully before setting it down and removing the arrows from the quiver and doing the same. When he'd finished and replaced the arrows, he gave them a shrug that required no translation and said something in a low tone.

Shira turned to Jet. "He says it is a fine weapon, but that business has been terrible, so he has no money."

Jet nodded. "Then he can't buy it?" she asked, stepping forward to retrieve the bow and quiver. "Does he know anyone who would be interested?"

Shira translated, and the man eyed the bow again. Another exchange, and Shira leaned toward Jet. "He says nobody he knows would buy it. Nobody has money. The economy is a wreck and people are struggling to survived. But he said if we have to sell it, he could offer us a little – far less than he knows it is worth, but all he has."

"Did he mention a number?"

"No."

"Ask him how much he would give us for it."

Shira did, and after considerable fidgeting and studying the bow, he named a price so low that Shira laughed out loud.

"That bad?" Jet asked.

"We're wasting our time. One of the arrows is worth more than that," Shira said, collecting the quiver and handing Jet the bow.

They were halfway to the doorway when the proprietor said something. Shira paused and slowly turned back to him. "He doubled the price and says that's the absolute best he can do," she told Jet.

"Ask him how much bus fare for two to Nairobi is, and ask him if he has clothes that might fit us. And we'll need food and water."

Shira relayed the message, and the owner made another face and checked his watch as though they were wasting his time.

Ten minutes later the haggling was done, and they emerged from the store in pre-owned robes, with bus fare and enough change in their pockets to buy a meal.

"He said the bus stops by the police station," Shira said. "Same block, but at the other end. There's one in the morning and another in the afternoon."

"Did he know what time the morning one leaves?"

"Not exactly. Nothing in Africa is ever exact. But he said we'd better hurry or it could be a long day."

They walked together in the direction the shopkeeper had indicated, drawing fewer stares now that they were clad like locals. They crossed several dirt streets and reached the police station just as the first cars of the morning began circulating. Shira was about to power past it to the small window with a sign over it announcing the bus depot when Jet grabbed her arm and hissed a warning in her ear.

"Stop."

"What is it?"

"Over by the corner – the man in the army hat. It's one of the kidnappers."

CHAPTER 42

Shira and Jet reversed course and hurried away from the bus station. Jet's mind was working furiously as they neared the next street, and her face was clouded with concentration. Shira's complexion had turned chalky when Jet had warned her about the kidnapper, and Jet maintained a grip on her arm to keep her from doing anything stupid...like running.

"If they're here, looking for us..." Shira said.

"We knew they were tracking us. The bus stop is the natural place we'd go," Jet countered.

"If they're watching it, we're screwed."

"Maybe not."

"What do you mean?"

"I wouldn't bother watching the bus if I were them. All I'd have to do was watch the ticket window. So the chances are that he's the only one here – the rest are probably looking around town for us."

"So what do we do?"

Jet was silent for a moment. "Looks like we'll be skipping breakfast."

"Why?"

She motioned to a man leaning against one of the buildings. "Because we're going to ask him to buy two tickets, and we're going to give him our food money and cigarettes to do it."

Understanding played across Shira's face, and she nodded and held out her hand for the money. Jet handed it to her along with the cigarettes and gave her some further instruction, and then Shira approached the man and had a brief conversation. He nodded and she slipped him the cash and smokes, withholding the last of the money until he returned, and then Jet followed him from a few feet away to ensure he didn't keep walking past the window and make off with the money.

The man did as they'd asked and paid for two tickets, and then retraced his steps to where Shira was waiting. He gave her the stubs and she handed him his fee just as a vibrant blue bus that appeared to be older than both of them trundled toward the depot. Shira began walking toward it when Jet called to her.

"You take a ticket and get on here. I'll board farther down the street – I'll flag it. They'll be watching for two women. Not just one."

"It's going to be hard to blend into the crowd," Shira observed. "We look just a little different."

Jet adjusted her headdress and covered the lower part of her face with it. "You might want to do the same."

Shira nodded and followed Jet's lead, and then made her way toward the bus, which was parked at the curb in front of the ticket window, all of its windows open as well as its front and rear doors. Six passengers were waiting for the driver to check their tickets – two men and four women, the females dressed in similar robes to Shira's. She waited until there was only one traveler left at the curb and took up position behind him, purposefully avoiding looking down the street at the kidnapper.

Jet brushed by her without pausing and kept walking. She crossed the street before the corner and continued along the way as the driver waited for any latecomers to arrive. She stopped three blocks from the station and stood in the shade of a building, waiting for the old bus to begin crawling down the road.

Her patience was rewarded in a few minutes, and she stepped off the curb and waved at the driver, nearly blocking the way. The bus groaned to a halt and she climbed aboard; ignoring the driver's sharp rebuke, she handed him her ticket. The man glared at it for a long beat, but ultimately had to let her take a seat near the rear, just behind Shira.

The bus picked up speed. Jet could see that the town was hardly more than a collection of ramshackle buildings strung along a main street, the size smaller than she'd thought when they had been walking. They were at the periphery in the time it took to blink, and then were passing huts built from mud bricks with thatched roofs. Children in the street stared at the Nairobi Express with eyes too big for their heads.

Hot air buffeted the interior from a cross wind created by the open windows, but it was still stifling even as the bus picked up speed. Jet blinked away sweat as the driver neared the paved highway, and stiffened when he took the shifter out of gear and began to slow.

A tree lay across the road ahead, and Jaali and three kidnappers were standing by it with AK-47s in hand. Jet whispered to Shira as she leaned forward and felt in her boot for the knife.

"Stay here. Play dumb, and don't do anything stupid," she whispered, and then she was up and moving to the rear door, which was still open to provide ventilation. Jet leapt from the bus, which was barely moving, and ran behind it so the chassis blocked her from Jaali's view. When the bus stopped just in front of the felled tree, Jet crouched behind the rear bumper, blade in hand.

Jaali yelled at his men and then pounded on the front door with his fist, rifle leveled at the driver through the window. One of the kidnappers moved to the open rear exit and pointed his weapon inside as the front door opened with a hiss. Jaali barked an order at the driver, who shut off the engine and descended the stairs to where he was waiting with his gunmen. The driver said something in Swahili, his voice quavering, and Jaali slammed him in the head with his rifle stock, knocking him to the ground.

Several of the passengers cried out in fear when Jaali climbed onto the bus with his men and began making his way down the aisle, leading with his rifle and radiating menace. Shira sat as still as a statue as they neared her position, watching out of the corner of her eye while the kidnappers checked every woman.

Jet rounded the back fender and crept on catlike feet toward the fourth kidnapper, who was blocking the rear doorway, brandishing his assault rifle with both hands. He sensed her approach at the last instant, but it was too late. Jet sliced through his carotid artery before he could react, and whipped his pistol free of his hip holster and then stepped aside to avoid the geyser of blood that painted the side of the bus red. She slipped the pistol into her waistband as the gunman crumpled backward on rubber legs, and barely caught his rifle before it hit the ground. He gurgled and clutched at his ruined neck, eyes wide in panic as his life seeped from him, and then shuddered and lay still. Jet pushed his corpse under the bus and, after peering through the doorway, flattened herself against the side and inched back along the rear fender.

Jaali grinned when he saw Shira. "You've caused me a lot of trouble," he snarled. "Where's your friend?"

"She…she didn't make it," Shira stuttered.

Jaali tilted his head at his men. "Make sure she's not hiding under the seats," he said. "As for you, we have a date with my boss." Jaali laughed, the sound as ugly as a fighting dog's growl. One of the gunmen lowered himself onto his hands and knees and swept the floor of the bus with his rifle before standing.

"Nobody there."

Jaali eyed Shira. "Adami's going to be disappointed, but I have a feeling he'll manage to console himself with you. He's got a soft spot for youngsters." He grinned again. "Maybe I'll get you as well for a few hours before he kills you."

Shira spat in his face. He laughed and backhanded her, knocking her head to the side. "That's good. Still got fight left in you even after all you've been through. I like that. We'll see how you feel after Adami gets done with you." He looked to the man beside him. "Get her out of here."

The kidnappers manhandled Shira off the bus, and Jaali kicked the unconscious driver in the ribs. He looked at the side of the vehicle, perplexed at the crimson spray drying in the sun, and then Jet opened fire from the rear bumper with the AK and cut him down with a burst that stitched across his pelvis, shredding flesh and bone before shattering his spine. He tumbled face forward onto the dirt and his rifle clattered on the ground beside him. Jet's next volley caught the gunman beside Jaali in the chest, and then rounds pounded into the metal by her head, the shooter who was holding Shira having loosed half his magazine at her on full auto.

Shira threw herself to the ground, her weight too much for the man's grip, and then Jet was emptying the AK into the gunman. The slugs knocked him backward like a rag doll, and fountains of blood sprayed from his back as rounds cut through him. His rifle flew from his hands and he collapsed in a pool of blood. Shira screamed, hands over her ears and her eyes screwed shut.

Jet tossed the spent AK aside and pulled the pistol from her robe, and then slowly walked toward Jaali, the barrel rock steady as she neared. His chest was heaving as he battled for breath, his eyes wide in shock. She stood over him, pistol leveled at his head, and his pupils fixed on her with pure hatred. He tried to speak, but only managed a rasp, and then he gasped and quieted, the lake of blood beneath him coagulating in the heat, his lifeless stare still on Jet as she flipped the pistol's safety on.

She moved to Shira and knelt beside her. "Shira? It's over. We're okay."

Shira mewled like a hurt kitten and opened her eyes, overwhelmed by fear and shock.

"It's over. They can't hurt us anymore," Jet said, and Shira nodded woodenly, as though barely understanding her words.

The driver groaned, and Jet looked over at him before returning her gaze to Shira.

"I need your help. We have to ask the passengers to haul the tree out of the road so we can drive to Nairobi. Can you do that for me, Shira?" Jet paused. "We don't want to wait around here for any of his friends to make it from town. They'll have heard the shooting, so we need to hurry."

Jet helped Shira to her feet, and they moved to the front door as the passengers watched them with terror and disbelief. Jet nudged Shira, and she pulled herself together enough to relay her request in Swahili.

"Tell them that these were bandits. Robbers," Jet said, when Shira was through. "And there are more of them, so if we're going to get away, they need to work fast."

Shira spoke again, and this time six of the passengers trooped to the front of the bus and disembarked to move the tree. Jet moved to the driver and examined him, and then turned to Shira, who was clearly still barely processing.

"Help me get him on the bus. Then we'll collect their weapons and get out of here."

"What about the others back in town? Won't they follow us?"

"Maybe. But they're probably on foot. And they probably won't want to have to explain this to the police, so my bet is they'll disappear." She looked over at Jaali's rifle on the ground. "If not, they'll wish they had."

"Shouldn't we go to the cops?"

"We will," Jet said. "Once we're back in Nairobi. I don't trust anyone right now." She faced Shira. "Do you?"

Shira shook her head. "I'll take the driver's left arm; you take his right." She hesitated. "You know how to drive a bus?"

Jet allowed herself a small smirk. "Always wanted to try."

CHAPTER 43

Paris, France

Dr. Chastain, Stafford's conduit at the Pasteur Institute, entered the office the institute had set aside for her use, his expression conflicted.

"We've got preliminary results on the tablets," he reported, his French accent pronounced.

Stafford sat back in her swivel chair and waited expectantly. "And?"

"The spectrum analysis was initially confusing, but once we understood what we were looking at, it made sense."

Stafford raised an eyebrow.

Chastain continued. "The active agent appears to be an experimental form of cancer therapy. That's the only sense we can make of it."

"Cancer? Why would the villagers be given…" Stafford said, and then stopped, her face clouding as the ramifications of their findings hit home. "It was a drug trial gone wrong?"

"That's what it looks like. Of course, that's speculation. But it's the only explanation that makes sense." He cleared his throat, took a seat opposite her, and smoothed the leg of his gray wool slacks before continuing. "This sort of trial would violate international law and is a crime against humanity, so you can expect that whichever company is responsible will have covered its tracks."

Stafford set the pen she was holding down on the desk and nodded. "That fits. It also explains why the military suddenly became unresponsive, if not obstructive."

"They were paid off, of course," the Frenchman observed.

"Of course." Stafford paused. "Can we pinpoint which company was likely responsible? The formulation has to be protected. Patent applications would give them away."

"I've already run a quick scan. It appears the culprit is Algernon Pharmaceuticals. They're headquartered in Israel, but have offices all over the world, including Africa."

She frowned. "Never heard of them."

"You can expect them to deny everything, of course, assuming you can get the U.S. to take it to the world court or the U.N. If I were them, I'd say that there was no trial, and that this is all an effort to smear their reputation."

"We have the blood sample to corroborate it," Stafford fired back.

Chastain scowled. "That news isn't so good. It had degraded too much to be of use. So what we're left with is a questionable sample of blood, bodily fluid swabs, and a handful of pills that may or may not prove that the company was doing off-the-radar trials in Africa – a common practice, I'm sure you are aware. It's officially frowned upon, but just as with organ trafficking, modern slavery, and every other unsavory practice, Africa is one of the epicenters for clandestine trials."

Stafford nodded. She knew of it from her time on the continent, but had never seen the results up close, nor so blatant – at least not that she knew of. She'd always assumed that the outbreaks of virulent diseases like Ebola and Marburg she had been sent to Africa to treat were naturally occurring, but there was no definitive way of knowing whether they were clandestine bioweapons trials gone wrong or not. She was aware of rumors of simian retrovirus experimentation in Equatorial Guinea, Cameroon, and Gabon, but had always dismissed them as conspiracy theories. Now she wasn't so sure. If the military of one of the largest African nations was willing to sell its rural population to the highest bidder for forbidden medical experiments, could she dismiss anything without serious consideration?

"They can't be allowed to get away with this," she said. "Dozens have died – perhaps hundreds. Someone is responsible; they need to be held accountable."

He nodded, but the set of his features wasn't hopeful. "That is your matter to pursue. I'm simply the bearer of bad news."

"I appreciate everything you've done for me," she said.

Chastain rose. "I'll get you the results of the analysis before the end of the day. What you do with them is your affair; however, I wish you luck bringing the responsible parties to justice." He hesitated. "My grandfather died in a concentration camp that was infamous for Nazi medical experimentation. I view this as no different – a cohort exposed to deadly substances without their informed consent is much the same as forced exposure. So I sympathize with the battle you face, and I hope you're successful."

Stafford watched him leave, and when he pulled the door closed behind him, she exhaled a tense breath and removed her cell phone from the pocket of her lab coat. She needed to inform her team that they were in danger if they flew in. She couldn't subject them to the risk of the military employing drastic measures to cover up the crime that had been committed. Once she confirmed that they weren't en route, she would report her findings to her superiors, and they would take the ball from there.

Whether they did anything meaningful or not was outside her control. She hoped that they would, but she'd worked with Washington long enough to be pessimistic that Nel and those like her would ever see justice.

It was the sad way of the world. All she could do was her job; and then, as with Chastain, it was out of her hands.

A thought occurred to her, and she made a note in her calendar to contact her friend with the *Washington Post*. If the government didn't take action, it wasn't out of the question for the results of her report to leak. At the very least, that might force the appropriate bodies into action, even if it was largely for show.

It was worth considering.

Someone should pay for robbing Nel of a future with the man she loved, as well as for the countless anonymous victims who'd been murdered with the drug. Even if it was a long shot, those responsible should be exposed to the antiseptic of sunlight and not be permitted to prosper in the shadows.

And Stafford had the power to direct the light their way.

CHAPTER 44

Nairobi, Kenya

Jet accompanied Elon through the passageway to the embassy, tired after her ordeal in the brush but glad that the mission was over, if unsuccessful at saving the pharmaceutical executives' lives.

The bus had taken five hours to arrive at the outskirts of Nairobi, where they had been met by Jabori, whom Jet had called on the wounded driver's cell phone when she'd gotten a signal. She'd decided it would be more prudent to forego an extended interrogation by the police, given Adami's influence, and Jabori had spirited them away before they hit town, leaving a bus full of passengers for the police to interview, assuming any of the travelers wanted to get involved – unlikely, based on what Shira had said about their distrust of the authorities.

Jabori had delivered Shira to the embassy and Jet to her hotel, where she'd collapsed into bed and slept for four hours before being awakened by the bedside telephone – Elon, requesting a meet at the coffee shop within the hour. It was dark by the time she arrived at the café, and Elon had already been awaiting her there, visibly more relaxed than during their prior exchange.

"I think I owe you an apology," he said as they climbed the stairs to the embassy.

"No need. Water under the bridge."

"Ahrens wants to see you and express his gratitude. He's...he's relieved Shira made it back in one piece. Especially given what happened...to the others."

She nodded. "Couldn't be helped. Although we don't have confirmation that Gabriel didn't survive."

"Few walk out of the wasteland here. My money's on him never surfacing."

"You're probably right. He shouldn't have double-crossed me in the field. He might be here today."

"I'm sure you'll detail all of this in your report."

"I will. But it's for the director's eyes only, and I doubt he'll feel up to sharing."

Elon nodded and lowered his voice. "What happened?"

"Off the record, he agreed to help me break them out and then disappeared instead of doing so. Not my favorite person right now. The others might have survived if he'd done his part."

Elon sighed. "Ah. I didn't realize."

"Too late to do anything about it now. Although one good thing that came out of this is that we know the identity of the kidnappers. This Adami character sounds like an especially nasty piece of work."

They reached the dusty office, and Elon led her down the hall to where the ambassador and Shimon Ahrens were waiting in the ambassador's office. Ahrens stood when she entered and approached her with open arms. She endured an embrace and then shook hands with the ambassador before sitting where indicated.

Ahrens cleared his throat and began to speak in a hesitant voice. "I want to thank you for everything you did. Risking your life, and saving Shira's. She told me about everything. Sounds like you used up several of your nine lives out there."

"That's the job. I'm glad we got her home safely. Sorry I can't say the same about the others."

Ahrens nodded. "Shira wanted to be here, but she's fast asleep. I thought it would be best to let her rest."

Jet shifted in her seat. "She's been through a lot."

"If there's anything I can ever do for you…" Ahrens began, but Jet cut him off with a wave.

"No need. We got her out of trouble. Now she just needs to stay out of it. Given that she was targeted by a local gangster, I'd suggest that you send her on an extended sabbatical somewhere else. Anywhere else, actually."

Ahrens nodded. "You read my mind."

When the meeting was over, Elon walked Jet to the Mossad communications room and left her with a secure line to the director. He answered almost immediately, his voice its usual gravelly timbre.

"I understand it wasn't as much of a milk run as we'd hoped," he began.

"You have a talent for understatement," Jet answered. "I'll file a full report tomorrow."

"Sorry it turned ugly on you. We had no way of foreseeing it, obviously."

Jet resisted the urge to snap at him. Instead, she settled for echoing him. "Obviously."

"The important thing is that you're in one piece. Unharmed, I presume?"

"Mostly. A few cuts and bruises and a hell of a headache. But nothing that won't heal."

The director cleared his throat. "Good." He paused. "Listen, I have something else that could use your delicate touch…"

She snorted. "You're joking, right?"

"This really is a minor item. But since you're on the ground in Nairobi, I figured we'd put the taxpayer's investment in you to use."

"This last…abortion…was also supposed to be a minor item, remember?"

"But this really is. It will require next to nothing from you." He hesitated. "I'd be in your debt."

Jet sighed. "What is it?"

"You may recall that we have a leak in the ministry. It was making headlines before you went on safari."

"Yes."

"We've identified the source. The documents were uploaded in Nairobi."

"Really? You suspect embassy staff, obviously?"

"Hard to believe. Everyone's thoroughly vetted. But we have a location from an IP address. I want you to go there and see what you can learn. They might remember something that can help us. It's an internet café. There are apparently many of them still in operation there."

"Yes. The infrastructure is…primitive. You see them on every block." She paused.

He gave her the date that the documents were uploaded and the time. "Probably from a USB drive using one of their systems. They weren't on long. Doubt they scanned hard copy."

"But you have no way of tracing how they got into the system in the first place?"

"That remains a mystery. But if it's one of the embassy staff…that would explain it. They would have access to the passwords. It's secure, and the info is classified, but nothing like our network."

"I presume you have an address."

"I do." He gave it to her. "This is a matter of some urgency."

"Why didn't you have Elon or someone here do it?"

"Given the circumstances, I thought it best not to use local staff."

Jet understood. With no idea who the leak was, he didn't know whom to trust.

"You want me to do this right now?"

"That would be best."

"I haven't even called my family yet."

"This won't take you long. Tell Elon to give you some money to spread around to the employees of the café. They'll probably fall all over themselves to cooperate with you."

"He's not my biggest fan."

"We already had a discussion about your earlier issues. He's on the same page now. You'll find him cooperative. Tell me if he isn't."

"Apparently Adami is holding a grudge. So it would be best if I left town sooner rather than later."

"I don't disagree. Make whatever arrangements you see fit."

"First-class tickets, you mean?"

A tense silence stretched before he answered. "Let's not go crazy."

She smiled and disconnected. The old man was strangely predictable in some ways.

227

Elon gave her the equivalent of two thousand dollars of local currency without comment. "Anything else?"

"I'd feel better with a weapon. I hear Nairobi can be dangerous."

"Then it's probably best not to linger."

"You don't have anything here?"

Elon's smile was frosty. "Contrary to pulp novels, we don't keep an armory in the embassy." His expression softened. "If you need something, I'd talk to Jabori. But honestly, it would be better for everyone if you just disappeared."

"I agree." She didn't tell him about her new assignment. If the director had wanted him to know, he would have told Elon himself, she reasoned. And for all she knew, he might be suspected of being the leak.

Back at the hotel, Jet changed into dark clothes, pulled on a baseball cap, and studied her reflection before smiling at herself and shaking her head.

She walked the six blocks to the internet café and stopped outside, eyeing the cheap sign over the single retail slot. Jet could see through the picture window that the clerk inside was cleaning the computers with a damp rag, and a glance at her watch told her that it was near closing time. The woman looked up at the door chime when Jet entered, and offered an apologetic smile.

"I'm sorry. All the computers are off. We're closed in five minutes. Maybe come back tomorrow?"

Jet looked around the space. There were a dozen older PCs, a glass display counter with power cords, thumb drives, and computer peripherals for sale, as well as some out-of-date software packages whose colors were faded from age. The distinctive mirrored dome of a surveillance camera was mounted above the cash register.

"I have a friend I've been trying to find, and I heard they might have stopped in here a couple of weeks ago," Jet said. "I've been trying everything to get in touch, but nothing's worked."

The woman looked puzzled. "I don't know anything about that."

"I was wondering if the camera's on all the time during business hours?"

The woman's eyes instantly radiated suspicion. "You'd have to talk to the owner about that. I just work here."

"Do you know how long she keeps the tapes? It's really important." Jet paused. "I could pay for any information." She removed a fat wad of bills from her pocket.

"You could get yourself killed walking around with that kind of money," the woman warned. "Better put it away before anyone sees it."

"If I could just take a peek at the tapes...what do they pay you here?"

The woman straightened her spine. "Lady, I told you, come back tomorrow and talk to the owner. Now I'm closing. Got to ask you to leave." She gripped the edge of one of the desks as though steadying herself. "Don't be flashing that money around. You'll get your throat cut. I'm serious."

Jet saw her initial line of inquiry was going nowhere, so she switched gears. "Okay. The truth is, I'm a private investigator. I need to find this person. It's important. There's an inheritance at stake."

"Going to be turning the lights off in a minute. Come back tomorrow and tell it to the owner. I don't know nothing," the clerk said, with a flick of her eye toward the camera.

Jet understood immediately. She nodded and walked to the door. "Okay. Sorry to bother you."

"No problem."

The shop lights went off five minutes later, and the clerk appeared at the door immediately afterwards. Jet approached her on the sidewalk after she'd locked up. The woman looked around nervously before nodding to Jet.

"What can you tell me?" Jet asked.

"I think she keeps the tapes for a month. On a server in the back. That's all I know."

"Alarm system?"

The clerk nodded. "It calls the police if someone breaks in. And there's a siren on the roof that goes off. Loud. We've had a few false alarms."

"Don't suppose you know the passcode?"

"Only to arm it. Not to open up. The owner does that every morning."

"What kind of alarm is it?"

The woman looked stumped. "How would I know? An alarm."

"Is there a back door?"

She nodded. "Off the alley. It's got sensors on it too, though. I can't give you the key. I don't have it. Sorry."

"No problem."

Jet handed her the equivalent of two hundred dollars, and the woman's frown turned into a smile. "The lady owns the place...she a nightmare to work for. That's why I have to play dumb for the camera. She think everyone stealing from her all the time. I'd quit, but I need the job." She paused. "I got kids."

"No problem. We never spoke. Have a nice night," Jet said.

"Server password is Possum."

Jet gave her another hundred dollars' worth of the local currency. "Anything else I need to know?"

"Never been here late at night, but can't think the cops are around much."

"Interesting. Be safe with all that money. I hear it's dangerous around here."

Both women smiled, and Jet turned and walked away, her hopes of getting a good night's sleep dashed.

CHAPTER 45

The streets near the embassy were nearly empty as Jet worked her way along the sidewalk toward the internet café, her black windbreaker and cargo pants heavy with the items she'd bought from Jabori earlier. He'd sounded less than thrilled to receive her call, but had perked up when she'd told him what she needed, and had agreed to meet her shortly after midnight with the gear.

Meanwhile, Jet had returned to the shop and staked it out, noting any police patrols that drove by over an hour – which was none. Reassured that this would be an easy entry operation, she'd circled the block and walked down the alley behind it, studying the tangle of cables overhead as she passed the rear of the café. The back entrance was a steel slab door with a deadbolt, and she'd studied the lock type for a few moments before nodding to herself and continuing to the other end of the alley, ignoring the stench of garbage from the bins that lined the way.

Now, at two a.m., the streets were empty, and the only sound was distant traffic from the clubs in the upscale areas and an occasional taxi going to or from a hotel. The city was asleep, and it was easy for her to believe she was the only one awake as she navigated the uneven slabs of the sidewalk. Two stray dogs across the street, their ribs jutting through their mottled coats, provided her only company.

She reached the block with the café and took a photo of the darkened front façade with the disposable phone Jabori had gotten her, struck by the remarkable confluence of events that had shaped her life. She looked both ways down the street and then crossed to the shop before continuing along the block and rounding the corner.

The alley seemed darker than before, the moon refusing to cooperate by providing decent illumination as it had the prior nights, and a low level overcast reduced its glow to a pallid echo of its wattage on the Highland Plains. She entered the alley, the soles of her Doc Martens silent on worn cobblestones that harked back to colonial days, and made her way toward the rear of the shop, stopping occasionally to listen for any sign that she wasn't alone.

The coarse brick of the building's rear face provided more than adequate handholds. She pulled herself up to a barred window and used the sill for a toehold to climb the rest of the way to the single-story roof. Coils of razor wire wound around the perimeter, and she used the wire cutters Jabori had provided to cut it, pushed it aside, and hoisted herself through the gap up onto the slab surface.

She looked around the edge of the roof and spotted the horn for the alarm siren. A snip of the wire cutters neutralized that threat, and then she was following the line from the telephone pole on the other side of the alley to a junction box where it connected to the building. Another snip of the phone line eliminated the alarm's ability to notify the police. Jet smiled in the darkness at the ease with which older alarm systems could be defeated – they relied on phone lines and wiring to work, and even a marginally skilled intruder could bypass them in seconds exactly as she had.

Jet checked around for any other potential threat and, when she didn't see any, returned to the roof lip and eased her body over the side until she was hanging by gloved fingers. She released the edge. Her feet dropped two meters to the alley, and she rolled to absorb the impact and then sprang to her feet and moved to the back door.

The lock posed little more problem for her than the alarm. Jabori's picks slid into the deadbolt with ease, and she brushed the tumblers with a slightly curved pick while exerting steady pressure with a flat one until the lock snapped open with a twist of her hand. The lock on the lever handle was child's play, and she had it open in moments.

Once inside the shop, she used the phone's screen for illumination, avoiding using the flash on the off chance someone saw the brighter light from the street. The camera server rested on a plastic milk crate on the cement floor beside a black metal desk with a ratty swivel chair. She approached it and sat in front of the monitor, and then typed in the password when the system prompted her.

The interface was intuitive, if clunky, and she was able to navigate the dates to the one the director had given her. She dragged the cursor at the bottom of the screen until she was at the time of the upload, and then backed it up until a few minutes before.

She watched the footage, which was low resolution but still serviceable, and after downloading the relevant file to her USB drive, she erased it and logged out.

The owner would find the alarm system deactivated and presume that burglars had tried to break in but had failed, given that nothing was missing. The police, if she even bothered to report it, would largely ignore the episode, and at worst fill out a form and warn her to add another deadbolt to the back door. The odds of her reviewing all of her security footage from the last month were so slim as to be nonexistent, and even if she did, the chances of her noticing a missing file were nil.

Jet closed the rear door and used the picks to relock the deadbolt, and then hurried along the alley to the street beyond, her hotel bed's magnetic pull calling to every muscle of her body.

CHAPTER 46

The morning rush hour was over by the time Shira had finished her breakfast and was preparing to start her day. She had at least five errands she had to run before lunch if she wanted to get everything accomplished, not the least of which was tendering her resignation at her job and wishing her boss well with finding a replacement. She had no hard feelings about working there and had been secretly relieved when her father had sat down with her over coffee and made her promise to quit, effective immediately.

She'd been surprised when he'd suggested that she pack and prepare to take an extended vacation to Israel, but hadn't argued with his logic that she might be a target for the crime lord's wrath. It wasn't worth the risk, and although she'd miss her dad, she was looking forward to getting back to civilization; the events of the last days had been overwhelming. The thought of relaxing by the Mediterranean with a good book made her smile, and she was still smiling when she walked out the front door and found herself face-to-face with Jet.

"Oh! God, you scared me," Shira said. "I'm so glad you stopped by. I didn't get a chance to thank you or say goodbye."

"I know all about the files you uploaded, Shira. I know everything. My only question is why?" Jet said, her tone flat.

Shira stared at her, dumbfounded, and then her eyes darted down the street to see if anyone was watching them. The bodyguard her father had hired to protect her was standing by the front gate, studiously regarding the street and giving her privacy for her discussion. "What are you—"

Jet cut her off. "Don't play dumb. I know that you got your hands on ministry documents somehow, and that you uploaded them to HonestyInternational."

Shira shifted from foot to foot. "How?"

"That isn't important. I've got footage of you doing the upload from Lorelai's. You're blown, Shira. It's over."

A tear worked its way down Shira's cheek and she wiped it with the back of her arm. "I...you wouldn't understand."

"Try me."

Shira's young face hardened and she clenched her jaw. "They're liars. All of them. They say one thing and then do another. In the meantime, people get hurt while they're playing their games. I wanted to...I saw how groups like WikiLeaks and whistleblowers like Snowden showed the American government to be lying constantly about almost everything, and I just thought...I admired what they were doing."

"Many people think Snowden is a traitor and Wiki is a propaganda tool."

She frowned. "Well, they're wrong. The NSA flat out lied about spying on the population, and Snowden blew their cover. So they had to admit they were liars and had been lying to the American Congress and the people for over a decade. And Wiki...they've never published anything that wasn't true. I thought...I thought that we needed something like that for our government. I couldn't watch them lying and getting away with it. I remember thinking somebody should do something, and then one day it occurred to me that I could be that someone." Her chin jutted out stubbornly. "I'm not sorry for what I did. If it makes them tell the truth, that's good for everyone." She exhaled loudly. "Except the liars, of course."

"How did you do it?"

"I accessed the network through my dad's computer, of course. I put a key logger on it and retrieved the password. He's not all that technical, so he never noticed. From there I uploaded a worm into the system, and it downloaded everything new that month on the network to my computer." She looked away. "He never suspected anything. This was my doing. He followed all the protocols. My behavior shouldn't reflect on him."

Jet shook her head. "Are you really that naïve? You think they won't hang him if they find out it was you?"

Her eyes returned to Jet. "What do you mean, if?"

Jet glanced at the bodyguard. "I need some coffee. Is there somewhere nearby we can get some?"

"Um, yeah. A block away."

"I thought about this all night, Shira. About what you did. I suspected your motives, but I wanted to hear it from you. You're lucky that nobody has been hurt because of the leaks, although that's not going to matter. What you did is treason. The government will consider you a traitor and treat you as such."

"So what? I'm not in Israel. I can apply for diplomatic immunity or something. Or I can just disappear. It's not like I'm some war criminal. All I did was prove that they're a bunch of liars who think they can get away with anything they want."

Jet sighed. "Shira, all governments are liars. That's what they do. It's not just ours or the Americans. It's the way the world works."

"Well, then, maybe there's something wrong with the world. Why should a small group of people be allowed to mislead the rest? This is our planet too. Who died and made them god?"

The security man followed at a discreet distance as they walked down the street. Jet was as conflicted as she had been when she first saw the footage of Shira – footage she'd already known would establish her guilt as soon as she'd seen the internet café's name on the sign. What Shira had done was criminal, but Jet could also understand her idealism and the childlike sense of fairness that the ministry routinely violated. She'd lain in bed after calling Matt and speaking with Hannah, and had asked herself how she would have felt if instead of Shira, it had been Hannah who had uploaded the files out of the same sense of right and wrong. Would she have done her duty to the clandestine group that was effectively blackmailing her into performing operations on its behalf? Or would she have found a way to forgive it and let her off the hook?

If Jet did her duty, Shira's father would be ruined, and a young, idealistic woman would spend her life in prison – assuming the government didn't decide to send someone like Jet to neutralize her without a trial. Would any good be served by that, other than the interests of those Shira called the liars?

A thought occurred to Jet as they neared the café. "Is there some way to disable the worm? For a computer specialist to find it and do it?"

"Uh, sure. I mean, if they knew the code to look for. But I wrote it so it would be almost impossible to find."

"You wrote it?"

Shira nodded. "I almost majored in computer programming. I'm still active with a lot of hackers. That's how I got some of them to cooperate in spreading this around. Hackers are largely young and hate the status quo – we see what's wrong with it. I mean, some are criminals, like total sleaze, but most do it to rebel against a broken system."

They entered the café, and the bodyguard remained outside. Jet ordered coffee for them both at the counter and then moved to a table by the window. Shira sat opposite her, and Jet fixed her with an intense stare. "You've ruined your life, Shira, and your father's as well. The state will never forgive either of you."

"But he didn't do anything!" she protested. "He's innocent."

"That won't matter. Examples will be made."

The waitress set their coffee in front of them and left. Shira's eyes were moist, and she had a hard time with the sugar, her hands were shaking so badly. "Have you told him yet?"

Jet sighed and took a sip of her coffee, black, as she preferred it. "No. I'm still trying to decide what to do about you."

Shira stopped what she was doing and studied Jet for a moment. "What do you mean, what to do? Aren't you...I mean, I figured you're part of the government, aren't you?"

"You mean one of the liars? No. And that's not important, anyway. What matters is whether your worm can be undone without revealing who planted it, and whether it would help anyone if you went to jail...or worse."

"I don't have to go back to Israel. There are plenty of other places to disappear."

"Shira, get real. Anyone can be found, no matter what precautions they've taken. It's way harder than you think." Jet paused. "But back to the worm. I have an idea how to fix that." She told Shira what she wanted her to do.

Shira nodded slowly. "That would work."

Jet drained her cup, the coffee rich and fragrant in her mouth. She set it down and slipped the USB drive with the footage from the security camera across the table.

"That's the video from the café. It's the only copy. I erased the master. Without that, nobody will ever know who uploaded the files. It'll just be one of life's unexplained mysteries."

Shira reached for the drive and rested her hand over it. "Why are you doing this?"

"Because in another time and place, I made decisions that could have been seen by liars as treasonous, too, instead of what was right for me. And I've paid for that many times over, but if I had to, I'd do it all again the same way. You remind me a little of myself." She stood. "Can you remember a local phone number?"

"I'll write it down," Shira said, fishing in her purse for her cell phone. She retrieved it and pulled up the contacts menu. "Shoot."

Jet gave her the burner number and then placed a couple of bills on the table. "Call me when you've had someone post it to 4Channel. Make sure it's triple untraceable, because you can absolutely guarantee that they're going to throw everything at it."

"That's easy."

Jet's eyes narrowed at her flippant tone. "Shira? Scrub that drive. Then throw it in the river or smash it with a hammer. You never want it to see the light of day." She looked through the floor-to-ceiling glass of the café's picture window and then back at Shira. "Maybe today's your lucky day because nobody should get to play judge and executioner out of the public eye. Maybe it's because I've gotten tired of that, or maybe I have been for a long time. It doesn't really matter why. What does is that you're lucky. So call when you've done as I've asked, and don't mess up the rest of your life. You only get so many chances."

Shira didn't respond, and Jet turned on her heel and walked out the door without looking back, her stomach a ball of acid, unsure whether she'd done the right thing but relieved now that she'd made her decision, and prepared to live with it and take this secret to her grave.

Shira watched the woman she knew as Claire leave the café. When she was out of sight, Shira pocketed the drive, her pulse triple digits as she considered what had just transpired. The woman had not only saved her life, but had done so twice, and she didn't even know her real name.

Whatever it was, she owed her more than words could express, and immediately after she destroyed the drive, she would write the post that would enable the ministry to find and eliminate the worm.

Her busy morning of errands would have to wait.

She smiled at the thought and rose. What had seemed so important an hour earlier were now nothing but nuisances she could deal with in her own time. The difference in her attitude was entirely mental and based on nothing more than her perception – nothing else had changed.

The waitress came over and warmed the room with her smile. Shira returned it and indicated the money Jet had left.

"Keep the change."

CHAPTER 47

Shira yawned as she pushed out the front door of her father's house. The tasks she'd committed to completing for Jet were done: the drive had been smashed into fragments with a hammer and the bits flushed down the toilet. She checked the time and looked at the sky, the deep turquoise marbled with clouds moving in from the mountains, the breeze cooler than usual, signaling the arrival of a storm later in the day. Her bodyguard was waiting by the front gate, as unobtrusive as a sumo wrestler.

Her thoughts were on what she would do next. She'd called her boss and told him that she'd be in before lunchtime to talk, and his tone had foreshadowed that he'd guessed why. His offices were half a mile away, and while she'd normally walk, with her time cut short from her unexpected errands, she'd allow herself the luxury of a taxi.

Her neighborhood was one of the best residential areas in Nairobi, with few pedestrians on the street and even fewer cabs, so she set off toward the main boulevard three blocks away, where she could easily flag down a driver. The bodyguard followed her from ten meters behind, hands in the pockets of his windbreaker. Neither of them registered the two men who darted onto the street behind them until it was too late.

The bodyguard was turning toward them and had his pistol halfway out of his pocket when a length of pipe wrapped in a towel slammed against his head, knocking him senseless. His gun clattered into the gutter as he fell to the ground. Another blow crushed his larynx, and he writhed and struggled to breathe before blacking out.

A van sped along the street and pulled level with Shira, its license plate smeared with mud and its side door open. It stopped with a shriek of metal on metal, and two more men jumped out, pistols in hand.

Shira's scream was cut short by a black cloth sack one of the assailants pulled over her head, and her struggle against the other's grip was met by a punch to the stomach that doubled her over. The men dragged her to the van and tossed her in like a side of beef as she tried to catch her breath. The pair that had taken down the bodyguard did the same with his corpse, and then climbed into the cargo bed as it pulled from the curb with a squeal of rubber. The side door slid shut and the van accelerated, rounded the corner at the next street, and disappeared from view, leaving nothing but a trail of exhaust and three pedestrian witnesses in its wake. One of them stabbed in the number of the police emergency line, but by the time the operator had answered and put him through to the appropriate desk, critical minutes had passed, and any hope of tracking the vehicle had been lost.

CHAPTER 48

After snatching a few hours of sleep, Jet had been summoned by Elon and was back at the embassy in the secure communications room, on the line with the director.

"So you didn't find anything that would tell us who the hacker is?" he asked.

"No. It was a dry run. I talked to the woman who works there, and she doesn't remember anyone special."

"What about security cameras?"

"There's one, but it's primitive, and the woman said they only keep the tapes a day or two – it's there to prevent pilferage by the employees." Jet hesitated. "I broke in, of course, but there's no trace of the file for the date in question." A truth – she'd erased it, so there wasn't.

The director cleared his throat. "Well, I have some good news. The techs who're working on this found a post on a message board bragging about how the leak was done. With that, they've been able to find and eliminate the malicious code."

"So it's a nonissue now?" Jet asked neutrally. Shira had called earlier to confirm that she'd arranged to have the relevant info posted to a widely followed board by one of her hacker contacts in Romania, so it was no surprise – the only one being how quickly the techs had pounced on it.

"Thank God." He paused, and she could hear him lighting a cigarette, his lighter's flick as distinctive as a fingerprint to her. "You've made arrangements to return?"

"Tonight."

"Very well. Safe travels."

Jet terminated the call and sat back. Her deception was now

official and her false narrative memorialized. Strangely, she felt nothing, no regrets or doubts, just an emptiness born of years of duty that had cost her everything and provided little in return. All she could think of now was reuniting with Hannah and Matt and putting this episode behind her.

She stood, walked across the small room to the security door, and tapped in the code to open it.

Elon was waiting for her, his expression even more dour than usual. "We have a problem," he announced.

"We?" Jet asked.

"Shira hasn't checked in. She promised her father she would, every couple of hours, to let him know she was fine. Her last call was at ten this morning."

"Did he try calling her?"

"Of course. Goes to voice mail."

"Maybe her battery's dead?" Jet wasn't about to tell him she'd spoken to Shira on the phone at eleven.

"We ran a trace on the locator chip. No ping."

"If it's completely out of juice…"

"Doubtful. Somebody disabled the battery." Elon shook his head. "Ahrens's at his wit's end. He hired security to watch her while he was at work, and the bodyguard also isn't picking up. Same story on his locator chip, too."

She nodded slowly. "So what are you going to do?"

"We don't have a response yet."

Jet's burner cell rang as they were walking to the ambassador's office. She checked the number and motioned to Elon to stop as she answered.

"Hello?"

"Claire? It's Shira."

Jet responded seamlessly, her voice unsurprised and calm. "Shira! What's up?"

"I realized I never got a chance to thank you for everything, and I wanted to see if you had a minute to get together? I went shopping and bought you a gift."

Jet thought quickly. "I'm sort of tied up until this evening. Meetings and reports. You can probably imagine."

The line hummed in her ear as Shira's end went silent, and Jet could detect the faint click of a mute button cutting out background noise before she finally responded. "Um, yeah, okay. That's fine."

"Where do you want to meet? At your house?" Jet asked.

"Oh, um, no. There's a park nearby. Any taxi would know it. Want to meet at, say, six?"

"Assuming I can get away. I'll call you back and let you know."

Another pause. "I'm in a bad area for cell service. Just text me or leave a message if it doesn't connect. I'll pick it up when I have a signal."

"Sure thing. I'll do my best to get away."

Jet hung up and looked at Elon. "She's under duress. My guess is Adami's kidnapped her and is forcing her to call. They want me, Elon, not her. They're trying to set up a meeting at some park." She thought for a moment. "I'm going to stall until it's dark. Do you have any assets who are competent snipers?"

Elon scowled. "Not really. Our field teams...that's not the sort of work they do."

Jet nodded. "I figured I'd ask."

"So now what? I'd better talk to HQ."

"Do that. I need some time to think."

"It's obviously a trap."

She gave him a skeptical look. "Oh, of course. But the question is how do we proceed? Have you made any progress on locating Adami?"

"Unfortunately, he's the invisible man. We've heard buzz that he's back in Nairobi, but that's all. Just street chatter. And the locals are useless. He probably has most of them on his payroll."

She removed her cell phone battery and slid that and her phone into her pocket. "They have contacts in the police department, so they've probably tracked this phone to the embassy. But why make it easy for them?" She paused. "This is personal. They're just using Shira to lure me. Our only advantage is that we know that. So the question is how to best turn the situation to our advantage."

"They probably won't kill her – she's valuable to them as a ransom candidate now that they've got her, assuming they know who her father is."

"True. At least, I hope so. But you can never be sure." She told him Shira's story about being in a bad reception zone.

"They're obviously keeping her off the air so she can't be tracked," he said.

"Which leaves the meeting."

"Let me call HQ and find out how they want to handle this."

"Fair enough. In the meantime, I'm going to need a clean phone, a computer, and someplace quiet. And you're probably going to have to come up with some serious cash before too long."

He held her stare without blinking. "For what?"

"Can't fight a war without supply lines and reinforcements."

"You have something in mind? Care to share so I can let HQ know?"

She shook her head. "Let's see what they come up with. In the meantime, I need to pull up satellite footage of that park and the surrounding area and figure out how to keep from getting killed."

"You're not thinking about actually going, are you?"

Jet gave him a flat stare. "If I don't, you'll get pieces of her in the mail. That'll be their next call if I don't show, and at that point any advantage we have is gone. So as far as I can see, I don't have much choice. But maybe I'm wrong, and HQ will pull a rabbit out of the hat. In the meantime, an office, phone, and computer would be a good first step while the big brains mull this one over."

CHAPTER 49

Jabori met Jet at a restaurant two blocks from the hotel with a kit bag containing the weapons she'd asked for. She handed him a brick of currency, carried the satchel into the bathroom, and inspected a suppressed Beretta pistol and three magazines of subsonic 9mm dumdum bullets, a switchblade with a black plastic handle, four police-issue stun grenades, and an FN P90 bullpup machine gun with extra magazines that at under two feet overall length would just squeeze into her backpack.

When she returned, she sat across from him and took a sip of her soda. "You find a shooter?"

He nodded. "Yes. Me."

"You've got experience as a sniper?"

"I'm a good enough shot, depending on the range. But my main strength is I won't sell you out." He sat forward. "I don't trust anyone else not to do that, given who you're up against."

She nodded. "You get the communication gear?"

He slid an earbud to her and a wireless hub. "It's good for up to two hundred meters. Tunable channels. Shouldn't be visible with your hair down."

"You know the area by the park?"

"Yes. There won't be many people out at dusk. It's off the beaten path. Perfect place to grab someone at gunpoint."

"What kind of rifle do you plan to use?"

"FN SCAR with a suppressor. Military issue. Should do the trick at that range."

"You won't have a lot of time to take them down, depending on how many there are."

"I won't need much." He motioned to the waitress and ordered a soda of his own. "Although the rain could make things more difficult. Let's hope it doesn't start until after we're done."

Jet went over the plan she'd developed with him to make sure he understood the finer points, not that there were many to shooting anything that posed a threat. When she was done, he nodded and drank his soda, his expression thoughtful.

"They're going to be ready for you to fight back," he said.

"Maybe not. They think they're going to surprise me. Hopefully that will work in our favor."

"Adami's going to send the best he has. They'll be ex-military, not street hustlers, so you can expect them to be tough to take down."

She regarded him. "Make sure you don't miss." She finished her drink. "I'll send a message in a few minutes confirming the meet. That will give you two hours to get into position and scout out the area. I'll do the same."

Jabori nodded. "No time like the present."

Jet paid for the drinks, and they walked to Jabori's car, where she transferred the contents of the weapons sack to her backpack.

"I'll leave most of this stuff with you," she said. "I won't need much besides the blade, pistol, and one grenade. I'll look less threatening if I'm not carrying anything."

"How are you going to hide the pistol?"

She unscrewed the suppressor, tossed it into the backpack, and slipped it into her waistband. "That should do the job along with a spare mag. I'll just carry the grenade."

"Pretty ballsy."

"I figure that will be unexpected." She paused. "I'm banking on it."

"One thing you haven't considered, though. Everything we're preparing for assumes they want to take you alive. What if they've given up on that and just want to kill you?"

Jet checked the time. "When they had us, they could have killed us at any time, but they didn't. Adami wants to do it himself. Do you know what he looks like?"

"I've never seen a picture, but he's supposed to be over three hundred pounds."

She smiled grimly. "If anyone like that shows up, then shoot them."

"I doubt he'd get his hands dirty in the field, especially after the shoot-out with the police. He's probably lying low."

"That's the hope. Guess we'll know in a few hours." Jet fastened her seat belt. "Let's get into position and look the area over."

Jabori started the motor. "We still haven't figured out how I'm going to get onto one of the roofs."

"There's a construction site on the latest satellite images, a hundred meters from the park. Three stories. What time do the crews work until here?"

"Usually five."

"Then piece of cake."

CHAPTER 50

The overcast sky was darkening as Jet walked toward the park, a baseball cap pulled down low over her brow and her loose shirt covering the Beretta nestled at the base of her spine. She carried a small metal canister in her right hand and her phone in her left. Her watch read six o'clock on the nose, and she and Jabori had watched a van park across the street from the park a half hour earlier as the area cleared of laborers, the working day over in the commercial district.

Jabori had bribed the security guard at the construction site a month's wages to make himself scarce and leave the gate padlock unlocked, and the happy man had shown no interest in why he might want access to the structure. There was nothing that could be readily stolen; the workers responsible for their tools took them home each night, and only large items like cement mixers were left at the location.

He'd settled in on the top floor of the half-finished building and was nestled behind a pile of bricks, his rifle jutting from it, the scope adjusted for appropriate range. Jet had watched the van with him and discussed the likely approach the kidnappers would take as she neared the statue of a Maasai warrior, in front of which she was supposedly to meet Shira. If there was only one assailant at the statue, she would allow herself to be directed at gunpoint to the van and, once there, would signal Jabori to open fire. If there were more, she would take them on in the park, and Jabori was to shoot the targets nearest her first and then take out the tires and strafe the van so it couldn't get away.

It wasn't perfect, but given the improvised nature, it was as good as any. If she'd had a day to plan, she would have done things differently, but she didn't have that luxury and so would work with what she had.

A light drizzle started as she crossed the street to the park, and Jabori's voice resonated in her earbud.

"So far there's just one target hiding behind the statue. I don't see any snipers, and he only has a pistol, so it looks like you were right that they're going to try to grab you, not shoot you here."

"That's reassuring. Unless the guy with the pistol does," she said.

"You give the word and I blow his head off."

They'd agreed on a code word for him to do so – Yaro. She was only to use it if it looked like the gunman was going to kill her. She didn't think that would happen, but wanted to be prepared in case she was wrong.

"I'm going silent from now on," she said.

"Roger."

The statue at the far end of the park was twenty-five meters away when Jabori's voice crooned in her ear again. "Van side door opening, but nobody exiting. They've spotted you." He paused. "Exhaust now coming from the tailpipe, so engine started. Driver behind the wheel. No sign of any weapons pointed at you that I can see."

Jet didn't answer and slipped her phone into the breast pocket of her shirt, walking easily, her body language giving no indication of her being on alert. When she reached the statue, she looked around with an annoyed expression and then walked to a nearby tree to get out of the drizzle.

A tall man with a goatee stepped from behind the statue and approached Jet, who had deliberately turned her back to the area. Jabori gave her a whispered play-by-play.

"He's making his move. Gun's in his right hand, held by his side. Doesn't look like he's planning to shoot you or he'd have raised it by now."

The man called out to her when he was five meters away. "You. Turn around, real slow, and put your hands up."

Jet had removed her baseball cap and had it in her right hand, shielding the flash bang from view. She complied with the gunman's order and pretended shock when she saw the man's gun.

"What is this? Where's Shira?" she demanded.

The man looked her up and down and motioned with the gun. "Walk toward the street over there. Nice and easy. No fast moves."

"Why should I? What did you do to Shira?" Jet asked defiantly.

"Because I'll gun you down where you stand if you don't. Now move."

Jet did as instructed, and the van pulled from its position at the curb and rolled toward her. Jabori murmured in her ear, "They're going to try to snatch you."

She reached the sidewalk and twisted to look back at the gunman. "You're never going to get away with this," she warned.

He grinned. "Shut up and get inside."

The van stopped beside her, and two men with handguns stepped from the cargo bay.

She released the handle of the flash bang and tossed her hat on the sidewalk by their feet. The clink of the cylinder hitting the sidewalk startled the men, and then the grenade exploded, temporarily blinding and deafening them, Jet's earplug having saved her right ear and the earbud having shielded the left.

Jet dove to the ground and Jabori opened fire, the pop of the silenced rifle muffled by the drizzle. The first round caught one of the van gunmen in the chest, sending him staggering back against it as a red stain spread across his abdomen. Another pop and the side window by the second man's head exploded. Jet freed the Beretta and brought it to bear on the stunned kidnapper who'd led her from the statue. His mouth hung open, and he had both hands over his ears, the pistol in his right hand pointing at the sky.

A shot rang out and a chunk of sidewalk by her elbow vaporized, and then two quick pops from Jabori's rifle took out the second man, who'd fired a wild shot at her. The van's engine revved and it began to pull away. A burst of rounds from the construction site shattered the windshield in a series of starbursts, and the front passenger tire popped and flattened. The van skewed back toward the curb, ran onto the sidewalk, and then crashed into a tree.

"All down except your man," Jabori said.

Jet motioned with her pistol at the remaining kidnapper. "Drop it," she yelled so he could hear her.

He glared at Jet as he drew a bead on her. Jet's Beretta bucked in her hand. Her shot caught him in the thigh, and the concave head of the dumdum blew a fist-sized chunk of flesh away as it expanded and exited the back of his leg. He screamed in pain and squeezed the trigger of his gun, and she felt a lance of pain along her ribs. She fired again and hit him in the upper shoulder, and his pistol went flying when he hit the sidewalk.

"Get down here and help me with him," she said to Jabori, her gun leveled at the downed kidnapper while she probed her side. Her fingers came away bloody, but she could tell from the pain that the bullet had only grazed her. Jet ignored the burn and struggled to her feet, pistol in hand. She crossed to the kidnapper and kicked his weapon away, and then peered down the Beretta gunsights at him. Agony was etched across his face and his eyes were clenched shut; blood was pooling beneath his leg and shoulder.

"Where's Adami?" she asked him.

The man shook his head, never opening his eyes.

"You either tell me, or I torture it out of you. Your call."

"I...don't...know..." he managed.

"Lying won't do any good. You're not leaving me any choice."

His eyes snapped wide at the snick of the switchblade opening. Jet examined the wicked blade with interest before looking at him. "You'll live if we tie off your leg and get that shoulder looked at. If not, you'll bleed out. But not before wishing you'd died a dozen times."

"He'll...kill me."

"Whereas I'll definitely kill you if you don't tell me what I want to know." She held his stare and shrugged. "Did you know there are dozens of nerve points where this blade will make the pain in your leg and chest seem like seaside vacations?"

Jabori came at a run and stopped when he saw Jet. "Your shirt's soaked with blood."

"We'll wrap it in the car. We need to get our friend in as well so we can have a nice chat with him. Tie off his leg and then pull the car around before the cops arrive."

"What are you going to do?"

"I'm going to start with his ears," Jet said, wielding the knife with a flourish.

By the time Jabori made it back, Jet was standing over the kidnapper, watching him die, his ears and nose on the sidewalk beside him. She turned at the sound of the car approaching and walked over to it after wiping the knife clean on the man's shirt.

Jabori stared at her when she climbed into the passenger seat.

"I have the address," Jet said. "It's a junkyard outside town."

"How can you be sure he didn't lie?"

"He gave me the same address each time. Nobody would last through what I put him through and be able to remember a fake address."

"And…is he dead?"

"He will be in a few minutes. Not much blood left in him." She winced and touched her side. "You have anything we can wrap my wound with? It's not terrible, but I can't afford to be distracted. We don't have a lot of time before this hits the radio, and it's possible someone will tip off Adami."

"Or that he's monitoring the police band." Jabori put the car into gear and sped down the street. "I'll stop at a pharmacy and get some gauze and tape."

"Thanks for the backup."

"My going rate just went up."

"You're worth it. But after you patch me up, I'm taking the car, and you're out of it."

He eyed her. "I can help you if you need me to."

She shook her head. "No. This will go better if it's just me."

He shrugged. "You're the boss. Offer's open."

"Find a drugstore or a supermarket. Antiseptic ointment would also come in handy," she said through gritted teeth.

"Got it," he said, and thumbed his smartphone to life to find the nearest pharmacy as sirens keened in the distance.

CHAPTER 51

The wrecking yard was located near the sprawl of the Kibera slums, a poverty-stricken, disease-infested area southwest of downtown where taxis were reluctant to venture at any time of the day or night and the roads were awash with sewage and mud. Jet drove as fast as she dared, given the road conditions, her side throbbing beneath the wrap of bandage and salve and one eye glued to Jabori's phone, which she'd commandeered along with his car.

The buildings degraded along with the pavement as she wended her way toward the yard. Newer modern structures gave way to ramshackle dwellings clustered together in the dark, streetlights an undreamed of luxury, the dirt roads now treacherous bogs in the strengthening rain. Jabori's wipers beat a steady rhythm while doing little but smearing water and mud across the windshield, and she cursed every time she had to slow at the last second to avoid breaking the axle in a pothole that could fit a piano.

She stopped a long block from the wrecking yard and zoomed in on Jabori's phone, memorizing the layout in satellite view. The yard consisted of a wagon wheel shaped out of car chassis with a tin-roofed central building in the middle, with spokes of clear space she took to be access aisles between the vehicles. She assumed that there would be guards posted around the yard, but given that they weren't expecting an attack, she was confident that she could evade them in the dark and the rain.

Jet stepped from the car and strapped on her backpack after removing the suppressed P90 and seating one of the fifty-round magazines before chambering a round. She set the compact machine gun on the driver's seat, water streaming off her nose and chin, and screwed the suppressor onto the Beretta's barrel. The pistol would be her preferred choice due to the silencer, but if things went south, the P90's firepower at close range would prove devastating.

The weight of the flash bangs and extra magazines in the backpack were reminders that if she couldn't rescue Shira using stealth, she had sufficient weaponry to take on a small army.

She checked the safety on the Beretta and, after slipping a pair of magazines into her back pockets, scooped up the P90 and eased the door closed, the rain cool against her skin. A flash of lightning brightened the cloud cover, and three seconds later, thunder boomed in the distance. Jet stuck to the muddy road shoulder, thankful that the unpaved stretch of industrial road was empty in the downpour. When she reached a fence that ran along the perimeter of the yard, she crouched low and peered through the corrugated metal sheets fastened in place, looking for guards.

She didn't spot any standing in the rain, and then she looked along the fence to the yard entrance, where two men were sitting in an SUV backed into a driveway blocked by the vehicle. Because of the truck's orientation, they hadn't spotted Jet, and she inched backward until she reached the fencepost that marked the corner of the lot. Once out of view of the SUV, she tested the fence and cringed at the scrape of the metal sheet against the chain link, but reminded herself that in the rain sound wouldn't travel far — not to mention that the patter on all the wrecked cars sounded like a miniature anvil chorus.

Jet slung the P90's nylon strap over her shoulder and slid the Beretta into the thigh pocket of her cargo pants, and then reconsidered, removed it, and pushed the barrel down into her waistband, the suppressor hard against her left buttock. After another glance around, she gripped the fence links in her hands and heaved herself up, using the gaps for toeholds for her boots. At the top, she took a moment to eye the yard and then swung herself over, thankful for whoever had strung barbed wire between the poles and skipped every third stretch.

Her boots landed with a splash in a pool of brown water, and she had the Beretta in hand before she straightened. The graze along her ribs burned like liquid fire from the friction of her maneuver, but she willed the pain away, now laser-focused. She crept along the fence line until she came to one of the access spokes and peeked around the corner. Seeing nothing but sheets of gray rain washing along the opening, she moved into the aisle formed by crushed cars stacked atop each other, the rectangles of compressed metal and plastic the size of a small desk.

A sneeze sounded from the far end of the passage, and she ducked into a gap between two stacks. She held her breath as footsteps splashed toward her position at a slow pace, the Beretta gripped by her side. A man with an AK passed the cavity where she was hiding, close enough so she could reach out and touch him. He continued past, not registering her presence, and Jet remained motionless until the sound of his boots in the puddles of water receded, leaving only the steady thrum of rain on the metal above.

She felt in her side pocket for the switchblade and snapped it open, and rather than darting toward the central building and hoping to avoid detection, she waited with it in hand. A minute later the boot steps returned, and Jet pressed flat against the crushed cars, knife at the ready.

The gunman again walked past her, not noticing her, and when his back was in view, she made her move. She stepped from her hiding place and drove the spike of a blade into the base of his neck at the C5 vertebra, and twisted when it reached the hilt.

The sentry dropped heavily, the only sound a whoosh of final moaned breath, and Jet caught him before his body hit the ground. She lowered him carefully and toed his weapon aside, and then dragged him into the gap where she'd hidden and laid him facedown in the mud. Another flash of lightning illuminated the access way, and she looked down the aisle to the building barely visible in the rain; and then the sky exploded with thunder so deafening the ground beneath her feet trembled.

She tossed the AK into the gap by the dead guard and picked her way along the cars until she was at the end of the row, the central building only twenty feet away. An ancient forklift hulked by a roll-up entryway, beside which stood an exit door fashioned from the same pot metal as the fence.

Jet scanned the area and, seeing nobody, dashed across the open space. She'd just reached the forklift when she heard male voices from around the corner of the building. Two men in plastic rain parkas appeared, rain coursing from the brims of their hats and their assault rifles hanging from slings rather than at the ready, reinforcing her impression that news of the bloodbath at the park hadn't reached them.

Yet, she thought grimly.

The men trudged past the forklift, conversing in low tones, and Jet resisted the urge to pop a nearly silent subsonic round into their heads from point-blank range. Another blinding flash of lightning lit the surroundings, and one of the men spotted her out of the corner of his eye and spun toward her with a cry of alarm.

The Beretta popped twice, the reports drowned out by the blast of thunder that followed the lightning a moment later, and Jet dragged both men into the shadows by a cluster of drums and wedged their corpses behind the containers. She did a quick search of their pockets and, finding no radios, straightened and worked her way along the wall to the exit door.

She twisted the lever handle and pulled the door open, grimacing at the creak of rusting hinges, and then she was inside, the snap of the rain on the tin roof like a thousand snare drums rattling arrhythmically in the night. She found herself standing in a dark hallway that grew lighter at the far end, the doorways on either side black as pitch. She inched along the corridor, pistol in hand, and paused at the sound of conversation – a deep baritone seething with anger and the unmistakable sound of Shira's voice.

"I had nothing to do with Yaro's death, or the woman. How could I have known that the company would send in some super commando?" Shira asked. "You can't hold me responsible. We had a deal."

"The deal died with my son. He'd still be alive if it wasn't for your little scheme," the baritone snapped.

"I delivered like I said I would. Adami, you're a man of your word. Don't do this. I did everything I promised, and you've got millions to show for it."

"And piles of dead fighters. This wasn't what I agreed to. My son's dead, and you're going to pay. With your life if you continue testing me."

"So all of this was for nothing? I went through hell, and you're going to stiff me out of my share of the ransom? You can't be serious," Shira said, her voice tight.

Jet peered around the corner and saw a mountain of a man in a black silk jogging suit, a cigar clamped between his teeth and a pistol clutched in a fist the size of a ham, standing by Shira, who was seated on a metal chair, her wrists bound to the arms with yellow nylon packing straps.

Jet had heard enough to piece together what was happening, and was stepping from the hall when Adami saw Shira's startled gaze and spun with surprising agility for his size. Jet fired six times in rapid succession, not wanting to give the big man the chance to shoot back, and four of her rounds struck home, one tearing half his throat out, and the final shot drilling through his forehead and blowing the back of his skull against the far wall.

The floor shook when he hit it and the light went out of his eyes as he fell. Shira stifled a scream at the bloody mess only footsteps from her. She looked up at Jet like she'd seen a ghost, and then exhaled in relief and looked at her wrists.

"Thank God," she said. "I figured you'd know I would never ask to meet you at a park. I can't believe you made it. He was going to kill me."

"I heard. Sounds like your business arrangement fell apart," Jet said, her voice glacial.

"I…nobody was supposed to get hurt. It was supposed to be a straight financial deal – they grab the drug company guys, the company pays, they walk away. I…it was a way to finance the resistance, is all. They've raped Africa for generations. It was a way to take something back and make them pay."

"Sure it was," Jet said, disgust dripping from every word. "But things didn't turn out that way, did they?"

"Which wasn't my fault. If you hadn't killed Yaro–"

"I never killed him. I told you. His men shot him while they were trying to hit me."

"It doesn't matter. Everything changed when you arrived. It messed up the whole thing." She pulled at her bindings. "Untie me. They could walk in any minute."

"How many are there?"

"I don't know. Ten? Fifteen? I wasn't counting." Shira pleaded with Jet, "Come on. Please. This isn't funny."

Jet nodded slowly, her emerald eyes hard. "No. It isn't. I imagine it wasn't funny for David to be some crocodile's lunch or for Noam to get shot like a dog, either."

"I had nothing to do with that."

Jet shook her head. "I can't believe I covered for you with the surveillance tape."

Shira's eyes widened. "You…you can't leave me here. They'll kill me. Seriously. They will."

"I believe it," Jet said. "Where's the money?"

"I don't know. He didn't say. Not here, if that's what you're asking."

Jet checked the time and nodded once to herself, as though making a decision. She looked around the room, her gaze lingering on the dead gangster, and then crossed to a doorway and looked inside. Shira's face was a mask of fear as she watched Jet walk away, and she twisted her neck to follow her until she couldn't see her anymore.

"You can't let them kill me," Shira blurted, her voice strangled. "You can't. Please. Oh, God, no, please, I'll do anything…" she wailed, her final words incoherent as she began to sob.

Jet didn't answer, Shira's pleas answered only by the steady hammering of rain on the roof and the sound of Jet's boots moving down the other hall.

CHAPTER 52

Jet returned from the hallway and flipped the switchblade open. Shira snuffled at her reappearance, her eyes red and glistening with tears. Jet glared at her and shook her head in annoyance.

"Shut up. Not another sound or I'll slit your throat myself," Jet threatened.

Shira nodded, and Jet slipped the blade beneath the right wrist strap and sliced it with a brutal pull. Shira gasped and Jet cut away the other strap. When Shira was free, Jet stepped back.

"We're still in serious trouble. Put his jacket on and we'll make a run for it," Jet ordered.

Shira made a face. "It's...covered in blood."

Jet didn't budge. "Doesn't matter. The rain will wash it away. But it's black, and your top's white, so put it on and not another word."

She watched the younger woman follow her instructions and wrestle with the jacket. Shira got it free and pulled it on, the sleeves hanging like pant legs from her arms, the jacket the size of a small tent on her. Shira gagged at the smell of blood and sweat and vomited near the dead gangster, remaining bent over and retching until there was nothing left to throw up.

"Okay. Here's what we're going to do," Jet said, ignoring her plight. "I've got a car nearby. We're going to sneak to the fence, climb over it, and hopefully avoid getting killed."

"What if someone sees us?" Shira whispered.

"Then we don't avoid getting killed," Jet answered, and pointed at the hall. "I've already taken out three of them, and the storm is working in our favor, but I'm not going to lie, it's a crapshoot. Once we're outside, you've got to match my speed and keep up, or you're on your own. Understand?"

Shira spit bile to the side and nodded meekly. Jet checked her watch again and drew a deep breath. "All right. Follow me. And not a sound."

They crept the length of the hall, and Jet stopped at the door. She pressed her ear against the metal and listened for a half minute, and then turned her head toward Shira.

"Once we're outside, there's a forklift to the right. Almost directly opposite it is one of the aisles between the wrecks. That's the one I came down. Unless they have roaming patrols, there shouldn't be anyone guarding it."

"Shouldn't I have a gun or something?" Shira whispered.

"Have you ever shot one?"

She shook her head.

Jet put her free hand on the door lever. "Now isn't the time to try to learn."

"But—"

"You're more likely to shoot yourself in the foot than one of them. Just follow me as close as you can and do exactly as I say, no questions or hesitation. If we're lucky, we'll make it out alive." Jet paused. "Ready?"

Shira nodded, and Jet slowly turned the lever and pushed the door open a few inches to see outside. The rain was still coming down hard, and the ground was slick with standing water, the air heavy with moisture and the smell of ozone. Jet held still and craned her neck to listen and, when she didn't hear anything, pushed the door open farther and slid through the gap, crouching low.

Shira trailed her into the rain, and they waited by the forklift for their eyes to adjust. When Jet could make out shapes without straining, she pointed to the access aisle across from her and edged around the forklift, Shira right behind her. Jet took a deep breath and bolted through the rain, and was nearly at the mouth of the aisle when Shira slipped and splashed facedown into the mud with a cry of alarm. Jet spun and retraced her steps, her eyes blazing fury. She jerked Shira to her feet and half dragged her to the passageway, Beretta in one hand and the sleeve of Shira's jacket in the other.

They raced together toward the fence, and when they reached the outer perimeter, Jet stopped her with her forearm and raised the pistol in warning. Shira froze beside her, and they waited in the downpour as voices faded in and out from nearby. Seconds ticked by and they heard boots moving toward them — two or three men, by the sound. Jet thumbed off the Beretta's safety and took a step backward, nearly colliding with Shira, who stood her ground with her eyes glued to the opening.

Jet held her breath, ears straining over the sound of the rain drumming against the cars and the sheet metal of the fence, but nobody appeared. Another flash of lightning illuminated the area, casting Shira's face in a spectral light, and when the boom of thunder split the sky, Jet whipped around the compressed cars in a crouch, leading with the pistol.

And saw nothing.

The men had turned down the next aisle, their footprints in the mud already filling with water.

Jet twisted to Shira and pointed at the fence. Shira nodded understanding and moved to a space between the sheets of metal and hooked her fingers through the links. She climbed to the top and was swinging a leg awkwardly over when Jet opened fire with the Beretta, the weapon spitting death at a trio of gunmen who'd reappeared in the adjacent aisle, drawn by the clamor of Shira's ascent.

She emptied the magazine, hitting all of them but not before the closest one got off a volley from his AK, the explosive rattle of the unsuppressed rifle deafening to Jet's ears. The shots went wide, her rounds having found home in his chest, and Jet swung the P90 into action and squeezed off a ten-shot burst, stitching the fallen men where they lay.

Shira dropped to the ground outside the fence, and Jet jammed the empty Beretta into her waistband and ran at the barrier, throwing herself as high as she could before her hands locked onto the links. She scrambled over in an instant and was lowering herself on the far side when a flashlight beam flashed near them from the SUV.

"Stay down," Jet warned, and when the flashlight swept the

ground by the corner post, she ducked around it with the P90 and opened fire at the two gunmen from the SUV, who were trotting toward her, weapons at the ready. Three six-round bursts from the P90 cut them down where they stood, and then Jet had Shira's sleeve and was urging her forward, pushing her down the road while running behind her, ready to empty the bullpup at anything that moved.

They reached the car half a minute later, and Jet quickly fished another P90 magazine from her backpack and exchanged it for the nearly spent one. Shira threw herself into the passenger seat and Jet slid behind the wheel. After two sputtered coughs, the engine caught with a rev, and then they were skidding down the flooded road, headlights extinguished until they made the main road, Jet's eyes checking the rearview mirror every few moments.

Nobody appeared to follow them, and Jet flipped on the lights and cut her speed to a more sensible pace. Shira was shaking from shock, staring straight ahead, her expression rigid. Jet didn't say anything until they were on pavement, and only then did she turn to her.

"We made it."

Shira nodded dully. "Jesus."

Jet drew in a long breath. "Here's how this is going to play, Shira. I'm going to drop you off at your house. I want you to pack a bag, kiss your father like you mean it, and tell him you're leaving in the morning, going somewhere safe. Then I want you to disappear. Drop off the radar. I don't care where you go or what you do, but I don't want to hear your name again. It will never be safe for you here with Adami's crew out for blood, and you don't deserve to go home to Israel. So go do charity work in the jungle, or join the Peace Corps or the Foreign Legion, but vanish for good. You've got a lot to atone for. Good people died because of your little scheme, and no matter what you tell yourself, they'd be alive right now if not for you."

"I told you nobody—"

"I heard you. But this isn't a negotiation. I stuck my neck out for you, which if I'd known everything, I'd never have done. I can't take that back, but I'm not about to let you put your father's career in jeopardy or let you live easy in Israel after the stunts you've pulled. You don't want to do as I say, Adami's men will hunt you down, and if they don't get you…I'll tell my superiors and the drug company about what you did. At that point, it's even money that you get a visit from someone like me when you least expect it." Jet paused. "You don't want that."

"So I have no choice."

"That's right. I could have left you tied to the chair, and you'd have been gang raped and then cut to pieces. But I didn't. So you could say I own your life. The first time, with Jaali, was business. This isn't. So either do as I say or you're going down hard, Shira. That's the only way this is going to play. Don't make a stupid choice."

Shira swallowed a knot in her throat and nodded once.

After ten minutes of careful navigation, Jet pulled to the side of the road at a deserted intersection and stowed the P90, and then drove the rest of the way to Shira's house in silence, the only sound the monotonous beating of the wipers and the occasional beep of Jabori's phone signaling an upcoming turn.

CHAPTER 53

Tel Aviv, Israel

Jet slid her key into the condo lock and opened it with a soft click. She stepped into the small foyer and smiled at her daughter, who was playing in the dining room at the far end, sun streaming through the window and warming her as she worked at one of her dozens of coloring books with crayons.

"Mama!" Hannah cried, dropping the crayons and running down the hall.

Jet stooped and hugged her, smiling with her face buried in the little girl's hair. Matt's head appeared around the corner and he padded toward them, giving Jet some time with Hannah before arriving.

Jet lifted her daughter in her arms and stood, and Matt hugged the two of them. He pulled away, noted the discoloration on the side of her face that her makeup had been unable to mask, and frowned.

"Rough one?" he asked.

She set Hannah down and kissed him. "No worse than usual. I'm fine."

He considered her for a moment. "You already deliver your report?"

She nodded. "All done."

"So we have you all to ourselves?"

Jet ran her fingers through Hannah's hair and patted her head, and offered Matt another smile, this one betraying the fatigue she felt. She sighed and looked away, her chest suddenly tight – this was what she wanted her future to be, not an endless string of missions, one of which the odds said she wouldn't return from.

She drew a deep breath and handed him her bag, her lips a tight line.

"For now."

About the Author

Featured in *The Wall Street Journal, The Times*, and *The Chicago Tribune*, Russell Blake is *The NY Times* and *USA Today* bestselling author of over forty novels.

Blake is co-author of *The Eye of Heaven* and *The Solomon Curse*, with legendary author Clive Cussler. Blake's novel *King of Swords* has been translated into German, *The Voynich Cypher* into Bulgarian, and his JET novels into Spanish, German, and Czech.

Blake writes under the moniker R.E. Blake in the NA/YA/Contemporary Romance genres. Novels include *Less Than Nothing, More Than Anything*, and *Best Of Everything*.

Having resided in Mexico for a dozen years, Blake enjoys his dogs, fishing, boating, tequila and writing, while battling world domination by clowns. His thoughts, such as they are, can be found at his blog: RussellBlake.com

Visit RussellBlake.com for updates

or subscribe to: RussellBlake.com/contact/mailing-list

BOOKS BY RUSSELL BLAKE

Co-authored with Clive Cussler
THE EYE OF HEAVEN
THE SOLOMON CURSE

Thrillers
FATAL EXCHANGE
FATAL DECEPTION
THE GERONIMO BREACH
ZERO SUM
THE DELPHI CHRONICLE TRILOGY
THE VOYNICH CYPHER
SILVER JUSTICE
UPON A PALE HORSE
DEADLY CALM
RAMSEY'S GOLD
EMERALD BUDDHA
THE GODDESS LEGACY
A GIRL APART

The Assassin Series
KING OF SWORDS
NIGHT OF THE ASSASSIN
RETURN OF THE ASSASSIN
REVENGE OF THE ASSASSIN
BLOOD OF THE ASSASSIN
REQUIEM FOR THE ASSASSIN
RAGE OF THE ASSASSIN

The Day After Never Series
THE DAY AFTER NEVER – BLOOD HONOR
THE DAY AFTER NEVER – PURGATORY ROAD
THE DAY AFTER NEVER – COVENANT
THE DAY AFTER NEVER – RETRIBUTION

77128190R00168

Made in the USA
San Bernardino, CA
19 May 2018